HARDBALL

HARDBALL

AN EROTIC NOVEL BY
BY T. HITMAN

alyson books
los angeles | new york

© 1999 T. HITMAN. ALL RIGHTS RESERVED

MANUFACTURED IN THE UNITED STATES OF AMERICA.

THIS TRADE PAPERBACK ORIGINAL IS PUBLISHED BY ALYSON PUBLICATIONS,
P.O. BOX 4371, LOS ANGELES, CA 90078-4371.
DISTRIBUTION IN THE UNITED KINGDOM BY TURNAROUND PUBLISHER SERVICES LTD.,
UNIT 3 OLYMPIA TRADING ESTATE, COBURG ROAD, WOOD GREEN,
LONDON N22 6TZ ENGLAND.

FIRST EDITION: SEPTEMBER 1999

01 02 03 a 10 9 8 7 6 5 4 3 2

ISBN 1-55583-533-3

LIBRARY OF CONGRESS CATALOGING-IN-PUBLICATION DATA
    HITMAN, T.
        HARDBALL : A NOVEL / BY T. HITMAN. — 1ST ED.
        ISBN 1-55583-533-3
        I. TITLE.
    PS3558.I8384H37 1999
    813'.54—DC21   99-31353 CIP

COVER ART BY BEAU.

This work of sweat-drenched jock fiction is respectfully dedicated to the boys of summer and to Scott Brassart for having the balls to throw out the first pitch.

FIRST INNING

The itch in Tommy Bruno's nuts just wouldn't go away. It might have been the rain, which was falling so hard on the tin roofs of the spring-training camp it sounded like classic-rock drums, a type of music that kept his heart racing, his blood pumping—in his ears, in his legs, in his nuts and the seven-inch rod hanging half hard over them.

It might have been the start of spring training, the antici-pation of long strenuous sessions of running, sweating, and working every muscle to the point of exhaustion. That kind of sweating always made Bruno's nuts swell, tingle, and itch. But this time—with the cartilage in his right knee that had ripped, healed, ripped again, then healed again—he doubted it was his first week in Florida at the training camp that ig-nited his balls, keeping his cock half hard half the time and rock-hard the rest.

The room was hot despite the open door and cool, wet air billowing through its outside screen. The small cabin seemed to close in even tighter when the rains began falling in tor-rents around the camp. The stink of sweat from half a dozen pairs of discarded baseball shorts, dirty socks, and mostly from Bruno himself hung heavily in the room.

Bruno glanced around the cabin at the double bed with its

harvest-gold spread bunched up near two hard pillows, the television and VCR, the dingy brown rug, a chair, and two mismatched bureaus. The one nearest the bed had a big square mirror.

He avoided the mirror at first and glanced into the tiny bathroom on the other side of the room's only other furniture, a shabby bedside table with a phone on it. But the quick image he'd seen reflected—and the itch in his nuts—pulled him back. Bruno took a reverse step to stand eye to eye with himself.

It wasn't the rain, the start of baseball training, the sweat that always gathered on his sac, or even the sight of himself that was burning his nuts. He realized it was all those things combined, along with a looming 40th birthday and the divorce.

"Shit, Bruno," he said aloud. His voice, almost a whisper, came out sounding sad against the rain. "You're getting old."

He leaned in and looked long at the image in the mirror. It was hard to deny it. He wasn't just handsome but damned handsome, and at the moment it didn't hurt to admit it. Sure, the hair over his ears was silvering slightly, but the rest of his neat short military cut was dark and perfect. The crow's-feet near his eyes only made his bedroom gray-blues sparkle even more. The rough 5-o'clock shadow wasn't scuzzy but worked to show off his white teeth and square jaw even better than when he shaved.

Bruno flashed himself a three-alarm smile and shook his head, if just for a moment. He looked better, just shy of 40, than he had at 20.

He pulled the sweaty gray T-shirt from where it was tucked into his faded jeans, and as he slowly slid it over his head, his hairy, muscular arms flexed. The sight of his chest—the dark bronze dime-size nipples crowning his neatly shagged pecs, his ropy muscled abdomen with the thin line of damp hair cutting him down the middle—made him remain near the bureau a second longer.

But then the happiness was gone. Bruno's smile faded into a frown.

Veronica—"Ronnie," Bruno's ex-wife—couldn't have cared less if he'd let his muscled body sag into a heap of tires.

"Fucking bitch," he spat, balling the sweaty shirt and wiping it under his furry armpits, then over his forehead. He deeply inhaled the clean, musky smell of his sweat.

The truth was, Ronnie hadn't cared about Bruno's pride and joy, his body, for a long time. She didn't like sex. He'd needed it. The itch in his balls had been a fucking monster even then.

Ronnie and Bruno. It seemed like a good marriage at first. She was from the Midwest; he was from Massachusetts, home of the Seaside Top Socks. If she hadn't been so stingy and given out a little more of her tired pussy, they might still be married.

Bruno thought of Ronnie strolling toward the bed they'd shared in Seaside, her "come towel" ready—and the sound of her bitching when she rolled over on the wet spot if she missed even one drop of his potent swimmers with it. "You're a thousand miles away, Ronnie," he said with a disgusted sigh. "And you still make my nuts itch."

Bruno flipped his middle finger in the imagined direction of Illinois and swore.

The rain falling outside up-tempoed. The itch in Bruno's nuts grew worse. It pulled him back to his reflection.

The half-hard cock rubbing denim started swelling to its full seven inches. There was no point in trying to stop it, so

Bruno didn't bother. It hadn't helped in the past to deny his cock or the itching in his nuts, and no amount of palm-driving sessions over a dirty movies, magazines, or memories of the fuckfests in his teens and 20s ever totally kept it down. Right after coming, it went back to its half-hard state.

"Fuck you and your come towel," Bruno said with a sarcastic huff. He kicked off his worn leather deck shoes, stood sideways in the mirror, and watched the bulge snake down his right leg. He popped the button, unzipped the fly, and pushed the jeans down over his gray baseball underwear.

Yes, his body was better now than it had been half his lifetime ago. *So what if it's getting older?* he thought. It certainly wasn't old. His hairy jogger's legs rippled with muscles from his concrete calves to the firm areas of inner thigh his baseball midlengths covered. Even the scar cutting across his right knee, a furrow through the dark hairs on his leg, was attractive in its own way. After all, men and scars went together.

Even his big feet were sexy. He kicked his left leg up on the dresser, flexed the toes on his size 12, and marveled at the way the dark sweaty hair on the top of his foot shined in the room's dull light. He had handsome feet, classic like the feet on statues, with well-shaped big toes and the second digit being the longest.

Bruno rubbed the big toes, scratched at the sweat between them, then sniffed his fingers. The strangely attractive stink of a man's fresh foot sweat filled his nose.

With that, he righted and turned, pushing the baseball shorts down over the hard muscles of his hairy, almost 40-year-old ass. He balled one fist and slammed it against concrete.

"You still got it, old man," he said, revolving back so that he faced the mirror. He tucked his thumbs into the elastic waistband. The coarse shag of man hair slid under his fingertips. By now Bruno was rock-hard. The hot steel head of his cock pressed against his thumbs.

"You still got it."

He reached down, fumbling in the fly front. The gray cotton had grown damp with his muskiest sweat. He pulled the material aside, freeing his nuts. Bruno's sac spilled out, his two big low-hangers dangling under the tent in his baseball underwear. Their heady smell mixed with the other sweat odors of feet, armpits, and the clean perspiration running in tiny rivers down his chest and hairy legs.

Bruno wrapped his fingers around the root of his sac and marveled at the fullness and size of his nuts. It was no wonder the itch never went away. "You got big nuts, dude," he said. He shook them by the root. The balls in the mirror—the left hanging lower, heavier, than the right—rocked under Bruno's big hand. "And you ain't wanting in the cock department, neither."

He groped the other hand into the hair-filled open fly and felt up the hard rod until he had it by the head. He released it from the baseball underwear, letting it hang with his nuts in all its glory.

He'd measured his cock on one of the palm driving sessions he'd had with his baseball glove and some spit. Ronnie would never be caught dead doing such a thing—men didn't get their cocks measured in rural Illinois. The long tube was now at its full seven inches, its arrow-shaped head stretching its lone eye each time he pumped it. A thin line of clear drool seeped from the piss slit, oozing down onto his big bare right foot. Except for the callus under the head caused by his thumb and the way he held it when jacking off, like the rest of Bruno, his cock was perfect. From the blue veins on its underside to the hair running half its length, the arrow-shaped stretched head, and the way his big come-filled bull nuts dangled below it, it was easy to understand why it was always hard.

"Look what she abused," he said as he spit on his right hand, wrapped his fingers around it, and began to stroke in slow, hard pumps. Bruno growled as another trickle of clear nut juice slipped from the head, splashing his foot. "Looking good, Bruno. You got a great bod, a big sac of nuts, and a decent tool. It's time you found someone who can appreciate a big jock who loves to fuck around the clock."

Bruno watched his cool hand-and-cock action in the mirror until the reflection of an old pair of sweat socks and stirrups stole his attention. With his steaming, itchy nuts and wet cock hanging from his baseball underwear, he sat on the bed, grabbed the dirty socks, sniffed them, then put them on. He stretched the stirrups up his calves before rolling over to the bedside table. He pulled open the drawer and grabbed the jar of eye-black before returning to the mirror.

He applied two black lines at the top of each cheek. Standing in his stinky socks, pouring with healthy sweat, Bruno smiled at the vision of his hard cock and bull nuts hanging from the gray baseball underwear.

"You've come a long way since little league," he said with a cocky shake of his head. He wiped his hands off on the baseball underwear before resuming his pile-driving session on the stiff rod.

It didn't take long; it never did. By that point Bruno's cock slit was dripping like a leaky faucet. He teased it just under the head, tickling the trigger of sensitive nerves with his fingertips. The dripping goo went from clear to milky white. A second later the rush of fire hit him.

Bruno arched his back, curled his toes in the stinky socks,

stretched, and growled as the cannon in his cock went off.

"Ah, shit!" he thundered. It felt like his cock doubled in size in his hand. Bruno watched in fascinated excitement as the first shot flew from the piss slit and hit the mirror. "Yeah, that's it!"

The second sprayed the top of the dresser. Like it always happened, Bruno's hand slipped back on the third. A geyser of hot juice squirted up his chest, hitting him under the chin. Drops of heavy load dripped down into the dense tangle of coarse man hair filling his open fly. The fourth shot, a smaller version of the third, fell back onto his nuts. The fifth was a gush. The sixth, with his orgasm subsiding, a trickle.

"Uh," Bruno groaned. The hot juice clinging to his fingers soaked the already wet material of his baseball underwear. The tremors racing through his muscles made him go to one palm on the come-slick dresser for support as the room spun around him. His fingers slipped over the slick wood. There was load everywhere.

Bruno sucked in a deep lungful of air, shook his head, spattering drops of sweat from his forehead onto the nasty spunk puddles coating the dresser, then just as deeply let it out. Every part of his body came down from the high of shooting his load—every part of him except the itching in his nuts that kept his cock stretched out after he wiped his hands on his socks and baseball shorts, and that was a fire not likely to be put out soon.

The knock at the open screen door startled Bruno into easy view. With his still stiff cock and glistening balls hanging from his fly, Bruno whipped around, sending a trickle of spent load flying onto the carpet in front of him. On instinct he yanked his big bull nuts and spent dick back into concealment. The action made him see stars. Bruno yowled in pain. "Fuck!" he bellowed as he faced the mysterious knocker.

"Mr. Bruno?" a deep but youthful voice called from the rain. Bruno slid a big hand into the steaming heat in his underwear, shifted his cock and adjusted his meaty balls. When he could see again, Bruno peered out the screen door.

The bedraggled beanpole with the mop of dark hair was Ricky Catalano, the new batboy. He was tall and skinny, an Italian-looking 19-year-old kid with big feet and a goofy smile whose Top Socks uniform never quite seemed to fit properly.

"How long you been standing there, kid?" Bruno snapped. He felt his face flush with the embarrassing realization that Catalano, who'd been nicknamed "Cat" by the team manager, had seen him jacking off.

Catalano shook his head. The baseball cap was plastered to his head. "Long enough to drown in this piss." Cat smiled and hefted the bundles in his hands into clear view. "I'm here to pick up your dirty laundry and bring you extra towels."

Bruno glanced at the piles of stinky socks and come-stained underwear scattered across the room, then at the clothes he'd donned during his latest pump session. He sighed before waving Cat in. The screen door banged loudly in place.

The skinny batboy stood motionless inside the doorway while Bruno gathered his dirty laundry into a bunch that filled his nose with the acrid stink of stale sweat. He extended the underwear and socks. Cat put the bag containing fresh towels down and pulled out a laundry sack bearing the number 31, Bruno's number. He curled his nose as the baseball shorts and sweat socks fell in.

"How you like it, kid?" Bruno asked as he peeled off the

stirrups and dropped them into the mess.

"You don't have to call me kid, Mr. Bruno. I'm 19."

Bruno grinned. "And even though I'm gonna be 40 by the end of next month, you don't have to call me Mr. Bruno. Bruno is OK. All my friends call me Bruno."

Catalano's face flushed. "Great, Bruno. You guys treat me real well. You know, I have your '92 MVP baseball card!"

"Is it worth anything?"

"To me it is." Catalano went silent, but continued to grin.

Bruno balled a fist and waved it playfully at the batboy. "Anything else?"

Catalano's dark chocolate eyes shifted toward Bruno's abdomen. "You want me to take those too?"

Bruno glanced down. With another deep sigh he peeled off the socks on his feet, then righted. He lowered his musky baseball shorts, exposing his rigid, wet cock and the low-hanging sac of bull nuts swinging beneath it. The cool air from the open door gusted over his hot, bared balls.

There was no mistaking the batboy's reaction to seeing Bruno's nuts and cock. Cat suddenly glanced nervously away, a guilty look on his face as he accepted Bruno's rank shorts and dropped them into the laundry sack. Saying nothing more and giving Bruno the back of his Top Socks uniform that proudly proclaimed BATBOY in bold black letters, Cat stumbled on his awkward feet to the door.

Bruno's deep baritone stopped him from immediately leaving. "Kid, take those towels. I don't need them."

His back still to Bruno, Cat slung the laundry sack over one shoulder. "They ain't for you, Bruno. They're for the new guy, that third baseman from Cincinnati."

Bruno reached down and scratched his sweaty balls. "What?"

Taking a noticeable swallow, Cat glanced over his shoulder. "Weare. Tim Weare. You and he are bunking together. That's what I was told—to deliver extra towels for him." With that and a pair of baseball underwear soaked with Bruno's spunk, Cat slipped back into the rain, leaving the handsome outfielder alone with not only the itch in his nuts but some unanswered questions.

☆   ☆   ☆

Cat moved quickly beneath the overhang. He passed Number 11—the blond-haired blue-eyed All-American second baseman, Scott Bradley—on his mad dash to the laundry shed.

"You got any towels on you, Cat?" Bradley asked with a good-natured clap to Cat's free shoulder.

Cat stopped in place. The laundry sack slipped off. The confused and excited haze coloring his senses worsened with Bradley's request. Cat tried to swallow, only to find his mouth had gone completely dry. "Nuh-uh," he eventually choked out.

Even through Cat's darting, nervous eyes, it was obvious the tall blond had been jogging in the rain. His slightly curled hair was soaking and slicked back. Bradley's muscular, hairy legs and arms, packed tightly in a pair of drenched navy-colored shorts and a matching T-shirt, were beaded with drops of water. Whether it was sweat or rain, the crystal droplets clung sensually to each hair on Bradley's legs and made the heat in Cat's mouth burn more uncomfortably.

"Wrong run," Cat eventually answered, forcing a smile. "This ain't the clean stuff."

Bradley nonchalantly peeled his wet T-shirt over his head and kicked off his black high-tops. He flexed his damp toes and smiled before reaching for his sneakers. "Towels, bro, when you got a sec," he said in a good-natured voice.

"Will do," Cat promised before resuming his mad dash to the laundry shed.

He nearly dropped the keys twice fumbling for the one that unlocked the small building's door. The smell of bleach, soap, and a lingering musky trace of sweat from dirty laundry billowed around Cat with a strangely pleasurable familiarity as he thrust the door open. He quickly locked it behind him after flipping on the light. The overhead fluorescent threw its pale glow on the industrial washers and heavy-duty driers, the folding table, the plastic tubs of laundry powder and bleach, and the old recliner near the shelves of white towels. The only window in the cinder-block walls, a tiny rectangle, had been closed from view by a transistor radio. It was all as he'd left it, knowing it was the one safe place where he could unwind the stiffness between his legs.

Catalano shucked his uniform pants down to his ankles and dropped the white briefs with them. His hard skinny cock—a cock that matched his wiry body, with its dark shaft, thin pink head, and black hair running up both its sides—was already leaking come.

Cat wasted no time. Plunking down in the chair, he spit in his palm and started fisting his tall, thin shaft. With each upward stroke of his hand, a pearl of precome oozed out.

"Bruno," Catalano sighed between gasps for air.

He stopped long enough to reach into the bag of smelly clothes and withdrew the handsome outfielder's sperm-covered gray baseball underwear from the tangle of sweat socks and stirrups.

They were still wet.

"Oh, fuck," Catalano huffed. He buried his nose in the cotton and deeply breathed in the acrid smell of Tommy Bruno's nuts and cock. The unmistakable odor of stale jock load filled his nostrils.

After a few sniffs Cat sucked on the wet stain. The taste drove him over the top. Biting down on Bruno's smeared load, he shot one, two, three strings of his own come into the air. It came back down in his hair, on his chest, and on the pair of stinking briefs clenched between his teeth.

Cat released his long, spent dick, spit out Bruno's smelly underwear, and mopped up his mess.

"Shit," Cat swore, inhaling deeply. Before he pulled his uniform pants up, he sampled his own load off the big guy's shorts. It didn't taste bad.

With a satisfied sigh Cat crossed to the machine. He dumped laundry soap and powdered bleach on the reeking socks and underwear, then grabbed a stack of whites for Bradley.

If I'm lucky and move fast enough, Cat thought as he closed the door behind him, *I might catch him in the shower*.

☆   ☆   ☆

The driving rain made twilight come an hour early; the outside lights snapped on, illuminating the far-off baseball diamond, the locker room and shower outbuildings, and the small residence cottages of the Seaside Top Socks' Florida baseball camp.

Bruno pulled on a fresh pair of boxers. He liked boxers—they were kind to his big nuts. He slid his comfortable jeans over them, slipped his bare feet into his worn leather loafers, and finished with a skin-tight navy-colored T-shirt bearing the team's insignia.

His intention had been to order a pizza, grab some beer

from the fridge in the lunchroom, and hit the sack early—
after another round of playing with his tool. But Cat's revelation changed all that.

He'd planned on getting some serious pussy while in Florida and fucking it endlessly in the small room. Having a hot-
dog roommate would shoot that plan in the ass.

Mitch Hudson, the Socks' team manager, didn't like his
boys going to town during training camp, though most of the
men did, married or not.

The room was small enough; there was no way a cot could
fit in, let alone another bed.

With a disgusted shake of his head, Bruno shut the door behind him and walked into the wet twilight. He was sure, with a
pissed-off scowl on his face, he could make Mitch see reason.

Mitch Hudson smiled through clenched teeth, threw his
head back, and thrust in once more. The tight muscles in
Mike Young's asshole sucked his cock better than any mouth.

"Fuck, Mitch," Young said in his deep Southern drawl. "I
think I'm gonna shoot!"

Hudson pulled back so that only the head of his unsheathed six-incher was speared in Young's butt. The juice
from Hudson's piss slit had painted his star left fielder's pink,
slick hole with milk. Each time he slammed back in, his fleshy
dick head teasing Young's prostate, the other dude went wild.

"Gonna...come!"

Hudson reached a meaty, scar-latticed hand around
Young's hairy chest and swept it down his ropy abdomen,
where it disappeared into dense cock hair. Young was jacking
himself but good. Something hot and wet slapped Hudson's

hand. "That's it, Mikey," he growled. "Show Mitch how much you like his cock in your butt."

"Ugh!"

Hudson pulled out, just to the edge. Young's stretched ass lips squeezed tight. The overwhelming feeling drove Hudson back in. "Do it," Young gasped in his drawl. "Jack my fucking cock. I want it, man!"

Hudson thrust in again, harpooning Young with all his solid, muscular weight. The hands hugging Mike Young's steely, hairy abdomen found new homes—one on the low-hanging meaty sac of nuts Hudson's balls kept slapping against, the other around the short, stiff rod Young let go of. "Yeah," Hudson groaned. "That feels so good!"

"You're telling me. Shit!" Hudson thrust in again, making Young break into staggered bursts of "Fuck!" and "Gonna come!"

Hudson beat the cock in his hand, pulled back, then pumped in again. A new wave of wetness slid between his fingers. "You're right, Mikey," Hudson said as he leaned down and sucked Young's ear. "You are gonna come. Do it, guy. Shoot that juice in my hand!"

Young lifted off the couch, taking the silver fox with him on his back—no small feat. He groaned, then yelled at the effect Hudson's attack on his asshole and dick was having on him. "Here it comes!"

"Shoot it, boy," Hudson ordered. "Shoot that fucking spunk in my hand."

Mike Young's cock erupted in hot white foam, all over Hudson's fingers.

"Do it, Mikey," Hudson continued. "Piss that load all over me."

"Fuck!"

The other man's shooting sent Hudson over the top. He pushed in one more time and felt his cock catch fire in

Young's tight, hairy stud cunt. Hudson shot for what seemed forever into his left-fielder's hole.

When it was over, Hudson swore and collapsed with his cock still inside Young. He felt his load oozing past the tight seal of the other man's ass. As he and Young kissed, their tang trickled in his hands and dripped from the left fielder's stretched shit hole, down onto both their balls, between their legs.

It was just the way Hudson liked it.

"Your hole is tighter than my wife's pussy," Hudson said. The come in his hands loosened the gold wedding band on his ring finger.

Young chuckled. Hudson passed his sticky fingers through the other man's neat military buzz cut and traced strings of cool sperm into his matching mustache, the stubby trace of a beard in the making.

Mike Young was a handsome guy, easily six feet and a few inches tall without one trace of fat in his 200 pounds of solid muscle. He had strong arms and legs with just the right amount of hair on them, big feet, a tight asshole, and a smaller but adequate rod that fit perfectly in Hudson's mouth.

They'd done it the first time on the road, five years earlier, before Hudson's graying hair had gone totally silver, making his sleepy blue eyes appear all the more dreamy. In those days Hudson had been a player, a first baseman. They were drunk and feeling good. Hudson's wife didn't seem to want to keep up with him. He was a guy. Guys had cocks that needed constant attention. Mike Young, a first-round draft pick new to the Top Socks that spring, had understood.

They'd helped each other to the bathroom, leaning on each other, touching each other. It was the cardinal sin: two jocks getting each other off. Men like Mike Young and Mitch Hudson didn't fuck each other. Oh, no. They ate pussy and sucked tit. They took two women to bed at a time, made other women eat their wives and girlfriends and got off watching them. That was expected. That was normal.

But the two men knew how to get each other off and continued to, keeping it separate from anyone else. They took care of each other when the wife and girlfriend refused to put out. They weren't selfish. Sometimes Mike took the ride, sometimes Mitch. And the fact that it was their secret seemed to get them off more intensely, right under the noses of the macho players who thought they were fucking two women at once.

Hudson wiped his face on Young's military buzz and reveled in the way it felt on his bare sweaty chin. "Fuck, Mikey," he groaned. He settled against the other man's neck and showered the salty, perspiring skin with small kisses.

He thought about all those other times—Atlanta, Boston, Oakland, Miami, Cleveland—him and Mikey Young getting each other off. There were times when only a man could make another man feel satisfied. A smile blossomed on his face as he dreamed behind closed eyes of the ways Mike had satisfied him. His rod, still buried to the hilt in Young's come-stuffed shit hole, stirred.

Hudson was about to pull out, give Mikey his turn in the saddle, when a heart-stopping knock sounded at the door.

"Hudson," the unmistakable baritone of Tommy Bruno thundered. "I want a word with you!"

☆   ☆   ☆

A low swear parted Hudson's pursed lips. Mike Young's southern twang echoed the manager's "Fuck!"

Hudson jumped up, spraying stale come across the bed and the left fielder's hairy leg. He reached for the cotton bathrobe slung over the nearby desk chair. "Just a minute!" he yelled as he haphazardly pulled it on.

Young stretched ass-up on the bed. "Get rid of him," he said, breathing heavily.

Hudson smiled. He was about to pull the bathrobe's belt tight, covering his hard, reawakened cock, when he realized the hand he'd jacked Mikey off with was still wet. He considered wiping it on the dark blue cotton robe but, with a sigh, brought his fingers to his lips and licked off the salty goo. "Yeah, I'll get rid of him, all right," he said in a purposefully low voice. With that Hudson knelt down, roughly spread the sweating cheeks of Young's muscled ass, and rammed his face into the swampy region around his tight, wet hole. He slurped up the tangy combination, his own spunk and the oily sweat from Mikey's butt. "Just so I can fuck you again."

He licked the left fielder's inner thigh, then swiped a hand across his mouth. When he rose his big, spent cock hung from the bathrobe. Mikey was there, as always.

"Clean it up, you handsome cocksucker," Hudson ordered.

Mike Young and his hot pink tongue took orders well.

The fist pounding the door, rattling the tight metal venetian blinds, drove them apart again.

"I'm coming!" Hudson bellowed, then in a low voice, as he tried to tie the belt around his waist, said, "Literally."

Young rolled onto his back, leaving his deflated cock and tightened nuts hanging in open view. Fuck, Hudson wanted him! The heat between his legs sent his bone tenting under the bathrobe. First he had to deal with his other star outfielder.

"Keep it down," he whispered to Young as he crossed to the cabin door. "The noise, not your prick."

☆   ☆   ☆

If not for the fact he'd heard Hudson shuffling around the room, Bruno would have left, gone back, and hit the hay pissed. The poorly lit room, the tightly drawn venetian blinds—the place looked empty.

Then he heard footsteps, and the door parted, but only slightly. Mitch Hudson—his perfect silver hair in a neat military cut, his pale blue eyes and athletic, hairy body barely covered by a cotton bathrobe—filled the space between the door and frame, barring any view inside.

Bruno, dripping wet under the ineffectual overhang, grinned. He was popping his rocks, he thought. Probably had just plugged some tight snatch, and he'd interrupted his boss's pleasure. If he wasn't getting it, Bruno didn't want the dude in charge getting it, either.

"Yeah, guy," Hudson said in a low voice. He curiously avoided direct eye contact, something Bruno immediately recognized.

"What's this about some Cincinnati limp dick bunking with me? Fuck, Mitch, I'm living in a footlocker as it is."

Hudson sighed and held up a big restraining hand. "Before you start busting my balls, it's only until that new pitcher gets shifted to the farm team so he can get some more practice in."

"Bust *your* balls?" Bruno said. "What about *my* balls?"

"He's a good guy. You'll probably end up being best buddies by the end of the season. I believe in a buddy system."

"A buddy I don't need—some young pup who's gonna keep me up at night talking, playing that rap music shit, and spanking his meat. Put me in with one of the older guys—Roger or the Cowboy."

Hudson's eyes darted nervously to the left of the door, to the small sofa where a ten-gallon hat crowned a discarded pair of jeans and cowboy boots. "Not possible," Hudson snapped.

"Just live with it, Bruno. I got bigger concerns to take care of now."

"I'll bet," Bruno growled in a menacing voice. His eyes lowered to the tent in the other man's navy bathrobe.

Hudson followed Bruno's eyes. At the same time he felt the hot rod between his legs slip out of the poorly tied cotton flap. The wind did the rest by pushing the flap further aside, exposing the big pink cock and swollen sac of nuts beneath it. Hudson took a heavy swallow, only to choke on the parched heat that had gathered in his mouth.

"Yeah," Bruno said after a silence that came when Hudson went speechless. "You got big things, but I got bigger. Go take care of that, Mitch." He thumbed the direction of Hudson's boner, then walked away, back into the rain.

The cool air gusting over Hudson's raging hard-on chilled the steam in his sac. Bruno's words played in his ears as, true to the promise, he returned to his secret lover, who took care of the big thing hanging between his legs.

☆   ☆   ☆

Bruno woke with a renewed sense of purpose. His anger fueled the itch in his big nuts. He went to the park at the crack of dawn and did five miles around the field in the misty, cold drizzle, but he barely felt it. The soaking sweat coating his balls did little to put out the fire burning inside them.

He did 100 jumping jacks outside and swung the bat with his nickname emblazoned across it an equal number of times at balls that were never pitched. By the time he returned to his cabin, the rest of the Top Socks prospects were either stumbling to the lunch room for coffee and breakfast or jogging in the drizzle, which seemed to be letting up.

Soaked with the kind of sweat that turned muscle to marble, he passed the Top Socks' star pitcher, Roger Twain, "the Thunderbird." The big guy jogged past him clad in a pair of navy-colored sweats and a T-shirt bearing the team's insignia. "Bruno, baby," the Thunderbird effortlessly huffed between breaths.

"Hey, bro," Bruno said. They high-fived, then slapped each other's hard asses respectfully.

Bruno peeled his sweat-soaked canvas parka off as he approached the screen door. When it slammed behind him, he shucked his cutoff sweat shorts, kicked off his worn cleats, and stood in his jockstrap and damp sweat socks, which were undeniably gray with his musk. He did 100 sit-ups and 25 push-ups that made the muscles in his strong arms pump and swell so far out, he thought they would explode.

But they didn't, and as exhausted as he was, Bruno stood, proudly displaying the perfection of his body in the mirror. The pain in his muscles, his feet, and forearms paled in comparison to the image staring back. With a smile breaking on his hard jaw, relaxing his angry face, Bruno felt his cock spring to life again.

It unfurled over his sweat-soaked nuts, forcing his flimsy jock out. Without even touching himself Bruno watched his hard cock free his balls by tenting the jock. The hairy sac and egg-shaped nuts spilled between his spread legs, dangling fully. The sight pushed his cock to its total seven inches.

"Fuck," Bruno groaned. Jacking his meat was the perfect way to end a killer workout. It gave him the kind of release a shower, cold drink, or rubdown couldn't.

He teased his nuts with one hand and marveled at the velvety feel of the pouch they hung in. The other hand freed his bat from the jockstrap. His cock's piss slit stretched up and

winked at him, dislodging a pearl of clear precome that an upward stroke sent oozing down the top side of his cock, over his
finger, into his shag.

Bruno settled back on the bed, sweat socks and all, spit on
his palm, and started pumping. The stiffness in his right knee
and the ache in both shoulders and ankles only intensified the
excitement he got from beating his meat. The electric fire from
his balls and cock head radiated to every muscle and vein.

He imagined the time he and Ronnie had fucked standing
up in a crowded bar. It had been so dark, so tight. He'd gotten in under her dress and up her pussy so fast, she hadn't had
time to argue. It was the one time she actually seemed to want
his cock. The excitement, the danger—he remembered how
bad it had made his balls ache, not being able to pull his low-
hangers out of his jeans for fear of their obvious size getting
them caught. He'd done it, though, and had fired a bucket of
his load up into her. That had been some fuck all those years
ago, the fuck that conceived Tom Jr.

His son's face swam in the red haze of his memory.

Bruno's cock head oozed a sudden heavy river of fuck juice.
It shocked him so much, the image of Tom Jr., who had
Bruno's face, legs, cock and trademark come-packed bull nuts,
that Bruno shot his load before he was ready.

"Oh, shit!" He swore as a hot ribbon of spunk flashed over
his hairy chest, catching him square in the face. The second
flew into his open mouth. The next two landed on his chest.
As Bruno gulped—then coughed on—the mouthful of jizz,
his orgasm wound down, leaving his bag soaked not only with
sweat but also with come. It ran down his hairy inner thigh
and invaded the tight hole between his hard butt cheeks.

Bruno released his spent cock. The still hard shaft flopped
onto his flat abdomen. He wiped his balls with the gamy jock

but was forced from the bed when he realized how ineffectual his jock would be in cleaning up the huge come dump he'd unloaded all over himself.

With the taste of his own spunk still on his lips, Bruno plodded on aching feet into the bathroom, grabbed one of the fresh white towels Cat had brought for the rookie, and wiped his balls and chest clean of his seed—the same seed that had conceived Tom Jr. years before. Sweat poured into his eyes, stinging him as the shudder of the powerful orgasm subsided. His whole body began to ache. "Fuck," Bruno growled in his deep baritone. He leaned down and pulled off his socks. His jockstrap followed them into a smelly pile beside the hopper. He threw the come-stained towel onto the back of the seat. Ronnie would have been proud, he thought with a sarcastic huff as he turned the shower on.

Steaming hot, it worked on his muscles like magic. In a daze—not just from the steaming mist but more from the memory of that most incredible of fucks that had sent his rod spitting—Bruno soaped up his nuts, shagged the last of the stale load out of his cock by jacking it under the hot water stream, and washed the sweat caking on his perfect mass of muscles away.

When he emerged, wanting coffee and a hearty breakfast but so tired from both workouts he decided instead to catch a catnap, he dressed in a fresh jock and kicked up his bare feet.

Sleep came quickly, with disturbing images he hadn't thought about for a long time.

The vision of a classic Greek statue greeted him when the screen door banged back in place, stirring Bruno from a dirty dream he couldn't quite remember. The fact that it had been an X-rated dream was evident in the painful way the head of his cock had snagged in the elastic of the old, worn jockstrap, trapping his piss bone in a snare.

"Tom Bruno?" the Adonis said. He flashed a Cheshire cat's smile and perfect teeth.

Bruno reached down and slipped the bare elastic off his burning cock before replying. "Yeah," he eventually said. "You the rookie from Cincinnati?"

"The one and only. Tim Weare."

The other man's image came into better focus as he unslung his big Army-green duffel bag and extended a bear paw of a hand in a worn, black leather batting glove for Bruno to shake. Both men squeezed hard.

He was a tall guy, easily Bruno's height, and packed fully into a pair of worn jeans with a rip in one knee, white high-top sneakers with no socks, and a yellow tank top beneath an unzipped baseball jacket. He smiled from under a pair of expensive black visor sunglasses and a plain black baseball cap. The rookie looked solid, strong, and able, though he seemed more a boy than a man with his longer-than-major league dark blond hair and shit-eating grin.

"Number 13," Weare said with a respectful military salute. "Reporting for duty!"

SECOND INNING

Bruno stood and yawned, only to suddenly realize that the head of his hard cock was still in open view. He thought about tucking it back, but it wouldn't be the last time Number 13 would see his bat stiff during spring training, so he left it hanging. He even stroked it twice for effect.

Instead of saluting, Bruno extended the same hand he'd touched his rod with. The rookie shook it again without reservation. "Tom Bruno. Number 31," he said in his deep baritone. They shook once more, each man squeezing down hard enough to break the hands of lesser guys.

The statement made Weare's grin widen. "Thirty-one and 13. Hey, it's like twins, only reversed."

Bruno tipped his chin. The hard head of his cock snaked further along his stomach as he stretched. "Hate to bust your bubble, kid, but it ain't some twist of fate. It's Hudson's sense of humor. He likes to pair up a rookie with a veteran. Calls it his 'buddy system.'"

Weare shrugged. "Whatever works, buddy." He grinned another four-alarm smile, knelt beside his Army-green duffel bag, and unzipped it. He pulled out a neat stack of gray and navy-colored baseball shorts, a collection of clean white gym socks, and a pile of white briefs. "Which one's mine?"

Bruno narrowed one eye on the rookie and flashed his best hard-ass stare. His balls itched, tingled, and there was no more privacy in the cabin's cramped quarters to deal with it. "Let's get one thing clear, kid."

"Name's Tim, Mr. Bruno," Weare said in a genuinely innocent voice, oblivious to the anguish behind Bruno's mean face.

Bruno shook his head. All his anger suddenly fled. Against his will, he smiled, too. "That one thing, kid, is my name. It's Tommy Bruno. My friends just use the last one."

"OK, Bruno," Weare said. On his knees the rookie's smile grew even wider.

A shifting in the kid's eyes told Bruno that Weare had noticed his cock. His erection, standing at full mast, reflected off the rookie's black visors in clear view.

Bruno chuckled, grabbed his tool firmly and freed it from the jock. He cocked his head at the bathroom door. "Guess I need to drain it."

"Good idea," Weare said. "I've been dying to take a piss for hours."

"You drive down?" Bruno asked.

Weare nodded. "All night."

"You sure are energetic and chipper," Bruno said. He tucked his raging hard-on back into the paltry cover of his jock as best as he could. "You go first. I can wait a minute."

Weare stood with a groan and a grin and put his clean laundry on the mirrored dresser, seemingly oblivious to the whitewash on the glass behind it.

"Gonna be longer than a minute," the rookie said. He peeled off his visors and flashed two sunny blue eyes. The baseball cap followed, then the jacket. Weare's solid arms rippled in the well-packed yellow tank top. The rookie had the body of a Greek god. "Feels like I ain't pissed in a week."

The younger man moved into the closet-sized bathroom. Bruno's underwear and socks sat in a pile near the head. Bruno followed him to the door, where he studied Weare's perfect piss stance. The sound of splashing raunch echoed off porcelain in the room's tight confines. Weare let out a long sigh of relief as the torrential piss droned to a trickle, then nothing. With his back to Bruno, he shook his meat, tucked it into his jeans, and hauled up his zipper. Bruno filled the doorway when Weare turned around.

"Thought I was gonna bust a fucking nut," the rookie said.

Bruno nodded. "I hear ya." He thumbed the direction of his rank underclothes. "Don't think I'm a slob or something. I'm just not used to bunking with anyone. We got a new kid that does the laundry every day."

Weare nodded as he surveyed the socks and stirrups. "Hey, dude, this is your room. 'Sides, I'm honored to be playing beside the legendary Tommy Bruno. I think you're the nuts."

Bruno grinned. "Yeah, nuts I got—and big ones, kid. But when you're done buttering my balls, you need to take care of your own."

"What?" Weare asked.

Bruno pointed at the stain expanding across Weare's tightly packed groin, a wet spot centered where the rookie's cock head bulged.

"Ah, shit," Weare swore. "Guess I didn't shake it enough." He reached for the nearest towel, the one Bruno had smeared his morning load across. Bruno watched in a sort of horrified excitement as Weare wiped his forehead and face, then passed the towel under his arms into his shaggy pit hair, and finally rubbed the piss puddle with it. "You said they do the laundry for you?"

Bruno nodded.

Weare kicked off his high tops and stood barefoot on two big, handsome feet with hairy toes and well-manicured nails. He popped the button at the top of his jeans, hauled down the zipper, and pushed the faded denim along with a pair of white briefs with their wet stain to his ankles.

Clad only in his yellow tank top, the rookie stood. His bare legs looked like hairy tree trunks, and his swollen balls hung low in a silken, down-covered sac. The rookie's cock could have choked a horse soft. A drop of piss glistened on the head. Weare wiped it away with the towel.

"Sorry about that," he said, standing stupidly with his flaccid cock in the terry-cloth towel.

"Yeah, well you will be if you don't let me near the head," Bruno growled.

"The head?" Weare asked. His smile nervously relaxed as he glanced down at his soft meat.

"The crapper, dumb fuck." Bruno clapped the kid on the shoulder. "Go put your shit away."

Weare's grin returned. "Will do, Bruno."

The veteran closed the door behind him and hovered over the raised toilet seat. Weare's piss swirled unflushed in the bowl. Its raunchy smell filled Bruno's nose.

As little as it pleased him to admit it, Bruno liked the rookie. He seemed genuine, like a country farm boy, though he just as grudgingly admitted a guy with a cock and balls as big as Weare's probably saw more action than qualified him for innocence. The boy was an Adonis and probably got more cunt than a gynecologist.

Bruno smirked to himself as he inhaled a deep breath of Weare's piss. The musky odor made his cock harden fully. He spit on his callused palm and worked it under the trigger of nerves. The sound of the rookie banging around maybe two yards away while he jacked off with only the door separating them intensified the fire in his cock, the itch in his nuts.

He pumped his tool, slowly at first, then steadily worked it faster. The top side of the head was still a little raw from its last jacking, especially on the permanent hard-skin scar where his thumb always gripped his pole just under the arrow.

But Weare…

Bruno heard him close the bureau drawer, the same dresser marked with his spunk. Bruno imagined him clad in the body-hugging uniform of the Seaside Top Socks, trademark white with black letters, a uniform that would fit the kid's Greek-god body perfectly. Bruno thought of him as he jacked his cock in one hand and teased his sweating nuts with the other.

In his fantasy, Weare had on the team uniform that show-cased the baseball shorts a player wore underneath. He had his baseball cap on backwards and sported the black visor sunglasses. Bruno envisioned Weare kneeling between the legs of a gorgeous blonde model; he'd hiked her dress up to her waist and was teasing the damp triangle of her flimsy lace panties with a batting-gloved finger. "Oh, yeah," Bruno groaned.

Weare's infectious Cheshire-cat grin widened as he pulled the scant panties aside, revealing a shaved pair of wet cunt lips.

"I want to eat your pussy," Weare growled. He buried his face in the pink cunt, spreading the lips wide open with his leather-clad fingers as he took the first lick. After that he lapped and slurped like a starving man gone mad. He was so good at chowing on pussy, the model groaned and writhed like she'd gone crazy along with him.

"Finger it," Weare continued. When he pulled back, his mouth was slick with the wetness from her pussy. "Stick a finger in your cunt. I want to watch you get yourself off."

Weare licked his lips. True to his word, he watched.

Bruno lost it at the thought of him kneeling with the huge bulge in his Top Socks uniform, a bulge that showed every vein in his cock, each wrinkle in his ball sac. Bruno imagined Weare, with that four-alarm grin and Greek god's body, lapping the juice clean from his face.

"Shit," Bruno sputtered. He sensed his load building. As the fantasy about Weare ended, he lost control. It was so intense, like pissing, the sound of his come in the toilet bowl echoed with loud plunking noises.

With a growl, he looked down at the viscous string of semen trailing his rough fingers, leading to the milky white puddle swirling in a sea of Weare's piss.

Bruno sighed loudly and stretched, grinning with the same wideness as Weare had in his fantasy. He leaned down to where the rookie's piss-stained briefs sat in a heap near his sweat socks, grabbed them, and wiped his hands, cock, and balls on the kid's underwear.

He was about to throw them back in the pile but paused, eyeing the wet yellow stain. Bruno pressed his nose to the damp cotton and deeply inhaled the smell of Weare's golden juice, then tucked his manhood back into his jock and flushed the toilet.

☆   ☆   ☆

Weare had donned a pair of old sweats cut off at the knees, a matching gray T-shirt, and ankle-length white socks and had slipped his big feet into a pair of old white high-tops. He had one of his bats out. Bruno emerged in time to see him swing it in the tight space with a strength that caused the muscles in his arms and legs to flex powerfully. A muted hum

of displaced air greeted Bruno's return as Weare swung a second time.

"You want to work out together?" Weare asked, lowering
the bat. He rested the tip against the ample nut bulge in his
sweats.

Bruno moved to the mirrorless bureau and pulled the top
drawer open. "You all checked in?"

Weare nodded and adjusted the bulge under his wood with
one batting-gloved thumb. "Yep."

"Sure, kid." Bruno pulled out a full pair of navy-colored
sweats, a gray T, and a fresh pair of white socks. He pulled his
head through the shirt only to meet Weare's handsome blue
eyes in something of a scowl.

"I ain't a kid, Bruno. I'm 23."

Bruno laughed under his breath. He rested his bare ass on
the bed and slipped one big foot into a sock. "Twenty-three?
You're still shittin' yellow." He got the other sock on and
hauled the sweats over his jockstrap. "I got 16 years on you."

"But you also got the stats of a 23-year-old. You play the
game better than anyone."

Weare's comment made Bruno flush. He reached into his
sweats, adjusted his balls and the insatiable cock that never
got enough attention, then grabbed his glove. He slapped
Weare's solid ass with it. "Come on, kid. Let's play ball."

They talked about each other's impressive runs batted in;
the pitching staff's earned run averages; the other guys; the
Socks' home stadium, McKinsey Field in Seaside, Mass.; and
Mitch Hudson and his buddy system while jogging, stretching, hitting, and running bases.

The rain had subsided, leaving the field a sloppy, muddy mess, but the sun's appearance had all the Socks prospects out, like boys in Little League who played no matter what the weather dumped on them.

Curly Ellis, a big black mountain of a man, hit the ball with a crack of thunder. Dressed in a Top Socks practice uniform with a black rain slicker thrown over it, Curly looked more like a force of nature, an ebony rain cloud moving violently around the field. He wore his hair almost to the scalp, which lent his image an even greater fierceness.

Then there was Roger Twain, Number 23, the Thunderbird. His 95-mile-an-hour fastball, registered via the radar gun in digital numbers above the batting cage, had already split three bats in as many days.

Except for Bruno and Mike Young, the Thunderbird was the oldest in the Socks' regular lineup. At 32 he'd been a Top Sock for ten years. His Thunderbird pitching arm would keep him one for years to come.

Bruno watched Twain's classic windup stance and the symmetry with which he pulled in, threw his right foot out and up, then pitched the baseball at warp speed toward the batter beneath the speed clock. He hit it at 30 over the speed limit.

Mike Young jogged past with Number Seven, one of the team catchers, Damon Thorne. A short and burly man with big feet and hands, strong legs, and ice-blue eyes, Thorne's neat goatee and mustache, clipped in a perfect circle around his mouth, and his incredibly hairy body had earned him the nickname "The Werewolf." Thorne's penetrating eyes glistened along with the fresh sweat from under his baseball cap.

"Werewolf," Bruno said. He clapped Thorne's firm butt as he jogged by.

"Good to see ya, Tommy," Thorne huffed.

Scott Bradley swung hard in the batting cage. He grunted with each powerful swing. In the cage next to him, Hector Valenza, the team's shortstop, stretched with his bats resting close by. Valenza, a third-round draft pick from New York in his second year with the Socks, joined Bradley in batting practice. The two strong men moved a lot of air with their wood.

The new recruit in the bull pen, a blond kid with the face of a boy and the body of a man, fired off a knuckleball. With his neat military buzz cut and strong body, the guy was Midwestern farm kid, Bruno guessed, the kind who spent summers picking corn and hay and fielding fly balls. The image brought Ronnie to mind. With a disgusted sigh he turned away, focusing on the gray and gold sky. He started stretching in an attempt to forget, but the look hadn't been lost on Weare.

"You know him?" Weare asked, breaking silence.

"Know who?" Bruno huffed.

"Tuc Vandercastille, the pitcher."

Bruno shook his head. The new kid had nothing to do with it. "Naw," he said. "I was just thinking about my ex-wife."

Weare paused in his stretching but kept one hand on the top of his worn sneaker. "You divorced?"

"Yeah, the cunt. You would've thought her pussy was gold, the way she guarded it."

Weare laughed. Bruno laughed. The sound of baseballs being fired off like bullets and the crack of wood surrounded the pair with a comforting familiarity.

Bruno hunched on his ankles. He felt one of his meaty nuts slide out of his jock and spill down his hairy inner thigh. He narrowed one of his gray-blues on Weare. "What about you, kid? With that fuck pole you must be getting more than any of us."

Weare chuckled again. "I got a girlfriend."

"Bet she's hot." Bruno's cock began to stir. He shuffled on his ankles to give it more room. The jock had it pinned against his leg.

"Yeah. Her name's Barbara. She's got the sweetest pussy— it tastes like flowers, man," Weare unabashedly proclaimed. "And she's tight. Real fucking tight. Even so, I bet you can fit two cocks in her cunt."

Bruno shook his bulge openly. The hot poker of his cock head raged under the elastic along his leg. "Sounds like paradise, kid. I haven't eaten a perfumed cunt in a hundred years."

"Come on," Weare said with a shake of his head. "Big stud like you? You're the one who's probably fucking round the clock."

Bruno rubbed his rod nonchalantly against his hairy leg as he envisioned Weare going down on his girlfriend. That was when he felt the wet spot. A dark stain appeared over the bulge in his sweats. Sticky precome wet his fingertips.

"Shit, kid, we gotta stop talking about getting laid, or I'm gonna cream my shorts."

Bruno rose. Weare jumped up with him. The kid seemed totally comfortable with Bruno's obvious hard-on.

"I'm going into town to get some of that pussy you think I'm chowing on," Bruno said as they jogged past the batting cages.

Weare nodded. "You should, man."

"Mitch doesn't like us fucking during camp. He thinks it drains our aggressions. But kid, I'm gonna explode if I don't get off in something other than my baseball glove."

Weare playfully slapped Bruno's ass, then raced ahead of him. "Last one to the showers has to suck cock."

"Yeah, fuck you!" Bruno bellowed, putting a swift burst of

speed into his effort. Though he'd never admit it to anyone—
let alone himself—his right knee began to throb like hell.

The sweat flew from them as they raced to reach the open
door. The competition ended in a draw, with veteran and
rookie reaching the showers at the same time.

☆   ☆   ☆

Bruno's knee hurt like a fucker. After dinner he stripped to
nothing but his mid-length shorts and crawled into bed with
a plastic bag full of ice cubes for his knee. The kid had worn
him out.

After the first few minutes, with the small TV tuned to a
stupid sitcom and the bedside table lamp on, Bruno thought
Weare would keep him up all night. Surprisingly, after a
mumbled "G'night" that came with a yawn, the TV snapped
off, and Bruno felt the mattress sag to his left. A big, hot foot
brushed his atop the covers.

"Good night, kid," Bruno sighed. "And try to keep your
prick on your side of the bed."

Weare turned over and flashed that damned infectious
Cheshire-cat smile. Clad only in a pair of pale blue boxers, he
smelled of toothpaste and soap.

The rookie reached a big hand into the hair-filled fly and
scratched himself. "You ain't got to worry about my dick."

Bruno cut a loud fart. It wiped the grin off Weare's face
while restoring Bruno's. "'Scuse me."

"You gonna do that all night?"

Bruno chuckled as Weare reached for the lamp. A flick
under the shade bathed the room in darkness. "Naw. I got better things to do than that."

The darkness settled from black to a hazy gray, with a glow

cast by the outside spotlights. The itch between Bruno's legs
grew the longer he tried to deny it, his need to play with his
pole as it stretched under the snug-fitting baseball shorts.

He fought it with Weare so close, hoping the excitement,
the exhaustion of the day would claim the rookie early. The
ice had turned to water by the time Weare started snoring.
With a sigh Bruno dumped the bag of water into the waste
basket at bedside and did—outside of playing baseball—what
he did best.

It might have been the strange surroundings, a bed that
didn't feel like his own back in Cincinnati, or adrenaline that
woke Weare up. It might also have been the steady squeaking
of the bedsprings to his right.

It took him a while to identify his surroundings and the
phantom shapes in the gray haze as a bureau with a mirror,
the door to a bathroom, and a pair of sweats slung over a
chair.

Weare lay still on his back, facing the ceiling. The bed continued to tremble to his right, where Number 31 was. Something wiggled against the tips of hair on his right leg. It was
the hair on Bruno's left, starting first as a tickle, then pro-
gressing into an itch he wanted, needed to scratch. It didn't
dawn on him at first until the shadows stabilized. When he realized Bruno was beating his meat, Weare nervously glanced
down without moving his head. He tried to swallow but nearly choked on the heat in his mouth.

Bruno's hand and cock were a fast blur moving in the darkness. Every now and then the veteran outfielder would stop to
fondle his big nuts, leaving his boner standing like a flagpole

out of the fly in his baseball shorts. Then the handsome fucker would lick one hand, lube his cock, pass the other hand
over his flat, hairy abdomen, and return to his jacking session.

Worse than the heat in his mouth or the itch of Bruno's
coarse leg hairs teasing his own in rhythm to the squeaking
bedsprings, Weare felt something stir between his legs. With
a rising sense of embarrassment, even horror, he felt his own
big cock unfurl in his boxers. He winced as its head jutted out
of his fly. His tool was stiff and straining from the fact his hero
was beating off mere inches away.

He fought the urge to touch it and willed his hard cock to
relax, go limp. But try as he might, the more he thought about
it and the longer he watched Bruno pumping his slick shaft,
the more Weare's cock throbbed. He tried to stuff it back into
his fly, hoping Bruno would be too consumed stroking his
dick to notice. Touching it sent an electric shiver down the
trigger of nerves under his rod's head, a jolt that worked down
the hairy, sculpted column of his cock, into the root, lower
yet, to his swollen, come-packed nuts. It didn't stop there; the
hair on his muscled calves, already tormented by Bruno's
coarse shag rubbing against one of them, stood at attention.
Weare's bare toes tingled.

He sighed. It wasn't intentional, but he couldn't help it.
His shudder made the bed squeak worse than Bruno's palm-
driving session. A moment later the bedsprings stopped quaking. An unnatural silence settled over the room.

Weare knew it—his groan had alerted the big guy spanking
his privates a cock's length away that he'd been found out.
The jiggling bed squeaked to a stop. The hairy leg teasing his
steadied. The comfortable air grew warm, then breathlessly
hot. Weare carefully drew in a guilty breath as his heart started racing. The room smelled of sweaty men.

As he waited in a rising panic, the hand Weare had on his washboard stomach automatically sought his boxer's elastic waistband. By the time he realized what he was doing, the jab of pleasure made him gasp again. Listening to hear if Bruno had resumed his jackfest was suddenly a moot point; he'd slid his probing fingers over the elastic, into the hair-filled open fly where his throbbing cock anxiously waited. Weare let out a deep growl as he gripped the sensitive underside of his dick head and teased the hot, fleshy ring. He unabashedly reached his other hand to his nuts and rolled the fat egg-shaped balls in their sac. He pumped his meat a few times with slow, stiff strokes, alternately tugging on his bag. It felt so good, too good to resist any more—so he didn't try. Weare released the hand on his cock for a split second, just enough time to lap a wad of spit onto his palm. He then snaked it back to his boner and resumed jacking.

The stink in the air—feet, sweat, the musky odor of guys getting off—filled the broken darkness over his eyes with a thousand imagined sexual scenarios. He thought about Barbara and her flowery cunt and all the times he'd diddled it. He dreamed of the time he'd gone to eat it after they'd fucked and had tasted his own seed on the lips of her pussy. He'd shoved his face between them for a better drink of come and had ended up licking every drop. Since then he'd eaten himself out of her regularly and drank his come every time he jacked off. Weare liked—loved—his own spunk. There was something private, natural, and just a little dirty about a guy chowing on his own nut juice. Grinning widely to himself, invisible in the dark, he brought his meat-beating hand to his mouth and smeared his smile with the first sticky trace of what promised to be an enormous load.

His goo tasted strong and bittersweet. Even the precome

was too good to waste. Weare didn't masturbate often; he did-n't need to. But when he did, it was intense. With Bruno, his idol, who'd been doing the same thing with his hard cock, so close by, Weare's dick threatened to shoot a load the likes of which it hadn't done in a long time. That load came closer to arriving when, a second later, the right side of the bed started squeaking again. A long, hot sigh smelling of mint and Bruno's breath whisked past Weare's ears, down his finely haired chest, and into the swampy heat between his legs.

Bruno resumed jacking his cock.

"Ugh," the big guy growled.

Weare closed his eyes in a terrified, horny kind of excite-ment. The darkness turned his inner vision a fiery red. He shucked down his boxers. There was no sense in trying to hide it anymore, so he didn't bother.

"Yeah," he added, pumping his freed, sculpted cock in sync with Bruno's rhythm. In fact, doing together what all men did privately and few owned up to seemed to work them into a shared high that was a total turn-on. It was part brotherhood, part buddy system, even part something Weare had earlier chalked up to hero worship. He admired Bruno. He liked Bruno. Damn, part of him loved Bruno!

"Ah, that's sick," he said aloud at such a thought before he could silence the words. The charge carried in the sweaty air.

"No, it ain't, guy," Bruno huffed in a deep, reassuring voice. His big foot brushed Weare's leg and felt so damn good the rookie spread his own calves apart. Bruno's left size 12 settled on Weare's right. Weare felt the hot sac of the big guy's nuts roll on to his outer thigh. That did it, having Bruno's hairy balls on him. The rumble started in Weare's deepest core, an icy-hot itch that turned to a raging geyser. About the same time Weare's spurt erupted, he heard Bruno groan and swear in that unmistakable growl of a guy coming.

"Yeah!" Weare sputtered.

"Oh, yeah!" Bruno agreed.

The squeaking bed became a tidal wave of fast-motion over-the-top jacking. Weare's cock seemed to double in size in his hand. He did it the way he'd taught himself to, slowing the jack by freeing all the fingers holding his meat except the forefinger and thumb and spanking his cock head between them. Teasing his dick into a violent orgasm gave him more control over it. Weare aimed his bone at his mouth. The first squirt jetted up over his chest, spraying his pecs with sticky rain. The second caught him square in the mouth.

"Ah, shit!" Weare sputtered between gulps of himself, enjoying his own bittersweet taste. The third volley of come hit his chin. The fourth was a trickle, and the fifth, a puke. Bruno groaned again.

Something hit Weare on the cheek, what felt like an enormous drop of hot rain. He flicked his tongue toward the puddle on instinct. It was the final straw; with an exhausted, appeased grin, Weare curled his tongue and lapped the spunk his idol had shot into the air and onto his face. Bruno's jizz was salty and sour. "Fuck!" he exhaled. A heavy growl to his immediate right signaled Bruno agreed. The two men settled back, until their heavy breaths turned to appeased sighs. Weare brought the wetness on his hand up to his mouth.

He was about to clean his fingers off, doing his favorite tongue-bath routine, when he heard the slow, wet, lapping sound in the shadows where Bruno lie. He knew the sound well. There was no mistaking it when a guy was sampling his own seed.

After it subsided, a strange calm settled over the darkness, and with it came a jab of embarrassment Weare couldn't

shake. "Bruno?" he asked in a whisper. The lone word shattered the silence as if it had been a shout, making him seize in
place.

"Yeah, kid," Bruno answered in a sleepy growl.

"Um, like, you won't tell any of the other guys, will you?"
The veteran outfielder didn't answer immediately, not for
what seemed a damnable length of time. When he did, it was
preceded by a deep, gruff laugh. "Don't sweat it, kid. You were
just answering the call. We're guys. Guy's have cocks. Cocks
love being played with. All we did was act like guys. You got
nothing to worry about. Every guy on Earth pulls his pecker
and makes it shoot."

"But..." Weare persisted.

"Naw, kid. Don't worry. I ain't gonna tell. What goes on
between us goes on between us."

Weare exhaled a long sigh and wiped the line of perspiration from his forehead. The sweat was slicker than it should
have been; he'd wiped a string of stale, cooling come into his
hair. A moment later he reached down for the boxers he'd
snapped down to his ankles but never made it. The movement made Bruno stir. His big handsome foot and hairy leg
pulled away. Bruno rolled to one side—the side facing Weare.

That was when he felt the wet, fleshy pole brush the back
of his hand. Bruno's new position sent the big guy's spent
cock against him.

"Uh," the hunky veteran growled.

Weare slowly settled back. The hot knob slipped from his
hand and flopped against his naked outer thigh. Using his
feet, the rookie wiggled out of his boxers and sent them into
the broken darkness at the end of the bed. When he was done
he rolled buck-assed naked over to one side. His wet cock
dripped spent scum over his balls.

Strange as it was, he couldn't help but smile at how satisfying it had been to come with Tommy Bruno. "Bruno," he said. "I'm glad you're my buddy." As soon as he'd said it, Weare felt his face flush. The statement came out sounding stupid. He hadn't meant it as an insult.

Bruno answered by hauling up the sheets and blankets their pumping session had bunched to the foot of the bed. "Thanks," was all he said at first, though his actions spoke volumes. He covered Weare protectively, like a big brother or even...

Weare clamped down quickly on such thoughts with a shake of head.

"You're OK, kid," Bruno said with an appeased sigh. "Now get some sleep. You're gonna need it."

It was the last thing he muttered before a round of deep snoring. The Zs didn't keep Weare awake so much as the big, muscled arm Bruno unconsciously slung over his shoulder. Weare lay there, not daring to move. A hot and hairy hardness pressed against his tight, rugged batter's butt. Like their shared forbidden exchange, there was something comforting, fatherly, brotherly, something even more beyond that. They were, after all, buddies, assigned by Coach Hudson to look out for each other.

The brush of Bruno's chest against his back and the big guy's loud, steady breathing eventually lulled Weare asleep. He felt real good under the veteran outfielder's powerful arm, protected and accepted by the man whose '92 baseball card he carried in his wallet.

☆   ☆   ☆

The brush of Bruno's foot across his leg stirred Weare

awake. He slowly opened his eyes, at first not sure of his surroundings. The sun streaming through the door and the
swampy, stale air inside the cabin lent new meaning to the
term *bull pen*. When the reality of the previous night hit him,
a strange pang of guilt tied Weare's stomach muscles even
tighter. He licked his lips. Memories of tasting Bruno made
the salty taste go sour. He'd tongued another guy's load after
jacking off with him. The thought snapped Weare's eyes up
like shades drawn too tightly. He went up to his elbows in the
quarter of the bed Bruno's spread legs and manly body didn't
dominate. Number 31 was sprawled on his back, big hands
and sexy feet extended like four points on a torture rack.
With his chin resting on the top of his chest, he snored into
the shaggy jungle of hair surrounding his nipples. The center
of the sheet Bruno had hogged was tented a rough seven inches by the flagpole jutting under its thin white veil.

"Fuck," Weare whispered. His eyes focused on the hard
knob sticking up from between his new buddy's legs. The sour
taste on Weare's thin, dry lips vanished in a sudden numbing
rush of heat. Time seemed to slip out of sequence; at one
point he realized he'd been studying Bruno's stiff cock with
unblinking wide eyes. Weare tried to swallow, only to find his
mouth had gone completely dry.

Weare clamped his eyelids down to clear his vision. He
swallowed in an attempt to quench the uncomfortable thirst.
The heat hanging over the bed suddenly pitched the room
into a tailspin around the young rookie. Before he could stop
himself or even contemplate what the action meant, he
reached a trembling hand for the corner of the sheet and gave
it a nerve-racking tug. It slid down below Bruno's chest to his
washboard stomach and snagged in the coarse tangle of shag
just above his meat. The flagpole tilted, then righted.

"I don't fucking believe I'm doing this," Weare said aloud. The dryness in his mouth almost made him choke on the words. He attempted to swallow again as he carefully shifted on the rock-hard mattress, trying to be as quiet as possible. Bruno's steady snoring continued in an uninterrupted rhythm when Weare rolled over to face him. It would only take a quick, easy folding back of the sheet, and he'd be able to see it for himself; the big guy's hand had prevented him from fully viewing it during their wild bone-jacking session together.

Weare reached a shaky hand toward the sheet's edge; the other went down between his own legs. He had gotten so hard, his dick hurt. He quickly stroked it as he gently pulled back the covers. Bruno's stiff cock—its arrow-shaped head capped by a pearl of morning dew—flopped down head-first across his hairy stomach, leaving a trail of precome in a glistening line over his fur-covered belly button. Bruno's two fat bull nuts shifted under the corner of the sheet.

Weare exhaled a long, drawn sigh while shaking his head in disbelief. "Fuck, dude," he whispered. "You're hung everywhere."

The statement brought his eyes back to the rigid pole protruding between his own legs. His cock was thicker than Bruno's, but the big guy had an easy inch on him. Bruno's nuts were like no other man's, though Weare's were a pair to be reckoned with. The musky, unmistakable smell of sweaty balls wafted up from the bed. Weare inhaled it deeply. As he slowly jacked his cock, the hunger overwhelmed him. There was no more fighting it. He lowered his hungry mouth toward Bruno's nuts and inhaled. It was true: All guys had that smell on their sacs. Unable to stop himself, he extended his tongue and nervously licked the silky, shaggy pouch. He moved upward and buried his nose in the hot, swampy hair near Bruno's hard-on. Weare swore, then he did it.

He lapped at the hard cock. The salty taste was incredible! A gentle but firm lick filled his mouth with a taste of salt, sweat, piss, soap, and a hundred other things. It ended at Bruno's navel, where he cleaned up the big guy's precome. Its familiar saltiness drove him over the edge. Weare knew he needed more.

He shifted on the bed into a better position. Before he could talk himself out of it, he gripped Bruno's bat and sucked the head into his mouth. The spongy flesh turned rock-hard. For his effort Weare was rewarded by a mouthful of sticky juice, water for a thirsty man. He sucked until all at once the big guy jerked violently on the bed. Weare spit Bruno's dripping cock out of his mouth and jumped up. He seized in place at the bedside, fearing he'd been caught.

There, with his own hard, hairy cock hanging out in the open, Weare waited—waited for the fist of a pissed-off man who'd caught another guy sucking his straight man's dick, waited for the end of his day-old career with the Top Socks, and an end to his idol's respect.

But the end never came.

Bruno snorted, farted, and rolled over, burying his wet, excited spike under his flat abdomen. His bared asshole winked at Weare from beneath a layer of black hair. Weare held his breath as Bruno's low-hangers spilled out beneath his tight-looking hole. It horrified him because, as scared as he was, he wanted to eat Bruno's ass more than he'd ever lusted after any hole in his life.

The room stayed quiet except for Bruno's steady snoring. Weare's rapidly beating heart steadied. When it became apparent he'd gotten away with his forbidden taste of Bruno's cock, a proud grin replaced the rookie's terrified scowl. He returned to the bed and carefully placed palms on either side of the veteran's muscular, hairy calves, then carefully push-upped his way to the veteran's butthole. Slowly, with his eyes locked on the tight, puckered knot, Weare lowered himself toward Bruno's ass. He was about to steal a taste when Bruno's snore became a snort, then a deep, feral rumble. Bruno again rolled onto his back, spreading his legs and big feet. Weare quickly, painfully found his discarded boxers, then pulled them on. He tucked his straining cock inside them and stepped to the cabin's open door as Bruno's sleepy bedroom eyes greeted the day. Weare could only watch while the big guy yawned, rubbed his dreamy gray-blues, and snaked a hand around his perfect, still-stiff piss hard-on.

Weare stretched at the door in an attempt to appear innocent. He opened it wider. A fresh, cool gust of morning air swept into the choking musky guy haze hanging over the room. When he turned back, looking calm and guiltless, the mosaics of light spilling through the door frame made Bruno squint. "You're awake," he said in a purposefully surprised, jocular voice.

"Mmm," Bruno growled. As his sleepy eyes adjusted to the light, his handsome face with its two-day-old stubble broke in a slight, cocky smile. "Hard to sleep, specially with Little Bruno needing to be walked." He playfully jacked himself. As confused as he was, Weare watched, trying his best not to seem obvious.

Weare slung one arm over his head and braced the door in a cool tough-guy pose. "Does Tom Jr. wake you up like that every morning?"

Bruno released his rod, then swung his big bare feet and strong jogger's legs off the bed. "Tom Jr.'s my boy, though the tough bastard's more of a man than half this team. He turned

20 a month ago. Me and Little Bruno, however, are gonna have us a piss and a shower and maybe a little fun."

"Yeah?" Weare asked dumbly.

Bruno scratched his nuts and flashed a shit-eating grin. "Maybe we'll go into town tonight, Little Bruno and me, to get some of that cunny you think I'm overdosing on."

Weare smiled. "Coolness, man."

Bruno stood and stretched. His rock-hard piss boner stood up, away from his hairy stomach as he yawned. "You up to some breakfast and coffee before we bust our balls out there?"

Releasing his hold on the door, Weare nodded. He went to the dresser and hauled out a pair of sweats. "Sounds like a plan, buddy. Go grab a shower, and I'll rustle us up two cups of joe. How you take yours?"

"With buckets of cream," Bruno said.

The rookie's grin sagged into a nervous smile. "Sure thing, guy."

Bruno playfully slapped Weare's ass while pulling fresh briefs, a new jock, and a pair of sweatpants out of his dresser. With that and no more, he disappeared into the bathroom, leaving Weare alone. The sound of the big guy's piss splashing in the toilet bowl filtered through the thin door.

Weare waited breathlessly for a few minutes after that, until he heard Bruno growl. He knew the veteran had shot a big load. A moment later the shower came on. Standing alone and hard with his sweats in his hands, Weare felt a thin line of drool slip out of a corner of his mouth and scatter when he shook his head.

"This is crazy," he mumbled. "I sucked my teammate's cock. I licked his bag. I almost ate his asshole!" He looked down at the biggest erection he could ever recall having between his legs. "Bruno. Tommy Bruno. Fuck!"

He hastily hauled on his sweats, pulled a pair of white socks onto his big bare feet, then tucked them into his sneakers. With his head halfway into a fresh gray T-shirt, he threw open the screen door. The bright morning sun should have been a relief, but it only crawled worse on nerves already tensed beyond their norm.

"I know what I have to do," he mumbled under his breath. He was so consumed by his thoughts, he didn't notice the other man until the deep voice shocked him back to the moment.

"You say something, dude?"

Weare stopped dead in his tracks. He glanced slightly down to see Damon Thorne, the Top Socks' star catcher, stretching near his cabin. Weare forced a smile. "Just talking to myself, Mr. Thorne."

"Mister?" Thorne laughed. "I only got a few years on you, kid. It's Damon. There are no misters in the Top Socks. We're a pretty loose bunch."

"That's good to know, Damon." Weare said. The two men shook hands and playfully ass slapped each other's concrete butt cheeks. After that Weare hurried toward the pay phone. He had to make the call—quickly, before the heat between his legs drove him mad.

Weare's cock stayed hard for most of the day. It was bad in the morning when Bruno emerged smelling cleanly of soap and shampoo, dressed in his crisp, clean Top Socks uniform, and it didn't get better—not after a rigorous morning work-out, during which Mitch Hudson barked out orders like a mad dog, or in the early afternoon, when the Florida heat and a hot spring wind intensified the horny fire surging in his blood.

His cock, confined in a pair of skin-tight white baseball shorts, bulged painfully in his new uniform. Instead of going to lunch with the guys, he went back to the cabin, stripped down, and locked his ass in the head. His pile driving launched four steady pop-up shots into the air. After that his nuts began to cool off. Weare cleaned himself up by wiping the spunk off his chest and stomach with a pair of Bruno's nasty socks.

As the excitement faded, he sucked his own load off the toes of the socks that still smelled like Bruno, then mopped the sweat off his brow. He quickly dressed and joined the team back on the field. There he found Bruno, and together—rookie and vet—they got physical again.

THIRD INNING

Roger Twain did his classic windup and pitched. His fastball slammed Damon Thorne's catcher's glove with a thundercrack as the radar gun clocked him at 92 miles per hour. But halfway into the next windup, he suddenly doubled over in pain. "Shit!" Twain swore, dropping the ball as he tried to walk off the pain in his leg. "Fuck!"

Weare stepped into the on-deck circle, where Bruno had been swinging his bat. Bruno tapped the dirt from his cleats with the head of his lumber and leaned closer to the rookie. They watched Hudson cross to the mound with the team's trainer, Doc Hanson. A jumble of low whispers passed between them as the trainer began to rub the top of Twain's inner thigh. Hudson's hard face broke into a sweat. He slapped Twain's ass, and the Thunderbird began to limp away, supported between them.

"Aaron!" Hudson yelled. A mid-20s fastball pitcher Weare didn't recognize pulled on his Top Socks cap and hotfooted it across the diamond from the bench. He and Damon Thorne practiced throwing the ball with five warm-up tosses.

"That's Aaron Sweeney," Bruno growled. "Great curve ball, but watch out. He's a moody prick."

Weare raised his visor shades for a better look at the new

pitcher. Number 44 looked solid, a good six feet and maybe a few inches more, he guessed, of hard, low-fat muscles. Sweeney kept his blond hair in a military buzz cut, and even from a distance Weare could see the cold blue of his eyes. Sweeney's game face, even on a practice squad, was a mean one; his pouty pink lips tightened during the windup. He narrowed his eyes before blasting the last of his warm-ups at Thorne. One of the new guys, Hector Valenza, had been in the batter's box when Twain went down. Valenza again stepped up to the plate. Without blinking, Sweeney pitched, catching him with a strike. On the second pitch Valenza golfed the ball to left field for a single. As the shortstop peeled off his batting gloves at first base, Weare remembered Bruno's words. True to them, nobody learned faster about Sweeney's bad temper than Ricky Catalano.

"Batboy!" Sweeney bellowed.

Cat had been talking with Scott Bradley in the dugout when the tantrum began. It quickly escalated after Sweeney threw down his glove. He kicked it and a cloud of dirt off the mound.

"What the fuck?" Sweeney shouted. "Either get the bats or get lost!"

Catalano nervously trotted to the plate, looking confused and humiliated.

Weare saw Bruno had been right about Sweeney. "What an asshole," he mumbled under his breath.

Damon Thorne ultimately calmed Sweeney's rising anger by putting him in his place. "Cool it, Aaron. Cut the kid some slack."

"I'll cut him a new asshole if he pulls this shit during exhibition!"

"I said cool it!"

Thorne tore off his catcher's mask and narrowed his eyes as he crossed to the mound. "Pick up your glove and play ball. Don't bust the kid for no good reason!"

They focused on each other like opponents instead of teammates. Thorne eventually stared Sweeney down, who reluctantly picked up his glove, swearing something to himself. Thorne crossed back to home plate, slapping Cat's butt on his way past. "It's OK, kid. You're doing a great job. Carry on."

The Werewolf's words didn't end the confrontation. A second later Hudson unhooked himself from Twain's arm and returned to the diamond. "What's the problem here, girls?" It was a demand, not a question.

"Nothing," Thorne said, pulling on his mask.

"Oh, yeah?" Hudson growled. He focused on Aaron Sweeney. The handsome, arrogant prick of a pitcher glanced away.

"Yeah," Aaron said. "Nothing."

"That's what I thought." Hudson returned to the dugout. "Scott…" Bradley front-and-centered. "Help Roger get to first aid. I'd do it myself, but I obviously can't leave the kiddies alone."

Bradley nodded. He took Twain's arm. The big guy's face was a mask of pain, but together they buddy-systemed off the field.

Hudson turned toward Bruno and snapped, "You're up." Bruno flashed Weare a four-alarm grin as he hustled to the plate. Weare replaced him in the on-deck circle. "All right, men, let's play some ball!"

The door banged open, and Bradley helped Twain hobble in. A second after it closed, the phone on Doc Hanson's desk rang.

The team's trainer released Twain to Bradley and grabbed the phone on the second ring. "Hanson," he stated. "Yeah, yeah. I'm on my way." Doc hung up and spun around. "One of your new guys just took a pitch off the helmet."

"Shit," Twain said. "Who?"

"That rookie, Timmy Weare," Hanson said on his way out the door. "He's a strong boy. He'll be OK."

Bradley eased Twain onto the big chair near Hanson's desk. "What about Roger?"

"How's it feel now?" Hanson asked, turning around.

Twain's sweat-streaked red face was the best answer. "I think I pulled something south of my belt, Doc."

"Groin?"

Twain nodded.

"Help him get undressed," Hanson said to Bradley. "Then up on the examination table."

"And?" Bradley persisted.

"Do whatever it takes to make him comfortable till I get back. This shouldn't take too long." With that and no further advice, Doc Hanson was gone, leaving Bradley to his own means. He shrugged and turned back to the Thunderbird.

"You heard the man, big guy." He helped Twain over to the white-sheeted hospital table and made him rest his ass against its edge. "Keep your can there. Can you take off your spikes?"

Twain moved to try. He got no further than a hunch when a searing bullet of pain forced him back. He danced in place, swearing as Bradley helped him walk it off.

"OK, OK!"

"Aw, Fuck!" Twain howled. He settled his ass back against the bed, both cleats still on. The fresh line of perspiration that had broken across his brow said everything Twain couldn't.

"Relax, big guy," Bradley said in a soothing voice. "Doc's

gonna be back soon as he throws a few aspirin down that hard-headed rookie's throat. Let's get you comfortable till he does."

Number 11 squatted at Number 23's size 13 feet. Bradley took the Thunderbird's left foot carefully on his knee and unlaced his cleat. Twain drew in a deep breath.

"You OK?" Bradley asked.

Twain nodded. He forced a smile. "You won't be, though, when you peel that sneaker off."

Both men laughed. "I don't care, dude," Bradley said. "Everybody's feet stink in the Top Socks locker room." Twain's sneaker came off, revealing the sweat-soaked cotton of his big foot. So close up, Bradley got a faceful of the clean, athletic smell of Twain's toes. For effect—and to set the Thunderbird at ease—Bradley lowered his nose to their star pitcher's foot and took a good sniff. "Smells real nice—clean and healthy, the way a man's sweat is supposed to smell."

"Yeah," Twain chuckled, shaking his head. "You like smelling my feet?"

Bradley flipped Twain his middle finger and dropped Twain's foot. "Can't get enough of your stinkin' feet, big guy." He removed the other cleat quickly. When he lifted from his crouch, Twain had unbuttoned his uniform shirt, and seemed to have relaxed some. "How's the pain?"

Twain nodded. "On a scale of one to ten, it's down to five if I don't move, and that's being generous. This fucker's just twitchin' to hurt me."

Bradley narrowed his baby-blues on Twain. "You gotta drop trou, big guy, before Doc gets back."

The Thunderbird unbuckled his belt and hauled down his zipper. The uniform pants, like on most men in the majors, might as well have been spray painted on him. They remained firmly on his butt. "That's it for me," Twain said. "You're gonna have to do the rest."

Bradley nervously shuffled in place. "Like, you mean, get you out of your pants, dude?"

"You heard Doc. I can't do it without you, buddy." Twain's face twisted in a pain-riddled scowl, but he managed a grin. "'Sides, I won't tell no one if you don't."

"Asshole," Bradley said, matching Twain's grin. He gripped the unzipped pants, one hand at the front, the other around Twain's rear, and carefully lowered them off the Thunderbird's ass. Twain's stark white jockstrap was tight over his full cup and the baseball underwear beneath. Bradley couldn't help but notice, especially when he eased back to his knees to pull Twain's pants down off his ankles.

It wasn't that he hadn't seen the Thunderbird's horse cock and nuts hanging low from all that dirty-blond hair before, soaped up and soft most of the time, half hard others. That was expected in the showers. It was normal for a guy to casually size up his teammates in the locker room. Everyone did it. Bradley knew who was hung and who wasn't, who had bull nuts and who was average. The Thunderbird had been blessed with a pair of big ones, and from what he'd seen of his cock at a safe distance and now, so close to his face, he had a pretty good idea of what Twain sported in his cup.

Bradley took a heavy swallow. He carefully lowered Twain's uniform pants over his stirrups, then off his sweaty socks. Sucking in a deep breath didn't clear his head like he'd hoped. All it did was fill his senses with the clean, heady smell of another man's sweat. With a terrified glance down, he realized he was getting hard. His cock unfurled in the plastic cup protecting his privates. The pressure on his nuts grew overwhelming.

Just when it seemed he couldn't stand the itch in his balls

or his own confusion another second, Twain's pants finally came off. Bradley bunched them and stood, sighing as he rose. The movement allowed his cock a little breathing room.

"There," was all he could think to say. "Let's get you up on that bed, so Doc can fix your sorry ass."

Twain shook his head. "This is gonna hurt like a fuckin' bitch."

Bradley adjusted his cup. His cock, still hard, pushed into his nuts, making him wince. "You're telling me, pal."

"I think I should get out of my shorts before I try this," Twain drawled. It made sense, and before Bradley could argue the point, the Thunderbird tucked two thumbs into the top elastic band of his jock and underwear and shucked both down. This bared the thick fur along Twain's flat, hard abdomen and the patch of coarse man hair capping his crotch. Bradley tried not to look beyond the baseball shorts, jock, and cup snagged around Twain's knees, as far down as the big guy was able to push them. "You gotta do the rest, dude. Shit, if I go any further, I'm gonna see stars."

"Join the club," Bradley said. He swallowed again, forced a nervous smile, and reached a trembling hand toward Twain's sweat-soaked underwear.

The quiver in his touch didn't escape the Thunderbird's keen predator's eyes. "What's the fuckin' problem, dude? It's not like you're getting off on pulling my pants down."

Twain's swampy underwear and jock felt warm in Bradley's fingers. "No. No way, guy."

"You do like girls, don't you?" Twain asked in a matter-of-fact tone.

Bradley huffed sarcastically. "As much as you do."

"I'm married. It's different."

"You're also ugly," Bradley laughed. He eased Twain's

musky jock off his big feet, bunched it up, and whipped it at the star pitcher, catching him square in the face with his own nasty underwear. "If I wanted to fuck around with a guy, he'd be prettier than you!"

"Fuck you," Twain joked. He tossed his shorts into a pile on top of his uniform pants.

"Not in my worst and your wildest," Bradley joked. "Let's get that ugly, hairy ass of yours up for Doc to take care of, so I don't have to look at it anymore." He slung an arm around Twain's hot, bare shoulder. "At the count of three—one, two, three!"

With Bradley's assistance he hopped his ass onto the exam table. Bradley knew it hurt even before the Thunderbird roared in agony; Twain's entire face went white. The fresh sweat on his forehead rapidly turned clammy. Twain seized in place on the stretcher and pawed at his inner thigh.

"Fuck!"

"What?" Bradley asked. "Tell me what I can do, man!"

"Down under my ass, dude. Shit, Scott. I'm gettin' a mean charley horse!"

Bradley went on automatic. He'd seen the way the trainers stretched out a pulled muscle enough times on himself. He leaned down and gripped the Thunderbird's left leg by its hairy calf, arching it over his shoulder. Twain roared. "It's OK, big guy. I'm gonna take care of you!"

At first, he didn't notice the tears in Twain's pale blue eyes or his tightly clenched jaw with its forest of day-old stubble. He didn't see the direct result of his action to help the Thunderbird loosen up. The room began to spin around Number 11's eyes.

"*Shhh,*" Bradley said in a deep, soothing growl. "It's all right, big guy. All right…"

Twain's pensive mask relaxed. His breathing slowed. The painful tears in his eyes began to dry. When Bradley's peripheral vision restored, the first thing he noticed was how he'd been gently stroking Twain's hairy inner thigh and buttocks, rubbing the tough muscles like a seasoned pro. "How's that feel?"

Twain clamped his eyelids down. "Real good, buddy," he sighed in a relieved huff. As Bradley worked his fingers along the inside of the Thunderbird's leg, Twain growled like a contented bear. The slightest of grins replaced the look of pain on his face. "Oh, yeah. Real good."

The odor of man sweat filled Bradley's senses. He took a deep breath of the athletic smell while continuing to rub Twain's muscles, hypnotized by the closeness of their bodies. As his hand rubbed the star pitcher's inner thigh in a widening arc, Bradley's fingers slipped under Twain's firm butt and slid into his hairy crack. Twain spread his legs. The smile on his face intensified, and suddenly Bradley understood why. Twain's eight-inch horse cock had stiffened to its full size, snagging under the second baseman's thumb as it grew. "Aw, fuck," Bradley sputtered, releasing Twain's dick. He set it back on Twain's concrete inner thigh, feeling the other man's sweaty nut bag roll beneath his fingertips. "Dude, I'm sorry!"

"I'm not," the Thunderbird growled. "Keep going, pal. You're doing a great job."

Bradley tried to fight it, tried to think that he didn't like what was unfolding between them, but it was no use. Swearing under his breath, he gripped Twain's thick horse cock and jacked it from the hairy root to its straining mushroom-shaped head. Twain reacted with an open-mouthed groan and lifted his left butt cheek the slightest, pushing his cock into Bradley's masturbating hand. Bradley's other hand returned to Twain's crack and teased the puckered knot of the big guy's shitter.

"Your wife won't mind?" Bradley asked. Hoping she wouldn't, he stroked the Thunderbird's rod a few times for effect.

"No," Twain growled. "She'd probably thank you, not that she's ever gonna know. Do it, buddy. Just like Doc Hanson ordered. Do what it takes to make me feel good."

The star pitcher's invitation was all Bradley needed; the second baseman leaned down and took his first forbidden taste of Twain's cock. He licked its underside, his mouth filling with the clean, salty taste of another man's healthy athletic sweat. Once he'd bathed Twain's dick in spit, he carefully sucked its fat head and the first few inches into his mouth.

Twain responded with a deep growl. "You've done this before, son."

Bradley spit out the Thunderbird's horse cock. "No way, man! I swear, this is my first time." A flushed look overwhelmed Bradley's clean-cut, all-American boy face.

"Yeah, right," Twain sighed deeply. "I know a seasoned cocksucker when his mouth's on my dick."

"Nuh-uh," Bradley persisted. "I don't know what got into me, man. I don't suck cock."

The Thunderbird snaked a hand down and started jacking the cock Bradley had spit out. "Come clean, guy. Who was it? Your best buddy? Did one of your brothers catch you spanking your meat and give you the real thing?"

A horrified look crossed Bradley's face. "No way, man. That's sick!"

"I told you to come clean, pal. Was it one of your teammates, maybe back in the minors? Some guy with a fat, hard cock who knew how much you loved it and let you suck him off in the locker room because his girlfriend wouldn't?"

"I'm telling the truth!"

"Yeah," Twain cooed, a shit-eating grin on his face. "If you ain't lying about how much you like sucking cock, why are you still hanging around so close to mine?"

Bradley's Adam's apple knotted under the influence of a heavy swallow. He didn't counter Twain's accusation. In fact, he didn't say a word. He didn't need to. His actions spoke volumes.

Wordlessly, swiftly, Bradley went back to his knees between Twain's spread legs. With the big guy's fingers still wrapped around his cock, Bradley sucked it into his mouth. Twain released his bat and watched all eight inches disappear down the second baseman's throat. Bradley buried his nose in the Thunderbird's mossy-smelling pelt, where he stopped sucking long enough to take a deep whiff. He also took hold of Twain's big sweaty sac of nuts.

Twain grunted and smiled. "That's it, son. Show the Thunderbird how much you love sucking his hairy fuckin' cock. *Ungh...*"

Bradley showed him, all right. He sucked Twain's boner hard until he tasted the first sticky trace of the big guy's pre-come. Pulling back so that just the head of Twain's cock was on his lips, Bradley tongued the drooling piss slit, catching every drop.

"You like that, buddy?" Twain growled.

"Fuck, yeah," Bradley said. He did love the taste of Twain's cock, the feel of it in his mouth, the smell of clean jock sweat coming off the low-hanging balls beneath it. He resumed sucking.

At one point the young, blond second baseman glanced up. Twain's handsome, rugged face, his pale blue eyes and mouth with its day-old stubble, looked again as though he was in pain, but Bradley knew better. Seeing him so turned-on made the second baseman smile. He licked the wet head of Twain's cock, then ran his tongue over the other man's bag.

"Yeah, son, lick my fuckin' nuts," Twain grunted. Bradley sniffed and sucked on each of Twain's nuts, focusing first on the left, then the right. By the time he was done, Twain's balls glistened with spit. After Bradley had licked them loose and they were hanging as low as Twain's nuts got, he hauled the heavy sac up, exposing the tight, hairy hole at the center of the big guy's perfect, hard butt.

"Fuckin' do it," Twain urged.

Bradley started by licking the big guy's sore inner thigh, kissing his wounds as if to kiss away the pain forever. He teased Twain's asshole with wet flicks. The moist, hairy hole twitched.

"Aw, come on, dude. Eat my fuckin' butt!"

Bradley sighed out a hot breath between Twain's spread legs. "You want me to?" he teased. Twain grunted his answer as he fidgeted on the examination table, driving his cock into the second baseman's masturbating hand. "Anything you want, you big stud, but first there's something I want." Before Twain could ask, Bradley eased the star pitcher's big left foot between his hands.

"What're you doing?"

Bradley lowered his nose to the toe-damp cotton and breathed in the smell of Twain's sweaty socks. He growled the way Twain had, a deep, appeased sigh. "Fuckin' A, man."

Twain's eyes narrowed. "You like sniffin' a man's big stinkin' feet?"

"Yeah, guy. I got a thing for men's feet. Sniffin' 'em and more." With that he took the tip of Twain's foot, sock and all, into his mouth. He sucked on the sweat-soaked cotton.

Twain flexed his big toes against the second baseman's teeth. "Fuck," Twain chuckled. "That feels kinda funny—but good."

"Tastes good too," Bradley slurred around the big toe in his mouth. "You got hot fuckin' feet."

Without asking he eased down Twain's stirrups, then his socks, baring the big guy's handsome feet. He ran his nose and tongue around the Thunderbird's toes, paying homage to them. Twain bucked at the strangely pleasurable sensation wracking him from the ankles down, until it proved to be too much. Bradley continued to suck contentedly on the toes of his right foot as Twain yanked it up, getting a tongue across the top of his size 13.

"Enough sucking on my stinkin' feet, pal. Get your fuckin' face up here," Twain ordered. "And put that square fuckin' tongue of yours in my round hole!"

Bradley nodded. "A deal's a deal, big guy." He zeroed in on Twain's hairy asshole, spearing it with his tongue. The Thunderbird groaned as Bradley ate out his knot with hungry, wet licks. The second baseman teased the oily hole with two fingers, then used them to spread Twain wide open. Bradley dove in. With his tongue inside the star pitcher's can and both lips on the outside of Twain's hole forming a tight seal, Bradley ate away.

"Chow on it, boy," Twain groaned. "Eat out that shit hole, son!"

Bradley again glanced up between Twain's legs to see the big guy stroking his own cock. Bradley dove in deeper. He felt Twain seize in place from the sudden rush of heat.

"Yeah, boy," sighed the star pitcher. "I like seeing that Ivy League face of yours working on my privates. You're fuckin' handsome to behold, son. Real fuckin' beautiful."

Bradley lapped Twain's hole one last time before rising up a notch. He grabbed the Thunderbird's cock and forcibly jacked it. "You want me to keep going, big guy?" Twain growled an expletive. "Then you're gonna have to help me out."

Twain nodded reluctantly. "You give what you get. It's only fair."

Bradley moved closer to the examination table in an attempt to prevent the Thunderbird from reaggravating his pulled groin. Twain knew just what to do. He unzipped the pants of Bradley's baseball uniform and went fishing around inside. After some fumbling, Twain pulled out the second baseman's cup and had pushed down his jockstrap and midlength underwear. Bradley groaned at the feel of Twain's rough pitching hand around his steel-hard cock. His was as long as Twain's, though not as thick, and was capped by a straining pink head.

"Nice one, son," Twain said. He clamped his forefinger and thumb around its head and squeezed down. A thin line of syrupy precome seeped out. "What else you got in there?"

Twain freed two egg-sized balls covered in blond peach fuzz and rolled them in their meaty sac. With his other hand the Thunderbird resumed playing with Bradley's cock. Another pearl of precome slipped from its winking piss slit.

"Shit, buddy," Bradley huffed. "Don't just play with it. Suck it!"

"What the fuck," Twain said. Flashing his trademark shit-eating grin, he sucked it.

And sucked it.

They settled into an awkward sixty-nine atop the examination table, with Bradley atop the star pitcher. Twain lowered the second baseman's asshole onto his face and began tonguing it, slowly at first. Bradley focused again on Twain's cock.

"Yeah, suck that fat dick," the Thunderbird ordered between licks. "Show me how much you like it!"

Bradley again sucked on Twain's balls, taking the left one, then the right, and finally both at the same time into his mouth. He gently chewed on the wrinkled, hairy sac, swabbing it clean of the accumulated sweat caused by their hard workout in the Florida sun.

Twain took a final lick of Bradley's hole before sticking a finger up into the moistened knot. The second baseman bucked. "Shit! What're you doing?"

The Thunderbird eased a second finger in, teasing the other man's prostate. "I wanna fuck you, son."

Bradley spat out a shocked, "No way, dude! I don't get fucked. Least of all by that donkey dick of yours." Undaunted, Twain's fingering continued, with a third finger painfully joining the other two. Bradley lurched up but took it.

"Yeah, and neither of us chokes up on another guy's bat. Get that tight, pink cunt of yours down on my cock now that I've loosened you up!"

Bradley let out a muffled swear as his asshole slid off Twain's fingers with a sloppy, wet suctioning noise. Wordlessly, he worked his way down to the star pitcher's cock. He was about to sit on it when Twain stopped him.

"No, guy. Spin around so your cock is facing me. I'll take care of you. Shit, you're gonna take care of me!" Bradley assumed the position and sat down hard. The rush of heat was painful before it turned pleasurable. "Ease up, son," Twain grunted. He gripped his rock-hard bat and guided it in farther, stopping long enough to rub it on Bradley's nuts. "You can take it. That's it, slugger. Yeah, fuckin' take it!"

Twain's horse cock popped through Bradley's tight hole and slid in to the hilt. Twain gave a final thrust upwards, and he was buried to his balls inside the second baseman's ass.

The agonizing look on Bradley's sweat-soaked forehead relaxed. When his tightly shut eyes again opened, Twain's ruggedly handsome face again welcomed him back. "Fuck!" Bradley howled.

Twain grinned. "You can take it, son. That cunt of yours is tighter than my wife's. Ride it, buddy. Ride that big bull cock!"

Both men worked together, with Twain anchoring his hands on Bradley's legs. Bradley pistoned up and down on the cock lodged in his asshole. His own wood was so hard, it slapped his flat, fuzzy stomach, spraying strings of hot precome across his six-pack. True to Twain's promise, the big guy gripped Bradley's shaft and started jacking it, using the precome for lube.

"Yeah, Thunderbird," Bradley groaned. "I love your cock—in my mouth, up my fuckin' asshole. I love you in my cunt, dude."

"You want to be my special guy when we're out on the road and my wife's pussy is a thousand miles away? You and me? You want to be fuck buddies?" Bradley nodded and grunted a response. "I love your hole, pal." His next sentence came out as a mouthful of swears and grunts. He followed it with something Bradley had no trouble recognizing. "I'm gonna shoot it, man!"

Bradley picked up the pace, riding Twain's dick. The star pitcher's grip on his cock tightened. With sweat cascading into their eyes, stinging their vision and filling the room with a hot, musky haze, the smell and synchronicity pushed them both over the edge. Twain unloaded first, firing a blast of hot bull come up into Bradley's asshole. The big guy moaned loudly and squeezed down on the second baseman's cock. Bradley lurched up, partly because of the hot flood that had invaded his can, mostly because Twain's fist on his cock sent him into overdrive.

"Here it comes!" sighed Bradley. In one fluid motion, he freed his well-stretched asshole from the star pitcher's spent bat and leaned forward into Twain's open, waiting mouth. Bradley shot once, twice, a third, fourth, and fifth time, emptying both his balls down the Thunderbird's throat. Tugging on Bradley's nuts with his rough pitcher's grip, Twain forced out a sixth and seventh shot. The eighth was barely a trickle. The Thunderbird swallowed everything except what was left on his face when Bradley pulled out, and the second baseman took care of that when the two men kissed.

"Fuck, son, that was great," Twain groaned. Bradley showered the big guy's stubbled face with hot, small kisses. He was about to dismount when Twain took hold of his wrists. "Not yet. Up on my face, dude."

"What?" Bradley sputtered. A moment later Twain reached between his legs, clamped the second baseman by his butt, and forced him up. Once he was in place, Bradley felt a hot, wet breath tease his asshole. Four long, deep licks invaded his shitter as Twain cleaned up his own mess. That done, the layer of sweat on Bradley's face began to cool, and the room fell under a strange silence, one broken only by the sound of Twain's wet lapping. The sensation made Bradley tremble.

Twain finished quickly. He slapped Bradley's ass to signal he was done. The second baseman dismounted the examination table and the Top Socks' opening day starting pitcher. He spun around and lowered to the handsome face wet with both their come.

"Thanks, buddy," Twain growled. "I needed that."

The taste of Twain's cock made him linger a moment longer. When they parted he took a deep breath, then just as deeply let it out. "Last year. A good buddy," he said.

Twain narrowed his pale-blues. "What?"

"You asked who it was that turned me on to sucking cock. Last year. One of my buddies on the team. It happened after a game, when we were both feeling good. It just happened."

"Well, we're buddies now on this team, son. The closest of buddies."

Bradley grinned. "You know it, buddy." He retrieved his T-shirt and wiped the torrent of sweat off his forehead, patted it under his arms, between his legs, over his butt. He mopped up Twain, paying careful attention to his half-hard, spent cock.

"So, who was it?" Twain persisted.

Bradley grinned and shook his head. "I don't suck and tell. What goes on between me and a pal stays there and nowhere else."

"I can respect that," Twain said. "Anyone I know?"

With a chuckle and a sigh, Bradley hauled on his baseball shorts. Before he could answer, the sound of footsteps shuffling outside the exam room door filtered in. Doc Hanson strolled nonchalantly in, only to stop at the sight of Bradley's near-nakedness.

"Uh, Doc," the second baseman said. "I was kinda hoping you could give me the once-over when you're done with Roger."

Twain flashed a cocky grin at Bradley's quick thinking. It was a good explanation, even though it didn't necessarily cover the trail of sweat-soaked clothes or the sweaty stink in the air. But by the way Hanson handled both their nuts and fingered their assholes during the examination, they figured they had nothing to worry about.

☆   ☆   ☆

Bruno leaned in and sighed. "You look like shit!"

Weare flipped the veteran his middle finger. "Then why the fuck are you gawking at me like you want an autograph?"

"Must be that sick fascination you get when you drive by an accident. You tell yourself not to look, but you can't help it. Same thing."

Bruno took Weare by his stubbled chin and tipped his head so he could see the cut on his ear. "You think that hurts now, kid, just wait till tomorrow. With all that black and blue, you ain't gonna need any eye-black for a week."

"Thanks," Weare said. He boxed Bruno's hand away and stood. "I may look like shit from this shiner, but you look like a million bucks. What's up?"

Bruno, freshly shaven and smelling like expensive cologne, beamed proudly from the complement. "My dick," he laughed. He coolly unbuttoned his navy-colored jacket. The crisp white shirt underneath was tucked into his jeans. Bruno wore faded leather deck shoes and white socks on his big feet. "I'm gonna score some of that pussy you think I'm always getting."

"Dressed like that," Weare said, "you're gonna have to fight the babes off."

Bruno glanced at the rookie, who was clad only in a pair of white briefs that perfectly showcased his well-packed manhood. "I'm feeling a bit overdressed. Maybe I should shuck down to what you're wearing."

"Then you'd definitely score," Weare growled in a sexy voice. He playfully punched Bruno's flat stomach. "Get that hairy ass of yours out of here, big guy."

Bruno shook his head. "I don't know, kid. I feel kinda strange about leaving you here all alone with that 'Sweeney

Special' on your crown."

"I'm fine!" Weare bellowed. He spun the big veteran around with a show of force and marched him toward the door. "Go!"

Bruno dug in his heels, halting Weare's attempt. The rookie slammed into him. "If I didn't know any better, I'd swear you were trying to get rid of me."

Weare coughed and cleared his throat. "No way. I'm real touched by your concern, but I don't want to fuck up your plans. If you want to do something, bring me back a big piece of raw meat to slap over this shiner."

With his back still to Weare, Bruno hauled down his zipper and fumbled in his underwear. When he turned around his flaccid cock was hanging from his briefs. "Is this big and raw enough?"

"Fuck you!" Weare laughed. "Get the fuck outta here."

Bruno let it dangle in front of Weare a second longer, then stuffed it back in with his balls. "You sure, kid? I'll hang with you if you want the company."

"I mean it," Weare persisted. "Go!"

The musical sound of Bruno pulling up his zipper ended with a deep sigh that sent the big guy's clean minty breath into Weare's face. "I will. I just gotta make a quick stop and get me a chunk of a certain asshole before I score a piece of pussy."

The sweat of their day game had long dried when the forceful knock came on Aaron Sweeney's door. He'd purposefully not showered with the team or hit the sauna or hot tub in anticipation of the knock. Having planned it all very well,

Sweeney kicked his big feet, still in the same socks he'd worn at practice, down off the bed, stood, and crossed to the front door. His smile sagged when he saw it wasn't the visitor he'd been so eagerly anticipating.

Tommy Bruno's unmistakable brick shithouse of a body loomed in the shadows on the other side of the door, and he definitely looked pissed. "Aaron," Bruno growled. "I need to have a little talk with you."

The confident, cocky smirk on Sweeney's face vanished. "Ah, this ain't a good time, Bruno."

Sweeney felt Bruno size him up from head to toe on the other side of the screen door. He was dressed only in a foul-looking jockstrap, white socks, and his baseball cap, which he had on backwards. Bruno narrowed his eyes, and in a deep growl whispered, "Am I the only one wearing clothes tonight?"

The statement was just loud enough to be heard. "It's hot out, and I'm tired," Sweeney sighed.

"Yeah, well I'm a little tired too. Open up." Bruno's demand left no room for debate. Sweeney stopped puffing his chest and conceded. He opened the door. Bruno stepped into the cabin.

☆   ☆   ☆

Before he could chew Sweeney's ass like he'd planned to, the other man about-faced, turning his concrete butt and its frosting of fine blond hairs Bruno's way. "Make it quick," Sweeney huffed. "I'm not up to your company, Bruno."

Bruno tipped his head to one side and whistled a steady stream of hot air across Sweeney's shoulders. "You ain't up to nobody's. You by yourself again this year?"

"What do you think?" Sweeney snapped, turning back so that their blue eyes were locked.

"This is a team," Bruno said matter-of-factly.

"I'm not much of a team player. You know that."

"Well, pal, you play for the Top Socks, you stay aware of the guys out there who are guarding your back when you're on that mound. You don't go gunning for their heads at home plate."

The hard scowl on Sweeney's face twisted into a cocky grin. "That rookie?" He chuckled a deep, menacing laugh in Bruno's face. "It was an accident."

"I was there, asshole. Not only was it intentional, it wasn't funny. You clocked that kid good, you fuckin' head hunter."

The twisted leer on Sweeney's square jaw intensified. "So what if I did? Do you think he's never gonna get hit by another pitch in the big leagues? This ain't high school catch, pal."

Bruno leaned closer. He exhaled deeply again, this time right into Sweeney's face. "This is how it is," he said, matching the sinister grin on the pitcher's face. "He's a good kid. He'd be rooming with you, but he got lucky, and Mitch stuck him with me. Trust me when I tell you it's your loss."

"I'm weeping," Sweeney answered.

Bruno's eyes narrowed. "You're also on notice, Sweens. You fuck with the kid or any of the new guys' heads, you fuck with me, and you know I'll set you straight."

"W-o-o-o," Sweeney sighed, puffing his chest up again. "I'm shaking."

Both men locked eyes. It was Sweeney who darted his glance away first. He gave Bruno his back. Bruno followed and clapped Sweeney on the shoulder. The pitcher jumped in place, just the slightest, under the veteran's strong hand. "So, I see," Bruno huffed. "There's no head-hunting in the Socks.

You're warned, asshole," he said on his way out of Sweeney's bungalow. He would have left if Sweeney's words hadn't stopped him in place with his hand on the door knob.

"What," Sweeney said in a deep, threatening voice, "are you fucking him? You sticking your meat up that rookie's tight little hole, dumping your load down his throat?"

The sudden rage in Bruno's blood made him grip the door knob tighter. His first instinct was to whip around and tear Sweeney apart, plant one of his balled fists square in his cocky face, lay him flat on the floor.

But the night wind sailing through the screen door cooled his anger. There was a place for his aggression, and it was out on the ball field, batting fifth in the lineup, not in some training-camp bungalow with a prick who knew how to push people's buttons.

"Fucking asshole," he said with a sarcastic laugh, banging the door shut behind him.

☆   ☆   ☆

He was still quaking by the time he reached the gate of the compound. It wasn't anger alone that caused Bruno's hands to quiver and drained all the spit from his mouth. Sweeney's words played and replayed with his steps, until Bruno stopped altogether. Shaking his head as if to banish the asshole pitcher's accusation from his head, he leaned his ass against the laundry shed's concrete wall. At first he didn't hear the footsteps on the wooden planks outside the shed or the door closing in place. Cat's concerned voice shocked Bruno out of his stupor.

"Hey, dude, you OK?"

Bruno looked up into the batboy's face. "What, kid?"

"I asked if you were all right," Cat repeated. He unslung the empty laundry sack from over his shoulder and put a hand on Bruno's.

"Yeah, kid," Bruno said. He exhaled deeply and righted. Cat's hand slipped off him. "I'm OK."

"Good. Can I get you anything?"

Bruno waved the big bear paw of his right hand expressively. "No, just some space."

With a dejected shrug Cat picked up the laundry sack. "You got it, man." He took a step away, but Bruno stopped him.

"Kid," the big guy growled. Cat turned back. "Thanks." Bruno gave Cat's ass a playful slap.

The batboy's goofy face beamed in a grin. "You got it, Bruno. Anything, anytime, anyplace."

Cat hurried on. Bruno was about to follow suit, but the nagging repetition of Sweeney's words in his head wouldn't let him. The warm wind lifted, making Bruno sigh as it filled him with an intoxicating smell of freshly mowed grass and warm Florida air. He looked ahead, then behind, toward the imagined direction of the cabin where the rookie he liked— dare he think it?—loved was waiting.

☆   ☆   ☆

The knock caught Sweeney off guard. It was the one he'd been waiting for, but Bruno's unscheduled visit had KO'd the perfection with which he'd imagined executing his plan.

He was still standing, trembling, when Cat appeared at the door. Sweeney whipped around, eyes wide, gasping out loud from the suddenness of the batboy's knock. For a moment he couldn't be sure who looked more unnerved, the 19-year-old gofer on the other side of the screen door or him with Bruno's threat still fresh in his memory.

"M-Mr. Sweeney?" Catalano stuttered. That show of respect on the batboy's part gave Sweeney all the power he
needed. The sheer perfection of his plan restored, a surge of
icy-hot fire surged through Sweeney's veins. It stirred his
itchy, half-hard cock in his jockstrap. The batboy was going
to pay for making him look like an ass out there on the field.

Oh, yes. Cat was going to pay.

"Yeah," Sweeney spat. "You here for my stinkin' shorts?"

Catalano nodded, and his throat knotted under the influence of a heavy swallow. "I can come back," the batboy said,
his nervous voice an octave higher.

"No," Sweeney growled. "Why don't you come and take
them now. I got a bone to pick with you anyway." The caged
look on Catalano's face intensified as he opened the screen
door. "That's it, little Cat. You and me's gonna have us a
chat."

The screen door banged in place behind Catalano. The
way the batboy jumped told Sweeney everything he wanted
to know. He felt his cock harden fully inside his jockstrap. He
had the team's gofer scared, and it swelled his dick to its
fullest, a fact not lost on the batboy, who glanced quickly
down at Sweeney's pouch.

"I didn't mean—" Cat blurted out.

Sweeney moved closer, folding his arms. "You didn't mean
what?"

"To, um, piss you off out there today."

The hard-faced pitcher reached a hand down and openly
rubbed the bulge in his jockstrap. Cat's eyes nervously followed. They both watched as Sweeney's left nut spilled out
into view, taking part of the right one still trapped in the
sweat-soaked jockstrap with it.

"Gonna be a simple way to see that never happens again. You're the batboy and the little man in charge of doing little things like laundry. Me? I'm a big fish swimming in a big pond. I get the big bucks to throw 'em fast and furious, so don't you ever fuck with me, kid. I'm too big for a lump of shit like you to ever think of fucking with."

Cat held up a hand. "I won't fuck with you, Mr. Sweeney."

"That's right, asshole," Sweeney bellowed. "Mister, not Aaron. If anything, I'll fuck with you. You're here to clean the stink off my shorts, and don't forget it."

Cat, wide-eyed, slowly shook his head. "I won't, sir."

Sweeney smiled. "Right. Now that we got us an understanding, why don't you start by doing your job, laundry boy."

"OK," Cat mumbled. He took a quick scan around the room but came up empty-handed. Sweeney didn't have any dirty laundry to take.

"You got a problem?" Sweeney growled. He folded his arms and stood in an arrogant, cocksure pose at the door.

"Um, I need your dirty clothes, Mr. Sweeney."

"So take 'em."

Cat's eyes darted nervously to Sweeney's big feet and the pair of socks on them. As the implications began to set in, the batboy took a heavy swallow. "W-what?"

"What didn't you understand, little fish?" Sweeney unfolded his arms and skidded his feet in their socks closer to Catalano's. "Take my stinkin' socks off for me." A look of horror crossed Catalano's face. "Go on. I ain't got all night for this."

The second threat worked. Catalano knelt down and reached his hands toward the tops of Sweeney's socks.

"Hurry the fuck up, boy!"

"But—"

"Now!"

Cat's fingers wrapped around the hairy, concrete calf of Sweeney's right leg. The sock slowly lowered. Catalano rolled it down over Sweeney's ankle. With a final tug that sent a cloud of foot odor into his face, the dirty sweat sock came off, bearing Sweeney's toes. Sweeney flexed all five of them, inches from Cat's face.

"Do the other one."

Catalano slowly complied. He gripped the pitcher's hairy left leg and pulled down the sock.

"That's a nice place for you to be," Sweeney chuckled. "There, at my feet, to show you just where you fit in on this ball club."

Cat didn't argue. He yanked the sweat sock off Sweeney's foot and tossed it into the laundry bag with the other one. He was about to rise, but the pitcher's firm hand shoved him back down.

"You ain't done down there, fucker. My socks ain't the only things in need of a good cleaning."

Catalano glanced meekly up, only to see there was a hint of something foreboding in Sweeney's cold smile and ice-blue eyes.

"My feet," Sweeney ordered. "Get your tongue down there and show me some respect!"

"I can't—"

Sweeney seized Catalano's face in his hand. "You don't understand, fucker! Your ass is mine to do what I want with. I could get you thrown so far off this team, the only game you'll ever see will be on cable!"

"Please," Cat begged.

"Who you think Hudson's gonna listen to? One of his starters or some jock-sniffing, foot licking geek with a wise-ass attitude." Sweeney's mean grin returned. "I seen the way you

disappear into that laundry shack each time you got a bag full
of steaming jockstraps. I know what you're up to when you're
supposed to be washing 'em clean. If you're wise, you'll start
licking."

Sweeney released Catalano's chin. Defeated, the batboy
lowered to Sweeney's feet, where he took his first lick.

"That's it, fucker. Clean it off good."

Cat did as he was told. The tops of Sweeney's feet covered
his tongue with a salty taste. He lapped at the star pitcher's
ankles, running his tongue into the forest of dark blond hair.

"The toes, fuck nut!" Sweeney growled. Cat lowered. Here,
he was given a face-first noseful of a hard day's workout on the
baseball diamond. Choking down his panic, Cat spread
Sweeney's toes and licked the stink from between them.

"That's good. You take orders real well, fucker. I think we got
us a real understanding now, don't we?"

Cat gazed up from Sweeney's spit-shined toes. "Yes, sir."

"Good, fucker." Sweeney's attitude softened. He placed a
big calloused hand on Cat's face and lovingly thumbed the batboy's chin. "Maybe I won't tell the rest of the guys what I
caught you doing to my feet—loving them, kneeling at them.
Maybe, maybe not..."

Catalano shook free. "I didn't do nothin'!"

"That ain't for you to decide, fucker," Sweeney snapped.
The asshole he'd been earlier was back and in charge again.
"'Specially since I could report you to Hudson for what you
been doing in here when you should be doing your job."

"I do my job!" Cat argued.

Sweeney tucked a thumb into the elastic waistband of his
jockstrap. "The laundry ain't getting done. One complaint
from me, fucker, and your ass is history."

Cat's eyes trained on the bulging, sweat-soaked jock with

the big left nut hanging out of it. Sweeney twisted the elastic under his thumb. The right nut spilled all the way out to hang mere inches from Catalano's open mouth.

Wordlessly, his face covered in sweat, Cat reached for Sweeney's jockstrap. The sweaty pouch came down in one quick yank that freed the pitcher's fat six-inch cock. Sweeney's lumber snapped up into Cat's face. It was obvious what Sweeney really wanted out of him. Licking his lips, seeming torn by the inevitable, Cat hesitated a second longer, but that was all.

Without asking, Cat took Sweeney's bone by its hairy root and sucked its already moist head between his lips. Even Sweeney was surprised by the batboy's finesse. He let out a startled gasp but kept pace with Cat's sucking until all six straining inches were down the batboy's throat.

"That's it, cocksucker," Sweeney groaned. He grabbed Cat by the back of his head and rode his face, forcing his cock all the way down, pulling it back so that just the head was lodged between the batboy's lips, then shoving it back in again to its root. "Fuckin' cocksucker. I seen the way you been looking at me."

With his eyes shut Catalano gulped the hard cock. He was so intent on sucking it, he wasn't prepared when Sweeney hauled it out with a savage yank. Holding his cock like a bat, Sweeney slugged Cat across one side of his face with it. The impact sent spit and a trace of nut scum over Cat's left cheek.

"Not so fuckin' fast, cocksucker," Sweeney demanded. "I got plans for you that don't include me dumping my load in two seconds."

A guilty, flushed look overcame Cat's face. He lapped the juice off his lips and studied Sweeney's pissed-off face in anticipation.

"Cocksucker. Lick the sweat off my nuts."

Cat buried his face in the mossy hair around Sweeney's cock as the hard-assed pitcher released his grip on it. From there he moved down to Sweeney's pair of meaty low-hanging nuts, where he carried out the order. Cat sniffed and licked Sweeney's fresh-from-his-jock ball bag until it glistened with spit.

"Fuckin' dirty cocksucker," Sweeney continued. "Must drive you crazy to see so many hot jocks struttin' naked in the locker room. Get back on my rod."

Cat spit out the pitcher's left nut. "It ain't like that! I love baseball, dude. I ain't just here to be staring at all of you."

The batboy's denial drove Sweeney into overdrive. He reached down and gripped the belt of Catalano's uniform pants and, in one deft motion, flipped him onto the bed. "Liar. Show me how bad you want to suck on some major-league dick."

"I don't!" Cat persisted, holding up both hands. Sweeney moved menacingly over his prey. A swift yank on Cat's zipper and a tug of his pants at an awkward angle bared the coarse black cock shag under the batboy's flat stomach.

"Yeah," Sweeney said, running his hands over Cat's coarse patch, "I bet you like watching all the big jocks playing ball on TV, and now you want the real thing." He slid his hands into Cat's open fly and pulled down his underwear, releasing the batboy's long, skinny cock. "You ever want one of them big sluggers to suck on your bat too?"

Cat's voice trailed to a whispered swear when Sweeney took his dick by the shaft. As he watched in disbelief, Sweeney leaned down and lapped his tongue over the fleshy pink head of the dark-skinned cock. After a few licks Sweeney took it in his mouth, swallowing it to the root.

"Yeah," Cat grunted.

Sweeney stopped sucking and lifted from the spit-shined rod, letting it fall back on Cat's stomach. "Yeah, what?" he growled. "Is this what you jack off about at night? Me and the rest of the team sucking on your pencil dick or sticking ours up your ass?"

The excited look on Cat's face turned to terror as the implications in Sweeney's words set in. Before Cat could react the pitcher was back to his feet. Sweeney rolled Cat over and pulled the batboy's uniform pants down. A moment later he felt something hot—the pitcher's tongue—brushing him between his tightly clenched butt cheeks.

"Open up," Cat heard him order. "Show me that little cunt of yours."

Cat thought about struggling but knew it was no use. He buried his face in the pillow that smelled like Sweeney and surrendered, pushing back into the pitcher's face. There, on his stomach, he let Sweeney eat him out but pretended it was somebody else chowing on his hole—Bradley, that new guy, Weare, Bruno....

Bruno.

The illusion ended when Sweeney mounted his bare back. A rough shove and a head full of stars later, Catalano felt Sweeney's bat enter his moist, hairy shit hole.

"Bull's-eye!" Sweeney grunted, sending the word and his sour breath past Cat's ears. The batboy moaned a swear into Sweeney's pillow. With a renewed burst of enthusiasm, the hard-assed pitcher pulled back, slammed in, and settled into a steady fuck rhythm on top of the batboy. Each of Cat's yowls only spurred him on more. "You like this?" Cat didn't answer. "Tell me, fucker. Is this what you fuckin' wanted?"

"Yes!" the batboy howled.

That did it. Having broken all resistance, Sweeney thrust

in a final time. "Fuck," he growled. "Here it comes, you dirty cocksucker!"

Sweeney shot the first ribbon of hot come into the batboy's butt, then pulled out and rolled Cat onto his back. He dumped the second right into Cat's open mouth. "That's it, eat my pine tar!"

Still shooting, Sweeney swung around and slid his cock down Catalano's throat while taking the batboy's dick back into his mouth. The salty taste of Cat's pink-capped lumber made him thrust down hard.

Catalano jerked suddenly underneath him. A few sucks later Sweeney felt the batboy's cock double in size between his lips. He spat out the skinny rod and a rope of salty come, then watched in sick fascination as a fountain of jizz erupted from Cat's pink cock head. The second blast hit Sweeney square between his open lips.

Sweeney didn't say anything at first. He wiped his mouth on Cat's underwear and rolled off of his conquest. With his back to the batboy, he folded his arms and growled, "Get out."

Cat's face flushed in embarrassment. He hauled up his pants as best as he could, tucked Sweeney's jockstrap into the laundry bag, and plodded toward the door. He was about to run out of the bungalow, into the night, when Sweeney threatened him again.

"You tell anyone about this," the hard-assed pitcher said in a deep, dangerous voice, his back still to the batboy, "and you'll answer to me."

Cat nearly tripped over his own big feet scrambling out the cabin door. When he was gone Sweeney shut off the lights and slid back on the bed. The covers were still wet. He grinned to himself, kicked up his now bare feet, and silently plotted his next humiliation.

☆   ☆   ☆

Bruno paced back and forth near the walkway. On the ninth time he stopped fighting himself and surrendered. After all, he told himself, it was just concern for a fellow teammate and buddy, not some twisted, forbidden attraction that had canceled his night on the town. He just wanted to make sure Weare was OK, just like Doc Hanson had instructed. Then Bruno realized it wasn't Weare he was worried about explaining this to.

It was himself he hoped to convince.

"Aw, fuck it," Bruno swore under his breath as he stepped onto the path and proceeded back beneath the overhang, toward their cabin. He'd almost made it to the front door when he noticed that except for the vague glow given off from the bedside table's lamp, the bungalow was dark. A thin sliver of yellow light seeped from beneath the drawn shades. The front door was closed.

It didn't hit the veteran center fielder until he opened the screen door, innocently turned the front door's knob, and walked in on Weare, who was engaged in anything but an innocent night's activities.

"What the fuck?" Bruno swore.

⚾ FOURTH INNING

The first thing to greet Bruno's wide, disbelieving eyes made the half-hard gristle hanging in his briefs toughen fully. The itch in Bruno's nuts that never went away began to burn. What he saw packed the front of his faded jeans to capacity.

Weare jumped up from between the naked woman's legs. His slick lips glistened in the poor light from the tongue bath he'd given her wet, trimmed pussy. "Bruno," Weare gasped. The beautiful woman seized on the bed but remained with her legs spread, one of them arched, just enough to show how wet Weare's lapping had gotten her.

The room hazed suddenly around Bruno. He couldn't be sure what it was that pumped him up most, the sight of the woman's pink, clipped cunt or the fact he'd caught his rookie roommate eating it. Some unaffected part of Bruno's consciousness glanced down at the tent in Weare's white briefs. The rookie's underwear showcased to perfection the hard cock and fat bag of nuts inside the crisp cotton.

"S-sorry, kid," Bruno stammered between quick gasps for air. He shook his head to clear it. When the room again stabilized, the look of shock on Weare's face had changed. He'd flushed an embarrassed shade of red that matched the bruise Sweeney left him with.

"No, big guy," Weare shrugged. "I shouldn't have snuck Barbara in. This is your room."

Bruno exhaled deeply. "Barbara?" He turned toward the 24 karats of babe spread open on the bed he'd shared with the rookie. "Hi, Bruno," she innocently chirped, waving her fingers in a delicate, pretty way.

And pretty she was. Barbara was just the kind of woman—supermodel beautiful—Bruno had expected Weare to keep in his stable. He found himself staring at her tits and tiny nipples and the moist, pretty pussy beneath the triangle of trim blonde bush between her perfect, slender legs. It was so obvious, Barbara spread them even further, giving him a better look. Bruno growled and licked his lips.

Weare's hand on his shoulder snapped Bruno's focus off Barbara's spit-shined cunt and brought them, rookie and vet, eye to eye. "I mean it, pal. I'm sorry if we got outta hand."

Bruno playfully punched the side of Weare's rib cage. "You sneaky fuck! If Mitch knew..."

"Hey," Weare countered jokingly. "You're supposed to be out scoring some of what I was already getting when you walked in!"

Bruno swung around and took Weare into a headlock. "I was fuckin' concerned about that shiner of yours," he shouted as the two men struggled. "I didn't realize you had both heads covered."

"Asshole," Weare spat in a friendly growl. They pulled against each other and soon had moved into a position with Bruno bracing Weare's back. The veteran pressed one arm around the rookie's neck. The other ran along his rippled abs. The course tips of the hair at the top of Weare's briefs prickled under Bruno's arm.

"You fuckin' stud," Bruno grunted. He rested his chin on

Weare's shoulder and peered over at Barbara. She had one finger inside her pussy and was diddling her clit with another. "Yeah," Weare huffed. He brushed the side of his stubbly cheek across Bruno's shaved chin. "Who's the stud? Is that a baseball bat in your pocket or are you just happy to see me?" The eight-inch bulge between the center fielder's legs throbbed painfully into the rookie's hard-as-nails can. Bruno tried to shift to accommodate it, but all he succeeded in doing was to push it harder into Weare's ass. The sexy grin on Bruno's face softened into a look of confusion. "Both," he eventually whispered.

Weare took a big gulp. Before he could comment on Bruno's remark, Barbara drew both men's focus back to the bed.

"You two gonna butter each other's balls all night or take care of me?" She fingered herself faster. The titter in her voice let it slip that she was getting close. A breathless gasp escaped her beautiful mouth.

Weare brought his lips so near Bruno's, it was almost a kiss. "You want to join in, you big stud?"

Bruno's mouth suddenly drained of all moisture. He peered into the rookie's deep blue eyes. Despite the poor light, he had no trouble identifying the fire in Weare's baby-blues. "What?" Bruno asked.

"I'm not a greedy or jealous lover," Weare growled back, "or friend. You're my buddy and you're hurtin' for it." The rookie pressed back into Bruno's straining cock. "Why don't you hang with me and Barbara. She'd like it. I know she would."

"She?" Bruno huffed. The statement sent a wave of hot minty air past Weare's ears. "What about you, kid?"

"I ain't a kid," Weare said. He stopped struggling against Bruno's solid grip. "And I got the stones to prove it."

What happened next almost made Bruno shoot in his pants as he dry-humped the rookie's butt. Weare eased Bruno's hand lower on his muscled abdomen, down into the tangle of coarse hair at the top of his briefs. Bruno's fingertips worked beyond the elastic band on the rookie's shorts to touch hard, hot skin. He cupped Weare's cock beneath his palm and gave it a firm shake.

"Nothin' little about you, buddy," Bruno sighed. "Not your game, not your heart, and certainly not this dick."

"You noticed."

"Hard not to."

Bruno released his hold on the rookie's cock and reached lower. He teased Weare's sweaty nuts. Weare groaned. "Do it, guy. I want you to play with my balls. I want to see you eating out my girlfriend."

The three-alarm grin on Bruno's face widened to add a fourth. "Now you're talking my lingo, dude." He pulled his hand out of Weare's shorts and gave his fingers a quick sniff. They smelled like hot sweat. Bruno unbuttoned his jacket and tossed it onto the chair. His white T-shirt followed. Bruno used it to mop the sweat off his forehead and under his armpits, then dropped it into the pile of discarded clothes on the floor. He was ready. "Hey, pretty lady," he said, smiling.

Barbara pulled the finger out of her clit and teased her cunt lips. "Hey yourself, slugger. I hear you been looking out for Timmy."

Bruno lowered between Barbara's legs and kissed her inner thigh. "Yeah," he growled. The warm breath ricocheted off Barbara's pretty pussy and sent back, as Weare had promised, a flowery scent. "I been taking care of him. Why don't you let me take care of that." He withdrew Barbara's finger from her pussy and sucked it into his mouth. The taste drove him wild.

"Ah, fuck is that beautiful!" Starving for more, he drove his mouth across Barbara's moist hole, where he tasted Weare's spit and Barbara's natural wetness. She howled as he licked and lapped at her openness. Stopping to suck on her swollen clit, he replaced his tongue with the index finger of his glove hand. Also true to Weare's claim, she was tight. Bruno licked around her pussy, pulled out his finger to clean off the taste, then inserted it again. Bruno ate hungrily, exhaling growls across her cunt while finger-fucking it.

Bruno's cock grew so hard in his jeans, it hurt. He snaked a hand down to shift it into a more comfortable position and saw Weare. He'd been so consumed with scoring a piece of Barbara's pussy, he'd momentarily forgotten about the rookie.

Weare leaned against the mirrored bureau. His hard cock hung from the leg of his underwear along with both of his low-hanging nuts. Weare stroked his cock and was obviously getting off on watching Bruno in action with his girlfriend. "Fuckin' sweet, dude," the rookie sighed. He fisted his cock faster.

Bruno tipped his head in an expressive guy gesture. "Why don't you come down here, pal, so I don't feel like I'm hogging all this choice snatch to myself."

"Yeah, Tim," Barbara urged painfully from the edge of the eruption Bruno had her on the verge of. "Do it!"

Weare moved beside Bruno and slid up between Barbara's thighs and kissed the spit-warmed wetness of her pussy. The rookie's talented mouth caused Barbara to buck on the bed. She moaned a round of breathless swears as he traveled familiar territory, all those places he knew she liked to have him exploring inside her. Just when it seemed he'd make her come, Weare withdrew from her pussy. He turned toward Bruno, who was obviously enjoying the spectator sport as much as the rookie had. The vet's handsome face still glistened with his girlfriend's pussy juice. Weare smiled. "Now you join me," he whispered. "Come on, big guy."

Bruno leaned closer—but not to Barbara. Weare followed suit. Neither man was prepared for it. The kiss just happened. Both men tasted the other's wet, slick lips, tentatively at first, then deeper, a kiss hot with breath and tongue. Bruno lapped hungrily at the rookie's mouth. He was beyond questioning it or caring what anyone, including himself, would think when the dust settled. It was the hottest kiss he could ever recall, and it had come from a buddy, a teammate, a man.

The men parted and wordlessly resumed their positions near Barbara's waiting pussy. Bruno licked first. Weare's tongue settled on her clit, where his cheek and chin teased the side of Bruno's face. Both men converged on Barbara's open hole. Their tongues swabbed in and out, over each other. Bruno eased in a finger. Weare did the same. Both men used their fingers like a double dose of cock to push Barbara closer to the edge.

Bruno broke away first. He kissed Weare's mouth again. This brought rookie and veteran face-to-face. "I wanna suck your girlfriend's tits," he growled.

"Do it, dude," Weare urged.

Bruno eased onto the bed. Weare watched the big jock take Barbara in his arms. As they kissed, Bruno ran his glove hand over Barbara's perfect tits, stopping to pinch the tight caps. After that her stiff nipples disappeared, one at time, into Bruno's mouth. Weare resumed eating her pussy. The double action drove Barbara wild.

Bruno sucked harder. He would have kept going, but a hand on his leg snapped him up, off her tits. He looked down to see Weare rubbing his calf. Without asking, the rookie pulled off one of Bruno's deck shoes, exposing the big foot in its clean white sock. Weare freed him of the other shoe, then slowly peeled off his sock too. Bruno flexed his toes like a contented cat while Weare played with them.

"You got sexy feet, slugger," the rookie said, breathing the words in a hot gust over Bruno's toes.

Bruno grinned. "You think so?"

Weare pressed his nose against the veteran's right foot and sucked in a deep breath. "Fuck, yeah, dude." A second later he ran his tongue along the sole, winding it up to Bruno's hairy ankles, finally to his toes, where he sucked each one like it was a smaller version of the center fielder's cock.

"Shit!" Bruno grunted. "That feels fuckin' great, buddy."

"Yeah," Weare sighed invitingly. "This is gonna feel even better."

The rookie reached up and cupped the bulge straining in the front of Bruno's blue jeans. The pressure made Bruno groan a string of *Fucks* and *Oh, shits* as Weare unzipped his pants. The rookie eased them down Bruno's hairy calves and off his spit-shined feet. Soon, like Weare, Bruno was wearing just a pair of well-packed white briefs. The rookie took care of that too.

Bruno couldn't believe how good it felt when Weare started fishing in the tent of his briefs or after he pulled the elastic band down, exposing his hard cock, precome glistening on its piss slit.

Weare seemed impressed by the size of Bruno's bat. The rookie studied it for a few seconds, then wrapped his lips around its straining head. For one brief, amazing moment, Barbara, with her choice pussy, wasn't there in the bed with them. It was just veteran and rookie, Bruno and Weare, and a selfless, forbidden understanding that was part brotherhood,

part sex—and the hottest kind at that. The threesome became a twosome as Weare sucked Bruno's hard cock. "I don't
fuckin' believe you're doing that, dude," he moaned. "And
doing it so good."

Weare lapped at the sides of Bruno's hairy cock between
jacking it. He buried his nose in the veteran's shag and took
a deep breath of the musky-smelling bush before going lower,
to the come-packed bull nuts hanging underneath the center
fielder's seven stiff inches. "You got the biggest pair of low-
hangers I've ever seen in a locker room," Weare sighed.

The comment made Bruno's smile widen. "Yeah?" he
asked. Weare answered by rubbing Bruno's sac of nuts over his
nose. The rookie inhaled Bruno's smell of man sweat and
nodded. With Weare's attention now on his balls, Bruno
reached down and stroked his own cock. "You like the smell
of my bag?"

Weare growled his response. "Mmm. Does it feel good,
big guy?"

"It'd feel better if you sucked 'em."

It was all the suggestion Weare needed. He rolled the egg-
sized nuts over his tongue, then sucked the left one between his
lips. Spitting it out, he turned his attention to the right one.

The rookie's mouth felt so good on his balls, Bruno started
to jack his cock faster. "Aw, fuck," he growled. "Suck my
fuckin' nuts, dude. Yeah, I want it—want it bad!"

Weare continued at Bruno's urging. It wasn't the first time
he'd licked another man's bag, but sex with Bruno was the
best he'd ever had, with a guy or a woman. He wanted, needed Bruno so badly. He spit out the big guy's balls for a taste of
what his sac had so far kept concealed. Weare licked lower
between Bruno's legs until his tongue slid into the hot, hairy
tightness of the center fielder's asshole. Both men gasped.

"What the fuck?" Bruno sputtered.

Weare started eating Bruno's hole with the same hunger he'd shown for Barbara's pussy. The more he licked at the ring of tight muscles, the more feral he grew, until he was moaning hot air up into Bruno's can.

Spreading his legs to give Weare easier access to his butt again reminded Bruno that Barbara was there. She shifted with him on the bed, put one hand on his hairy chest, and groped his rock-hard cock with the other. She settled down near his dick and started stroking it. Being serviced by both the rookie and his girlfriend almost proved to be too much for the veteran.

"How could one man get so lucky?" Bruno sighed.

Barbara answered by running her tongue over his cock. "Tim's the best, that's how."

"I'll say," said Bruno.

The comment brought Weare's Cheshire-cat grin and handsome face up from the center fielder's asshole. He joined Barbara with a kiss over the head of Bruno's bat, but when their lips parted they both lowered down to suck on Bruno's cock together. In seconds the big slugger was dripping come like a leaky faucet.

"Do it, both of you," Bruno huffed, begged. "I gotta shoot!"

Barbara suddenly pulled up. "No," she groused. Weare too released his lip lock on Bruno's cock. Before Bruno could protest, Barbara gripped his chin and planted a kiss on his mouth. Bruno tasted himself on her lips. "Not yet," she said. I don't want either of you shooting till I'm ready."

"Are you ready?" Weare growled from between Bruno's legs.

"Close," Barbara chirped. She moved on top of Bruno and spread her legs over his face. Her sweet-tasting pussy settled against his mouth. Bruno spread her pussy lips with the fore-finger and thumb of his glove hand and resumed licking. He buried his face as deep as she could take it, and whatever doubts he'd had about what he'd entered into vanished deep inside the rookie's girlfriend's snatch. For what seemed the longest time, Bruno only came up for air. It wasn't until some-thing hot, hard, and wet rubbed the trigger of nerves under the head of his cock that Bruno released her.

Weare had shuffled onto the bed. He'd gripped both their cocks and was rubbing them, one sensitive underside against the other. A generous dose of precome from each man's piss slit provided the lube. Weare continued to hump his cock against Bruno's, but Barbara had different ideas: She sucked both cock heads into her mouth. Weare replaced his hand on Bruno's nuts and rolled the balls in their meaty sac between his fingertips, gently scratching the hairy skin.

The men were still in this position when Barbara rolled off Bruno's face. "Tim's been real giving," she tittered. "I think it's time he got some reciprocation." She slid off the bed and into the chair where Bruno had dropped his jacket. As both men watched, dumbfounded for a second, Barbara pulled the jacket around her shoulders. She sniffed at the collar for the scent of Bruno's cologne. "God, you smell great," she said, rolling her eyes. Bruno grinned and jacked his hard, dripping cock. "You," she pointed to the rookie, "get your ass on the bed, up near your handsome buddy."

Weare's cock bounced as he joined Bruno in the place where Barbara had been a minute before. Again they found themselves together, just two guys. Barbara was content to watch them.

For a brief and terrifying moment, Bruno wanted to punch the shit out of Weare and kick his own ass just as hard for having given in to it, for having fooled with another guy, and having loved it so much.

But that same attraction kept him rooted to the spot. He was so excited, nothing could have shoehorned him away from Weare's hot, sweaty nakedness. Weare reached an arm up over Bruno's shoulders and gently stroked the veteran's chest. Yeah, it felt good.

Damned good.

Slowly, both men moved their faces together. They kissed softly, deeply—lips, teeth, then finally tongues. When they parted, Bruno gazed into the younger man's eyes and knew from that moment forward, pussy alone would never be enough. There would be no going back.

"You ever done this before?" Bruno growled in a deep whisper.

Weare flashed a cocky grin. "You mean get off with a good buddy?" Bruno nodded. "Yeah," the rookie conceded. "Once or twice. Just never with as good a buddy as you."

The warmth in the rookie's eyes said it all. It was a look of sincerity and total adoration. It made the sweat pouring off Bruno's forehead flow faster. Bruno swabbed at the stinging torrent. The last thing he wanted to do was to let that moment end. "I'm honored," he said.

"What about you," Weare asked. "You ever do it with a buddy?"

Bruno considered what had been asked of him. He continued to gaze into Weare's handsome eyes and shook his head. "No, dude. But I think I can handle it."

Lifting to his elbows, before he could talk himself out of going further, Bruno moved down between the rookie's legs. Weare's cock snapped up, at full attention against his own stomach. Bruno took it in hand and gave it a few stiff strokes for effect, then lowered his face toward the rookie's bag of low-hanging nuts. He already knew what his own balls smelled like—that heady odor of man sweat from a good workout that never fully went away, even after showering. Bruno took a whiff of the other man's nuts and followed it with a slow, curious lick.

"That's it, big guy," Weare urged. "Show me how glad you are you didn't score in town tonight."

Show him, Bruno did. He licked at Weare's nuts, savoring their swampy taste, showing the same unquestioning respect the rookie had showered his with. While the concept of being so close to another man's cock had repulsed him at first, everything about Weare, including his dick, now filled Bruno with a hunger he'd never known before. "I'm real glad, pal."

Weare arched himself up to his elbows to watch as Bruno took his first taste of the rookie's cock. He ground his teeth and growled at the sight of big Tommy Bruno readying to suck a dick—his dick.

Bruno, who'd had his choice of women for most of his cock-hard life, now wanted nothing more than the rookie's bat. He closed his eyes and sucked the head of Weare's cock into his mouth. A few inches of dick rolled over his tongue, then Weare lurched up, burying two more down Bruno's throat. Soon the veteran's mouth was full of hard, wet cock.

It wasn't as bad as he'd thought. The rubbery, spongy flesh had a strangely pleasurable feel on his tongue. And the taste… Bruno had sampled his own come plenty of times. He'd eaten it out of his ex-wife's pussy or mouth during those rare times of marital sex or tasted it after jacking himself off in those long sessions when he'd been alone and needed it, so he knew what to expect. Weare pulled back, resting only the head of his cock on Bruno's tongue. The rookie's precome was salty and heavy. As Bruno took those first few sucks off his new buddy's bat, he figured it wouldn't take the rookie long.

Weare gripped the back of Bruno's head. He ran his fingers through the veteran's neat buzz cut and held on as if Bruno's cock sucking was about to launch him off the bed. Weare anchored his other hand on Bruno's stubbly cheek, growled, and fucked the big guy's mouth. Bruno went on automatic and sucked harder. The rookie swore something unintelligible, then grunted, "Do it, man! I'm coming!"

Bruno didn't know whether to keep going or spit Weare's cock out. Before he could decide, the rookie's cock sprayed a flood of semen more powerful and satisfying than anything Bruno had yet tasted that night. He gulped the rookie's spunk down. Weare thrust his pumping cock one last time into the veteran's mouth. Bruno continued sucking until Weare's moans went from pleasure to pain. Weare's dick softened. Bruno spit out the rookie's bat and licked it clean, making sure to get every drop. Once he'd done that, Bruno gave the rookie's tightening nut sac a few sucks, then satisfied his curiosity by taking a few forbidden licks of Weare's hairy asshole. Weare accommodated by spreading his legs.

"Fuck," the rookie moaned between gasps for air. The breathless swear spurred Bruno on. He groped Weare's balls and twisted them out of the way, exposing the rookie's asshole. He ran his tongue across the moist, puckered knot, showering it with hungry kisses, his last concession to what he and the rookie had shared. Bruno ate Weare's ass. The longer he did it, the more he loved it. Once he'd lubed the rookie's hole with spit, Bruno worked the same finger he'd used to fuck Barbara's pussy up Weare's hole. The rookie bucked against the pressure Bruno put on him but finally gave in. Bruno licked around his finger, tasting the fresh sweat between Weare's legs. The rookie perspired more as Bruno's finger worked its way to the second knuckle.

"You got a tight can," Bruno growled. "It's real fuckin' tight."

Weare reached down and toyed with his spent cock. He gave it a few shakes. The slippery meat toughened between his fingers. "I'm a man. You'd better believe it's tight."

Bruno smiled and thrust his finger in all the way. Weare lurched. Finger-fucking his ass was making the rookie's cock come alive again. Bruno pushed faster. In the seconds that followed, Weare's bat stretched out to its full six inches. His tight ball bag started to loosen. To help it along, Bruno ceased tonguing around Weare's hole and sucked in a mouthful of nuts.

The rookie pushed against Bruno's fuck finger. "I don't believe you're doing this to me, man," Weare sighed. "Shit!"

Bruno grinned and spit out Weare's nuts. "What would you rather have me fuck you with? My big toe?"

Weare stroked his cock and smiled. "You got such sexy feet, dude, I'd consider it."

Bruno raised to his knees. "I got a better idea, if you're man enough to take it."

"I'm man enough," Weare huffed.

Bruno gave the rookie's cock a final kiss before assuming position. "I know it, pal. I'm just giving you a chance to get out of having my cock in your ass."

The excited look on Weare's handsome face also showed the slightest hint of fear. Fresh sweat broke out on his forehead. Still, they'd gone too far to even think about heading back. Weare knew it and solemnly nodded. "Do it, big guy."

"You're sure?"

Weare nodded. "You're my hero, buddy. Put it in me."

It was all the invitation Bruno needed. He withdrew his finger and moved into position, aiming his cock between Weare's legs. Just rubbing the head of his bat over the spit-lubed and finger-fucked man's cunt sent a wave of excitement flooding through him. Bruno nudged his dick closer. "Here it comes, pal."

"Go for it," Weare said through clenched teeth.

The veteran pushed in. Both men let out a round of deep grunts. Weare opened up, and Bruno felt his cock slide in. Soon he'd buried all seven inches up the rookie's asshole. The pressure on his dick was incredible. He'd never fucked anything so tight.

"Thanks, buddy," Bruno grunted. He settled on top of Weare, who had gone tight-lipped, with a trace of tears in his eyes. But he had taken it, despite the pain. For that, Bruno would never forget him.

"Little Tom feels pretty fuckin' big right now," Weare groaned.

Bruno kissed Weare's face, the tears in his eyes, his clenched mouth. Bruno pulled back so that just the head of his cock remained lodged in the rookie's asshole. Then he shoved back in, fully.

They settled into a mutual fuck rhythm that knocked the headboard against the wall and made the old mattress squeak violently. The grunts of both men thundered through the room. They'd gotten so into each other, Barbara had to clear her throat three times to remind them she was still there.

"Boys," she said. Bruno stuffed Weare's ass with his bat before looking over the rookie's handsome face to the chair where his girlfriend sat. "I didn't mean for you to forget about me when I told you to take care of each other!"

Bruno took the hint. "We got two cocks between us, pretty lady." Holding Weare against him, Bruno rolled over, taking the rookie with him into a reverse doggy-style. The action sent Bruno onto his back with his cock still stuffed up Weare's shit hole. This put the rookie's cock up and ready.

Bruno's jacket slipped from Barbara's shoulders as she slid off the chair. She carefully mounted Weare's cock.

The rookie let out a painful grunt. The pressure from wanting to thrust up into Barbara's pussy and push back onto Bruno's cock was overwhelming. Weare steadied himself on Barbara's hips. Bruno, in turn, steadied his grip on Weare's thighs. The closeness proved to be too much for all of them.

Bruno unloaded first, firing five steady shots of hot come into the rookie's ass. This drove Weare into a frenzy. With Bruno still grunting beneath him, Weare felt Barbara's pussy clamp down hard on his cock. He shot his second load of the night into her as their group grunt powered down to a whisper.

☆   ☆   ☆

Barbara shook free and rolled off of Weare, onto the bed, leaving the men joined together.

Weare unhooked himself from the cock lodged in his asshole. He moved between Bruno's legs and took a gentle last suck of the veteran's spent dick. "Just cleaning you up, buddy," he said.

Bruno forced a smile but said nothing. After the fuck grunts ended, a strange silence settled over the room. The musky haze in the air gradually degenerated into nothing more than the stink of old sex. The taste of Weare's come, which had been so appealing minutes before, soured on Bruno's lips.

Weare oozed off the bed to stand on shaky legs. He took a few uncertain steps to the bathroom and emerged with a

towel, using it to mop up the cascade of stale sweat that covered his naked body.

"That towel reminds me," Barbara chirped. She stepped off
the bed and crossed to the bathroom door. "I need a shower."

She blew Weare a kiss, then winked at Bruno. He caught it
with a cocky tip of his head and a smile. The sound of running water left both men together in the awkward silence as
the implications of what had happened between them began
to set in.

Weare sensed it in the lack of words between them, the
look of guilt on Bruno's face. In an attempt to curtail it from
spreading further, he swabbed the towel over Bruno's chest
and carefully wiped up his sweat. "That was really hot, dude,"
he attempted.

Bruno growled out a single word. "Yeah."

Weare considered dabbing the towel over Bruno's sweaty
cock and low hangers but thought better of it. He dropped the
towel and settled on his side of the bed until Barbara emerged.
The smell of shampooed hair and fresh flowers from her per-
fume broke the guy stink in the room.

"Not that this hasn't been the balls, guys," she said with a
giggle, "but this girl's got a career and one hell of a long flight
home if I'm gonna keep it." She went to Bruno's side of the
bed first and planted a deep, wet kiss on his mouth. "It's been
real. Hope we can do it again."

"You bet," Bruno promised, flashing a tired three-alarm
grin. "You need a lift?"

Barbara kissed Weare deeper and wetter before answering.
"No, just someone to sneak me back out. I got a rental parked
outside the security gate."

"I got it covered," Weare said. He pulled on a pair of old
gray sweats, a navy-colored T-shirt, and slipped his bare feet

into his cleats without wasting time on socks. "Be back in a flash."

Bruno nodded but again said nothing. His eyes had a far-off, almost sad expression. The memory of his face followed Weare out into the night. He was still contemplating the center fielder's silence when Barbara's sporty rental veered away, out of sight, leaving him alone in the early morning haze.

☆   ☆   ☆

The walk back to the cabin seemed to take forever. Weare felt his heart racing as he neared the cabin's door. The room looked even darker than when he'd left it. Maybe, he thought, it was what had happened between them that had caused Bruno's silence or the fact that Barbara being gone would leave them alone in the bed with the uncomfortable possibility that history would repeat itself, not with two men and a woman but with just two men.

Weare approached the door.

Bruno was on his side of the bed, clad in a pair of white midlengths that glowed in the poor light spilling from the bathroom. The big center fielder lay with his back to the door, almost in a fetal curl. While his breaths were heavy, Weare knew the veteran wasn't sleeping.

It was all as Weare feared: Bruno's silence, the fact that he'd sacrificed his easygoing nudity for a pair of baseball shorts—like Adam, who'd eaten forbidden fruit and suddenly grown ashamed of his nakedness.

Weare peeled off his T-shirt and kicked off his spikes. He thought about shedding his shorts but, like Bruno, decided he'd bared enough for one night.

Before he went back to the bed, Weare smoothed out

Bruno's black linen jacket. He slung it over one arm and crossed to the bathroom for a hanger, stopping long enough to take a deep sniff of Bruno's cologne. It was intoxicating.

Don't go silent on me now, big guy, a voice in his head begged in silence. *Not now, when we've gotten this close.*

He hung up the jacket and returned to the bed. His weight on the mattress made Bruno stir. "G'night, pal," he whispered, forcing a smile.

With his back still to Weare, the veteran sighed, "Good night, kid."

It wasn't much, just a glimmer of hope that the Bruno he knew would be in bed with him when they both woke in the morning. Sleep didn't come easily; at one point the big guy's steady snoring lulled Weare into horny dreams that replayed the night's events over and over again.

Hours later, the rookie woke in the sun-filled room alone, with a raging piss hard-on.

Bruno was gone.

The sinking feeling Weare had gone to bed with resurfaced, only stronger. His rock-hard boner softened without him even considering giving it the usual morning attention. "Fuck," he huffed. "Don't do this, dude."

A hundred imagined scenarios flashed through the rookie's mind, visions of Bruno reporting the night's indiscretions to Mitch Hudson or, worse yet, their teammates. He envisioned the end of his short career with the Seaside Top Socks and a very embarrassing finish to what would have been a sweet career in pro baseball. Weare's cock went totally flaccid. The stale taste on his lips was like a punch to his gut.

He left the bed to drain his bladder but first brushed his teeth. Halfway through that, the screen door banged closed. Weare sucked a mouthful of water from the faucet and spit out a stream of minty foam. When he finished pissing, Bruno dominated the middle of the floor and was doing push-ups. His bare back glistened with sweat. Dressed only in a pair of dark gray jogging shorts that were just as soaked with perspiration, Bruno had shucked his black sneakers and white sweat socks. Some unaffected part of Weare's consciousness—the part that didn't feel guilty about appreciating a buddy's maleness—drank in the sight. Even the way Bruno's feet flexed as he push-upped his body into a mass of ripped muscles made the rookie want him more than anything else.

"Morning, dude," Weare said, attempting to sound casual despite the fact his cock had again swollen to its previous stiffness.

"Hi, yourself," Bruno said effortlessly between upward inhales. That and nothing more. He continued his routine.

Weare's cock got so hard, it snagged in the elastic of his shorts. He gave himself a shake to adjust it, then took a seat on the edge of the bed. "You're up pretty early. When did you go out?"

"At 5," Bruno said in an emotionless monotone. "I wanted to get a start on training. We got a game with the Matadors today."

"I know," Weare continued. "You should have woken me up. I would've gone with you. I could use a good jog around the camp."

"Then go jogging."

"I meant together, buddy," Weare smiled.

Bruno stopped his routine. He lowered to his elbows, brought a knee up, and solemnly rolled onto his back, for the first time giving Weare his face, if not his focus. Bruno's thunderhead-colored eyes darted away. "I didn't want to wake you. 'Sides, I had some things to consider." The veteran center fielder cupped his hands behind his head and arched his knees for a round of sit-ups.

"Things about last night?" Weare persisted. Bruno didn't answer and instead exhaled as he rose, inhaled when he lowered, and locked his dreamy gray-blue eyes on some peripheral target on the cabin wall. It was as the rookie had feared—the drop of the other shoe. Weare shrugged and slid off the bed to a place on the floor beside Bruno. "Come on, man. We got to get over whatever it is that went up between us when Barbara left. Call me selfish—"

"I thought you said you weren't a greedy or selfish buddy last night," Bruno growled.

"I am when it comes to you. I don't want to lose your friendship over this."

"You won't," Bruno said. "I told you I just needed to think things over."

Without asking, Weare moved into position at Bruno's ankles and steadied them. "While you're thinking about it, at least let me spot you."

Bruno didn't argue the point or fight Weare's hands on his feet. As much as he wanted to, Weare tried not to fixate on the beads of sweat that clung to the hairs on Bruno's legs. He didn't lick the slugger's feet like he had at the start of things. With Bruno so hot, so close to him, Weare wanted nothing more than to relive what it was they'd shared the night before, but he wouldn't initiate it. It was Bruno's turn to step up to bat.

Just when Weare thought the big guy was going silent on him again, Bruno shattered the pensive silence with a simple statement. "Barbara's real fine."

Weare smiled. "I told you she was."

"Next time I'd like to try that theory of yours out on her."

"My theory?" Weare asked, a dumb look on his face.

It was the first time that morning Bruno actually faced him.

"You know. About sticking two cocks up that tight cunt of hers, to see if she can take it."

"Two cocks," Weare said. "You mean you and me?"

Bruno went to his back and remained there. "Of course you and me."

The bulge throbbing between Weare's legs suddenly toughened. His grip on Bruno's solid jock legs loosened. He slid his fingertips up into the hair running up the center fielder's shin, rubbing the sweat in small circles. "That'd be hot, guy."

Bruno groaned, "Yeah, real fuckin' hot."

"Like last night." Weare lifted Bruno's leg. Suddenly, it was all right to be there, at Bruno's feet, tonguing the sweat from between his toes again. "I mean it, dude. If you need to pretend it never happened, I'm OK with it. I'll take full responsibility for the whole thing." He sucked Bruno's big toe the way he had his cock. Weare's looked up to see the veteran adjust the tent in his workout shorts. "It's all me, big guy. I'm the one that sucked cock. You were just being a gentleman by letting me suck it."

Weare licked and sniffed the stink off Bruno's toes. He lapped at the soles and tasted the salty sweat on Bruno's hairy calf.

"No, pal," Bruno said with a deep sigh. "It wasn't all you. Fuck," he groaned, "that feels good."

Weare grinned against Bruno's leg. It was the old Bruno he'd come to know and love in their short time together, the one who acted all guy even if he was having sex with another guy. "You like that, buddy?"

To cement the center fielder's answer, Weare reached between Bruno's legs and stroked his meaty bulge. He found the veteran already rock-hard. Weare teased his nuts, then slid his hand along Bruno's leg until his fingertips disappeared up into his shorts. Bruno moaned as the rookie toyed with his erection. "I really like it, pal."

"I guess." Weare released Bruno's cock and settled back at his feet, where he resumed sucking on the jock's sweaty toes. Perfectly content where he was, Weare would have continued without needing more, but Bruno upped the game's stakes.

"Give me one of yours," he growled, arching up to his elbows. Weare spit out the small toe in his mouth. "One of what?"

"Your stinkin' feet, dumb fuck. If we're gonna work out together, you can't go it alone."

Weare flashed his sexy Cheshire-cat grin and stretched out on the floor, moving into position beside the handsome vet. Soon, each man had one of the other's feet between his legs.

Bruno arched Weare's ankle and gave the rookie's foot his own version of a tongue bath. After a few wet licks, he brought Weare's foot down and rubbed it over the tent in his shorts. The rookie watched, fascinated, as Bruno freed his cock and balls from his shorts to rub them along the tops of the rookie's spit-lubed toes. Weare flexed his foot and teased Bruno's hairy nut sac. The big jock groaned, so Weare kept it up. "Fuck, pal, I could really get used to this."

Weare got Bruno's cock so worked up, he felt a drop of pine tar ooze between his toes. "You're a stud, man," the rookie said. "You want to get off a dozen times today, I'm gonna help you do it."

Bruno closed his eyes and sighed deeply. "Buddy, I'm so sick of being confused by all this. I'm done riding my own back. You want to be cock buddies? I ain't gonna argue. It feels too fuckin' good to let go of."

"Cock buddies," Weare said proudly. "Just two buddies taking care of each other when we pop wood."

Bruno grunted a swear as the rookie teased at his boner again with the warmth of his toes. "Let's stop talking about it and take care of our cocks, buddy." With that, he grabbed his bat and resumed jacking it on Weare's foot. The rookie followed Bruno's lead, and soon both men were masturbating with the other's foot.

They stroked in silence, stopping every once in a while to hawk a wad of spit on the heads of their cocks. Neither spoke. What passed between them did so in growled swears.

"Fuck," Weare said. He brought Bruno's foot up and slurped his own precome off the shiny hairs on the tops of the big guy's toes. "You ever drink your own load?"

"Sometimes," Bruno growled through clenched teeth. "I used to when I first started pumpin' it. Being married has a way of castrating those tendencies. I ate it a few times out of my wife, but Ronnie thought it was sick."

The veteran center fielder's voice was broken by excited gasps. He was getting close; Weare sensed it. More than anything, he wanted them to come together. He grabbed Bruno's sweaty size 12 and spanked his cock hard and rough against his instep. "And now?"

Bruno closed his eyes and grinned coolly. "Now I feel like a young guy again, like I'm beatin' off every ten minutes. I'm horny 24 fuckin' hours a day since you showed up."

The comment brought both men eye to eye. Weare felt his jaw drop as he buried his gaze in the veteran center fielder's gray-blue eyes, only to see Bruno stuck deeply in his. For one brief and burning moment, there was no world outside the cabin—no baseball camp, no game with the Matadors later that afternoon, just the line they had crossed.

"I fuckin' love you, dude," Weare grunted, stroking himself faster.

That did it. Bruno groaned Weare's name in a loud, thunderous bellow and unloaded on the rookie's toes. The sight of his first shot—a majestic string of hot, white ball snot—sent Weare over the top. He fucked Bruno's foot one more time before the heat in his nuts unloaded, blasting scum into the sexy dark hairs running above his ankle.

They continued as a second, third, and fourth volley erupted. Still shooting, unable to stop himself, Bruno pulled his foot off of Weare's pulsing cock and pulled it toward his face. He quickly bent his foot toward his mouth and lapped the spunk off it. Weare tasted hot and salty.

"Shit, dude," The rookie grunted. Like Bruno, he followed suit and flexed his own foot into his face so he could lap the veteran's come from between his toes. When it ended, they collapsed together on the floor. This time Bruno didn't go silent.

"Don't worry, buddy," Bruno said. "I'm over feeling guilty about being a guy."

Weare smiled and leaned forward, kissing Bruno's stubbly face. Their lips gradually met. Weare tasted both their come on the veteran's mouth. "I know it, dude. You need me, I'm here—any time, any place, and as often as you want it."

"You sure 'bout that?" Bruno sighed.

"Scout's honor." To reassure Bruno he slid his hands between the center fielder's legs. Bruno's cock was still half hard.

"Fuck," Bruno moaned. He spread his legs for a better view of things. "I told you, son—ten minutes later, and I'm primed to pump it again."

Weare stroked Bruno's bat a few times, then released it. "Sorry, big guy, but I got to get my ass to Doc Hanson's for a clean bill of health if I'm gonna help the team beat the Matadors." The rookie stood and aimed his nose into one of his armpits. "I stink. Want to take a shower?"

"Only if it's a golden one," Bruno joked.

Weare hauled down his underwear and bunched the musky, soiled cotton into the shape of a baseball and pitched it at Bruno. The sweaty missile caught him square in the face. "You're sick."

Bruno pressed his nose into Weare's nasty shorts and sniffed them. "You know it, dude."

"And I like it." Weare shook the last few drops of stale come onto the carpet before vanishing into the bathroom. As strange as the last two days had been, the rookie felt stoked in ways he couldn't describe. It wasn't just the team's first exhibition game; it was Tommy Bruno.

He ran the water until it was comfortable, then stepped in. The first place he washed was his nuts and spent cock. The action—and thinking about Bruno—started to stiffen him again. By the time he'd soaped his feet, pits, and asshole, his dick was hard. Weare had just begun to regret his decision to not suck Bruno off again when the shower curtain was suddenly pulled aside.

"What the fuck?" Weare gasped. His shock softened into a smile.

Bruno, sporting a full seven inches of lumber, stepped in. "Bend over," he growled.

Weare chuckled, "What?"

The answer to his question came not in words but actions. Saying nothing, Bruno took the soap from his hands, then grabbed Weare's ass. He worked a decent lather between the rookie's concrete butt cheeks.

"What are you doing?" Weare asked. "No fuckin' way, dude. You're too big!"

But he didn't fight it after Bruno assumed the fuck stance, standing up behind the rookie so that the shower nozzle sprayed both their faces. The head of Bruno's cock slid in.

Weare braced the shower wall in front of him. It hurt as much as the first time, but Weare wouldn't have traded places with anyone for a million bucks.

"It's been ten minutes, and you promised," Bruno huffed over his shoulder, through the hot spray and Weare's hearty grunts. "Time to prove how much you want it."

The rookie nodded. "I did give you my word, dude, didn't I," he said, grinding his teeth.

☆   ☆   ☆

Once the shower had washed away the grime, sweat, and soap, rookie and vet toweled dry. Their crisp, new Seaside Top Socks uniforms needed to be filled for the first exhibition game of spring training.

Bruno pulled on his midlengths, his jockstrap and cup, then his uniform pants. "What goes on between us," he said, adjusting his nut holder, "stays between us. You don't tell none of the guys, or all bets are off. I mean it."

Weare buttoned down his uniform shirt and tipped his gaze to see the dead-serious look in Bruno's handsome eyes. "I won't, guy." He countered the big guy's serious look with one of his three-alarm Cheshire-cat grins. "'Sides, if I bragged about how good your dick tasted, every dude on this team would want to choke up on your bat, and there'd be none for me."

"Fuck you," Bruno laughed. He picked up his glove and slapped Weare's tough ass, took two steps toward the cabin's door, but stopped. He turned back and moved his face close to Weare's as the rookie utility player fumbled with his sun glasses. He seemed hesitant and hovered in place.

Weare bridged the distance. Their lips met in a clean, breathless kiss. "I mean it, dude," Weare whispered. "I won't tell no one. This is between you and me, and I couldn't be happier."

Bruno nodded. They kissed one more time before Bruno pulled away. "I just hope Doc Hanson doesn't decide to stick a finger up your ass," Bruno joked over his shoulder on the way out the door. "He might recognize me up there."

"Me, too," Weare said, following him out. "He might get jealous."

☆   ☆   ☆

The warm spring sun made every inch of Bruno's skin tingle. As was the unspoken rule among the Top Socks, a player never hit the field in anything but a spotless uniform, and now the diamond was full of them. Bruno wore his baseball cap bearing the team's insignia of a sweat sock with black piping beneath his batting helmet as he approached the cages for batting practice. Jimmy Trout, the team's hitting coach who'd led Seaside to their famous '89 pennant chase, tossed balls for Bruno. The veteran center fielder spanked 17 hard out of an even 20 pitched.

After that he did calisthenics and stretching exercises with the regular lineup and some of the bench players. The rest of the team came together in a mandatory jog around the field. The Werewolf, Damon Thorne, kept pace beside Bruno.

"Hey, buddy," the Socks' chief catcher said.

Bruno had been so deep in thought about Weare and their new friendship, it took Thorne a second time to get an answer.

"Earth to Bruno. Anybody home in center field?"

"What?" Bruno panted.

The Werewolf grinned. "I asked how the fuck they were hangin'."

Bruno jokingly tugged at his cup. "You seen 'em. Pretty fuckin' big and low, buddy." The two men laughed. Shortly after that, the cocky smirk on Bruno's face softened into a sincere smile. "Good, Werewolf. Real good. Better than I ever thought."

"I just wanted to ask. You know, this whole divorce thing with Ronnie."

"Fuck Ronnie," Bruno sputtered, his smile persisting. "That divorce was the best thing that could have happened to me." He paused, shook his head. "Maybe the second best thing. Believe it or not, for the first time all year, that bitch ain't ruling my rod."

Thorne playfully clapped Bruno's ass. "Good for you, old man. See you at the old folk's home!" With an extra burst of speed, Thorne raced on.

"Fuck you," Bruno chuckled. "I got more youth in my left nut than most of this team!" In a show of energy few men in the majors could have duplicated, Bruno overtook him. He knew he'd pay for it later; his fucking right knee would scream in pain all night.

But Bruno realized he wouldn't be sleeping all that much at night anyway—not now, not with his nuts finally freed of the itch that had earlier kept him walking around with a 24-hour hard-on. The thought of Weare sent fresh adrenaline surging through his already pumped body.

"Fuck the knees, fuck Ronnie, and fuck the Matadors," Bruno spat when he and the Werewolf were 20 feet ahead of the team. "I got all I need now, you hairy cock knocker."

"That's the Bruno we know and love." As the others approached, Thorne formed a private wall with his back. "Did you hear about Roger? Day to day with that groin pull." Bruno shook his head and sighed in disgust. "Mitch is gonna keep that kid he was supposed to shift to Triple A."

"Vandercastille?"

"Yeah. Name's Tuc. He's being dumped on me. I gotta double up with him at the hotel when we play Philly."

Bruno clapped the Werewolf's shoulder as the team chugged by them like a powerful machine, oiled well with sweat and testosterone. "Don't be so quick to want out, Wolfie. These young bucks can learn a lot from us old bucks, and we just might find ourselves learning from them." The statement seemed all the more credible when, a moment after Thorne rejoined the joggers, Weare appeared in the dugout. Clad in his own spit-and-polished Top Socks trademark black and white, the sight of him captured Bruno's stare. Weare's handsome face seemed to light with a wide grin, too, at seeing the veteran center fielder. He stepped out of the dugout and into the sunlight. Then the rookie took off at a trot, his glove in hand, his perfect athletic body packed into his tight uniform.

Bruno knew then that he was in love, for the second time in his almost 40 years. But this was a love that stood alone.

"Clean bill of health," Weare proudly proclaimed.

Bruno almost didn't hear him. He was so happy to see the rookie, he temporarily forgot about the Werewolf, the Cowboy, that prick Aaron Sweeney, and two dozen other macho men on the field of dreams surrounding them. "Pal," Bruno said only to Weare, "there's something I want to ask you."

Weare plunked down his duffel bag and peeled off his shades. "Wow!" he sighed.

Bruno beamed from the complement. "It ain't much, but it's paid for and it's mine."

A quick glance revealed the pool beyond the window, the row of trees separating Bruno's house from the nearest neighbor, and all the accommodations inside that made a house a home: trophies, a framed poster depicting a scene at the plate from Bruno's '92 MVP season, comfortable leather furniture. "So what do you say? You want to bunk with me when we've got home games?"

The rookie went silent, but his actions spoke volumes. Weare kicked off his old sneakers, baring his big sexy feet. He braced the door with one foot, closing it, then spun on the other to face Bruno. Without saying a word or needing to, he reached for the big guy's zipper and slowly lowered it, freeing the heat in Bruno's underwear.

FIFTH INNING

The biggest thing Damon Thorne learned about Tuc Vandercastille other than that the lug-nutted pitcher had a knuckleball that could dance like a bottle rocket was that the 24-four-year-old couldn't keep his hands off the balls between his legs. The handsome rookie, sporting a neat buzz cut and growing a major-league goatee and mustache combo, seemed to be constantly toying with or adjusting the bulge between his legs.

"Can't help it," Vandercastille said when the Werewolf asked him if he had a case of jock itch or crabs. "I hate midlengths. I can never get my wang comfortable under my cup."

Thorne liked the hot-dog pitcher immediately, as Bruno had predicted he would. In the Thunderbird's absence Vandercastille was scheduled to open against the Philadelphia Pilots, with whom the Socks had a long-standing rivalry. The rookie, obviously nervous, had paced the room most of the night. They spent the morning pitching and catching. When Thorne called it quits, Vandercastille continued to ready himself for the big game with the pitching coach, Jim Trout.

Philly was hot for the opener, damned hot. Thorne shucked down to just his baseball shorts, minus the nut cup, and a pair of clean white sweat socks. As much as he liked Vandercastille, he was happy to be free of him, even if only for a few hours. The rookie's pacing had prevented him from jacking his tough, average-sized cock, something the Werewolf always did right before a game he was catching. It didn't take long for Thorne to spill his load. It never did. True to the nickname he'd been given, right before he blasted, Thorne teased just the head of his five inches and howled, spanking his nads over the edge. The first shot blew across the arm of the hotel chair. Having such an average-sized cock allowed the Werewolf more control than some of the bigger-dicked guys he knew. To intensify the sensation he rolled the heavy, come-packed sac of nuts over his spurting knob. The end result was a load blow that was so violent and fulfilling, it satisfied more than just the head of his cock. He jacked his dick between both balls until the sensitive, fleshy trigger of nerves was rubbed beyond pleasure to the verge of pain. Then, like any self-respecting wolf man, he lowered his head between his own legs and started lapping his balls clean of the musky juice he'd coated them with.

Thorne had sucked his own cock and balls regularly since Steven had taught him how to do it. Being athletic helped. Having a bigger pole to polish would have helped too, but Damon Thorne used what he had to his advantage. On more horny occasions than he could count, being able to suck his own balls and cock had come in pretty handy—during long, lonely road trips with the team, before the stress of catching a big game, even in bed as part of a great fuck. It never failed to impress whomever Thorne had hooked on Werewolf come.

He was almost done polishing off his hairy bat when the hotel door's computerized lock rattled. Thorne quickly tucked his spent, spit-soaked cock and balls back into his shorts as Vandercastille opened the door with his magnetic passkey. He too was covered in sweat and looked like he'd lost his best friend. The handsome rookie knuckleball pitcher peeled off his perspiration-drenched Top Socks ball cap and sighed.

"Hey, Tucker," Thorne said. He pulled his hand out of his midlengths and kicked his feet over the arm of the chair.

Vandercastille forced a smile, flashing perfect white teeth. His pale blue eyes glowed dully. "How's it hanging, dude?" the rookie replied.

Thorne scratched at his nuts for effect, but the truth was, it disguised his need to shift the still-hard, sticky lump rubbing against his hairy ball bag. "Pretty fuckin' low, guy. How'd it go?"

"As good as it's gonna get. Pilot Field's a big fuckin' park. Lots of corners. I ain't never pitched in anything so big."

"You're tough. You can do it," Thorne said, bringing his legs down. He'd planned on hitting the bathroom to get things south of his belt orderly in private, but right out of a scene from a dumb sitcom, the rookie shuffled in the same direction, and all they ended up doing was dancing into each other. The two men collided. It was unintentional, but the feel of his meat slamming into the rookie's bulge was overwhelming. "What the fuck!" he exclaimed. "Wanna dance?"

Both men saw stars. Vandercastille put a hand on the Werewolf's shoulder to stabilize them both. Thorne's right paw went unintentionally to the double bulge connecting them both below the waist. His fingers groped the rookie's meaty protrusion while trying to smooth the pain out of his own.

"Sorry 'bout that," Vandercastille said. "Luckily, I yanked out my cup a few hours ago." He reached his free hand into his Top Socks jacket and pulled out the plastic protector. "If we'd done that when I had this on, you might be on the floor singing soprano."

At such close range Thorne knew what it was he'd felt between the rookie's legs: cock, unobstructed by a cup. The

longer they remained pressed together, the bigger Vandercastille's manhood started to feel. Thorne took a heavy swallow, only to find his mouth had gone completely dry—despite
the fact he'd just swallowed down a bellyful of his own come.
In a cracked voice he scolded, "What the fuck are you doing
not wearing your plastic pud protector? You ever get cracked
in the nuts by a pitch?"

With a goofy grin Vandercastille stepped a pace back. The
Werewolf's fingers slipped off both their fronts. "I told you,
man. These fuckin' things are making my balls go blue. 'Sides,
my knuckleball floats in around 60 miles an hour." He took
off his jacket and hauled his Top Socks uniform shirt over his
head without unbuttoning it. The shirt took his black T-shirt
underneath with it. The smell of clean sweat and the rookie's
deodorant gusted around him. Thorne unintentionally took a
deep whiff of Vandercastille's smell as the rookie plunked his
ass in the same chair where he'd just jacked off. "It kind of
stinks in here," the knuckleballer said innocently. He kicked
off his sneakers and peeled his sweat-soaked white socks and
black stirrups off, flinging them into a pile between both beds.
Halfway out of his uniform pants, his handsome, youthful face
broke in a goofy smile. "Course, those socks ain't gonna help."
He dropped the rest of his uniform to stand only in his midlengths, the source of his irritation. He casually tugged at his
meaty bulge. "I'm going into this game wearing briefs. I
fuckin' hate these things."

The hot coals in Thorne's mouth suddenly ignited. "No
wonder," he choked out, eyes locked on the rookie's well-
packed groin. "Could they be any tighter?"

Tucker Vandercastille's midlength baseball underwear
looked like they'd been spray painted on the rookie's privates,
just like they were supposed to, only the new guy's full, heavy

manhood was mashed uncomfortably against his pelvis.

The rookie pitcher glanced down. "Yeah, these are fuckin' squeezing my nuts," he said, continuing to paw at his meat.

"I'll say," Thorne growled. Before he could stop himself, he reached out and cupped his hand over the rookie's. Tuc pulled back on his grip and gasped in shock. The Werewolf massaged his bat and balls, rolling the sweaty nuts beneath the underwear. "I'm a little jealous of them squeezing your balls. Here," he said, tugging on the elastic top of Vandercastille's midlengths, opening them up to expose a thick layer of coarse, dark-blond hair. "Let's see if I can help you with your problem."

The knuckleballer watched, too shocked to move, as his hardening cock poked its head out. Thorne quickly gripped him by the root of his bat and gave it a few stiff strokes before pulling his underwear down fully, freeing the rookie's low-hanging ball bag, which Thorne stroked with his other hand.

"Now that's what I call knuckleballs," Thorne said. He massaged Vandercastille's loose nuts while jacking him to his full eight thick inches. "How's that feel?"

"Better," Vandercastille gasped through clenched teeth. "I don't fuckin' believe you're playing with my cock, dude—or how fuckin' great it feels."

Thorne smiled. "No sweat, kid. This is Philadelphia, the city of brotherly love. You know anything about roadies?"

"What's a roadie?"

"That's what happens when a ball jock's on the road with a boner and nobody but his roommate to suck it. I can make you feel even better if you want."

Vandercastille sucked in a deep breath before replying, "Yeah."

Going to his knees in front of the hot-dog pitcher, the veteran catcher sucked the straining head of Vandercastille's eight inches into his mouth. The rookie's knees went wobbly; he put both hands on Thorne's shoulders to steady himself. "Fuck!" the young pitcher cried between gasps for air. "Holy shit. You're suckin' my cock. I don't believe you got your mouth on my wang, guy! What are you, queer?" The statement was followed by a loud, happy "*Ungh!*"

Thorne spit out the head of Vandercastille's rock-hard cock and took a deep whiff of his nuts before replying. "Not queer, just horny." He passed his tongue over the pitcher's meaty, sweat-covered balls, licking them like a hungry dog. "'Sides, would you care if I was?" The rookie grinned sheepishly as he toyed with his boner.

"Fuck, no," Vandercastille said. "It feels too fuckin' good. I just never expected to find you down on your knees in front of my dick before opening day, that's all."

"Good, now maybe you'll relax some. You're wound tighter than that knuckler of yours." The Werewolf grinned. "You ever do it with another dude?"

Vandercastille didn't answer right away. During his hesitation, Thorne stroked the rookie's cock, which began to ooze its first trickle of spunk between his fingers. Thorne brought hand to mouth and licked the come off—unlike the solid, salty punch his own come packed, Vandercastille's was sweet. "This ain't my first time," the rookie eventually answered.

"Yeah?" Thorne said in a husky whisper. "You ever done it with another jock?" Vandercastille nodded. Thorne kissed the rookie's piss slit for another taste of his gamy precome before rising to his feet. "You ever do it with another baseball player?"

Vandercastille's eyes darted nervously away from the Werewolf's penetrating blues. They settled instead on the obvious tent in Thorne's tight-fitting baseball underwear. Before

Thorne could grill him further, Vandercastille went to his knees in a reversal of their previous positions. He eased his strong pitching hand into the tangle of coarse shag underneath the top of Thorne's shorts. The Werewolf stood. His hard, stubby rod popped out, winking its straining eye. Vandercastille stared at it for a moment, stroked it slowly. Then in one deft swallow, the rookie gulped it all the way into his mouth.

"Shit, kid," Thorne moaned. "This ain't your first time."

Vandercastille slurped on the catcher's cock for a few seconds before replying. When he did he spit out the Werewolf's reawakened dick but wrapped his callused fingers around the shaft and head. "And you just shot your load, didn't you?" Thorne grunted an affirmation. "I can taste it on your dick, dude."

Thorne matched the sexy grin on Vandercastille's face with one of his own. "You're kneeling in my juice, man. Guess being locked in here with you and that big choke stick of yours got to me."

"Does that mean you've done this before?" the rookie asked, sliding Thorne's fleshy, sensitive cock head across his lips.

The excited leer on Thorne's face widened into a predatory smirk. "I told you—this is the city of bro love, little buddy."

"What?" Vandercastille asked.

Thorne pulled his shaft out of the rookie's hand and leaned forward, rolling his nuts over Vandercastille's mustache and goatee. "Shut up, Tucker, and suck on my bag."

"I got a better idea." The rookie gripped Thorne's midlength underwear by the elastic waistband and shucked them down to his feet. Once freed of the last of his clothes, the rookie backed Thorne to the edge of the bed and spread the catcher's hairy legs. The rookie then buried his face in the swampy, shaggy heat between the Werewolf's thighs. He licked and kissed, sniffed and sucked, until Thorne's cock and balls were glistening. Vandercastille licked his way lower, closer toward the Werewolf's asshole. "Fuck," Thorne sighed. "Dude, you thinkin' what I think you're thinkin'?"

Vandercastille answered by lifting the Werewolf's heavy ball sac and searching his way into the thick jungle of hair running between his butt cheeks. "This ain't hair, dude," the rookie said with a deep laugh. "It's fuckin' pelt!"

To help him out, Thorne reached a hand down and smoothed aside the thick brown shag, baring the pink hole inside. "I didn't get my nickname 'cause I bay at the moon, boy."

"That's for sure." Vandercastille licked around the tightly clenched knot between the veteran's concrete ass cheeks. Thorne's hole constricted and flexed with each flick of the rookie's tongue. The longer the knuckleballer worked around Thorne's hairy knot, the hungrier he seemed to grow for it. In minutes it ceased being a simple rim job; the rookie dove in with his mouth, lapping all the way, eating the Werewolf's hole with his own kind of predatory dominance.

The Werewolf threw back his head and howled for effect. Baying caused the rookie to pull back. Between Thorne's legs Vandercastille's grin glistened with spit. "You jonesin' on my hole?"

Vandercastille answered by running his tongue over the Werewolf's sweaty nut sac. "So what if I do? You like me eatin' it?"

"Fuck, yeah," Thorne growled. Up until the point when Vandercastille worked a finger between his well-lubed butt, it had been the truth. Without asking, the rookie shoved his fuck finger into Thorne's asshole, right to the last knuckle. Thorne jumped off Vandercastille's pitching hand. "Oh, no, kid. The Werewolf don't play that game!"

"No?" A menacing tone crept into the rookie's voice. "A moment ago you was all for me suckin' your root, dude."

"There's a difference between two buddies chowing on each other's sticks and butt fucking." Thorne tried to rise, but Vandercastille grabbed him by his boner, giving it a friendly tug.

"Not where I'm from. The buddies I sucked cock with grew to like taking my fat dick up their assholes."

Thorne again tried to move but not too hard. All he did was make Vandercastille milk a steady trickle of precome out of his cock. "I don't think so. I'm not taking that corncob up my asshole. You're too fuckin' big!"

Vandercastille chuckled as Thorne slipped out of his dick hold. Soon both men were playfully wrestling on the bed. "Come on," the rookie persisted.

Thorne fought with him, yanking his midlength underwear all the way down. He worked a dry finger up into Vandercastille's pink, hairy hole. The rookie's shitter was so tight, it spit his finger out like a bullet. "Holy fuck," Thorne gasped. "Your can's tighter than the team owner's wallet."

"Tightest fuckin' one you'll never get to fuck."

Thorne smiled. He liked the challenge. "Wanna bet?" With that, he buried his face between the knuckleballer's legs and took his first taste of the rookie's ass. Vandercastille's hole was still musky with the sweat from his extended workout, something the Werewolf went wild for. The longer he lapped, the less Vandercastille struggled against him.

"You hairy fucker," the rookie sighed. "I love having my asshole eaten out by a teammate."

Thorne stopped licking and rested his face on top of the pitcher's square ass. "Come clean, kid. Who have you sucked and fucked in the big leagues?" He reached between Vandercastille's legs and jacked on his fat cock to sweeten the offer. The handsome rookie shook his head. "Maybe one day we'll have us a three-way. He's someone you already know." "No shit?" Thorne said.

Now flat on his back under the Werewolf's spread, hairy legs, Vandercastille threw up his hands expressively. "I wouldn't bullshit you, dude. Me and one of the Top Socks done it during winter ball. We were both a little drunk and real fuckin' horny. It sort of just happened."

"That's fuckin' hot," Thorne said. His eyes took on a deep, far-off look, as if searching his mind and memory, through the lineup, for a face, for just who it could be.

"It was," Vandercastille admitted. "Fuckin' hot. It was so natural. Two guys without any strings or commitments. Just two men into being manly together."

The statement snapped Thorne's mental Q & A session with himself. "Speakin' of manly assholes," he growled, diving back between Vandercastille's spread cheeks. The rookie responded by sucking down the Werewolf's cock. Both men worked each other to the verge of shooting their loads, but before that happened, Thorne pulled his knob out of Vandercastille's mouth. "No more fightin' it, pal." The rookie shook his head solemnly and didn't. The Werewolf did a 180 until both men were face-to-face. "Fuck, you're handsome," he growled under his breath, sliding his well-lubed cock into the young pitcher's hole. They kissed deeply, hungrily, as Vandercastille unclenched the muscles of his ass, accepting his place beneath the other man. After that, the fucking began.

"You got a tight ass," Thorne grunted. He howled and thrust his five-incher into the rookie's can, settling into a steady rhythm. "Tell me who it was." Vandercastille shook his head, his teeth grinding together. Thorne pulled back so that just the head of his cock was lodged in the knuckleballer's ass-hole. He rammed it back in with all the zeal he could muster without shooting his load. "Tell me!" he demanded.

"Not until you give up some of that ass of yours," Vander-castille huffed. He bit down again as the Werewolf pulled out, plowed in again.

"Never," Thorne said. "I don't take it up the ass—and never one as big as yours, fucker."

Ramming the rookie's asshole made his thick slab spurt precome again. Thorne knew Vandercastille was getting close by the way the rookie's massive cock, directly under his ab-domen, flopped wildly with each thrust of his own bat up the knuckleballer's ass. The Werewolf looked down to see it spraying traces of ball snot across the rookie's six-pack. This sent him into overdrive. The eruption building in his own nuts came swiftly and violently.

Thorne pulled out. He quickly scooted up to the rookie's shoulders, aiming his cock square at Vandercastille's mouth. The rookie opened wide. The first blast of spunk hit the back of his throat.

"Aw, fuckin' suck it, dude," Thorne sputtered. The rookie didn't disappoint him. After Vandercastille gulped the second and third shots of semen down his throat, Thorne pulled out, leaving a breathless, hungry look on the pitcher's handsome face. "Take a load of this, buddy," Thorne huffed through gasps for air, a devilish grin on his face. As Vandercastille watched, the Werewolf leaned down to catch the last spurt on his lips. Then Thorne sucked his own hairy cock down his throat.

"Fuck!" Vandercastille grunted, licking his lips. "I ain't never seen nothin' like that."

Thorne grinned, growled, and continued sucking his cock.

Trickles of come dripped from around the corners of the veteran catcher's mouth. Vandercastille quickly rose up to meet him, and together they licked and sucked on the hard, spent cock between the Werewolf's legs. Thorne released his bat, and Vandercastille took a final slurp of its head. They kissed after that, sharing the mutual taste of musk on their lips.

"Fuck," Thorne said with an exhausted grin. "That was fuckin' intense!"

Vandercastille shifted beneath him. "It ain't over yet, dude. I'm getting close."

Thorne shuffled to one side on the bed. Streaked by sweat and as spent as he was, the sight of Tucker Vandercastille pumping on his rock-hard cock was too good to pass up. "Do it, kid," Thorne urged. He snuck a hand across Vandercastille's meaty sac and teased the rookie's balls. "Jack that fuckin' monster." He rolled the fat nuts in their low-hanging bag.

"Aw," Vandercastille gasped. "Pull on my fuckin' balls."

Thorne did the rookie pitcher one better; he leaned down and sucked on Vandercastille's nuts. This threw the rookie into overdrive. He bucked off the bed, each upward stroke leaving trails of precome across his flat, hairy abdomen. Right before Vandercastille shot, Thorne grabbed the fat eight-incher out of the rookie's hand and squeezed down hard, clamping his fingers in a choke hold beneath its slippery head.

"What the fuck?" Vandercastille yowled. He threw back his head as Thorne's viselike grip prevented him from coming but prolonged his orgasm.

Thorne aimed the crimson cock head at Vandercastille's open mouth, then relaxed his grip. A ribbon of hot liquid white gold flew out, catching the rookie square in his open mouth. "Eat it, knuckleballs," the veteran growled. "Eat that fuckin' load."

The second blast shot right onto Vandercastille's tongue. The rookie gulped his own juice until the pressurized spurt trailed to a trickle. Once Thorne had gotten a taste for himself and had cleaned up the mess, he settled beside the rookie atop the soaked bed covers, panting for breath, more than satisfied.

"Where'd you learn how to do that?" Vandercastille asked, shaking out his spent manhood.

Thorne stretched and yawned deeply. "Do what?"

"Suck your own cock."

The Werewolf's predatory blue eyes narrowed on the rookie's pale blues. "Someone taught me."

"Who?" Vandercastille persisted.

Grinning, Thorne reached down and teased the rookie's balls. "Who chowed on your meat in the Socks?"

"Touché," Vandercastille conceded.

"Touché nothing, pal," Thorne said. He stood off the bed and shook his cock dry. "Call that a little good-luck suck for the game."

"Thanks, man," Vandercastille responded with a smile. "I'm gonna need it. This rivalry between the Pilots and the Socks is bigger and older than both of us."

Though he didn't admit it, butterflies were taking flight in Thorne's gut too. "You're gonna do an ace job, kid. Just don't let them Philly hot dogs fuck with your confidence. Your job is to throw strikes and not walk anybody; ours is to smack the balls their pitchers send our way outta the yard."

Vandercastille nodded. He rolled over onto his stomach and arched his ass. Thorne playfully, respectfully slapped it in a familiar buddy gesture. He was about to walk away when he noticed a trickle of stale come clinging to the hair on the rookie's bag.

"Get some sleep, kid. We've got a big game to win tomorrow."

☆   ☆   ☆

Vandercastille's knuckleball dazed the Pilots through seven and a half innings. By the time the middle relief pitcher took the mound, the rookie had surrendered only two singles and a base on balls. The Socks' slugging offense had the Pilots down four to nothing when the call to the bull pen was made.

"This is fuckin' beautiful," said Bruno. He hefted his bat and headed for the on-deck circle. "That kid's golden."

The Werewolf could only agree. He slapped the veteran center fielder's concrete ass as he moved up the dugout stairs. "Yeah, Bruno. Tucker Vandercastille has one hell of a knuckleball."

Thorne trained his shades on Timmy Weare, Number 13. The other rookie on the team had worked the count full to three balls, two strikes. Weare cocked his head to the dugout for signs, but before looking back to the mound, Thorne noticed the rookie tip his head toward the on-deck circle, where Bruno was swinging his big bat. Both men exchanged a knowing buddy smile. The gesture was not lost on the Werewolf. He'd seen that look between buddies before.

Weare lined the next pitch through the gap at second base. It was a close play, but he hustled his ass safely to first, beating out the throw. A deafening mix of boos from the loyal locals drowned an equally sincere round of cheers from the Seaside faithful scattered throughout the bleachers.

"Number 31," the announcer proclaimed. "Center fielder Tom Bruno."

Bruno stepped up to the plate, assuming his classic slugger's stance: legs spread, knees bent slightly, his grip choking the bat. The first pitch was low and away, but he chased it. His swing chopped it foul down the third base line. A fastball right at the knees was called the second strike. Bruno stepped out of the batter's box and swung a few practice swats before resuming his stance. With Weare already at first and Scott Bradley coming up next in the rotation, a hit from the veteran center fielder would be a big one to potentially pad their lead.

"Come on, dude," Thorne growled under his breath. "Use that bat of yours like it was your cock and bring your buddy home with it."

Bruno's next swing caught a piece of the ball, fouling it in the dirt at his feet.

"Do it, Bruno," the Werewolf urged. He clenched both fists on the dugout ledge. "Do it for the Socks—and that rookie you're jonesin' on!"

The next pitch, a breaking ball, looped over home plate. In perfect concert Bruno lashed out, putting all his strength into the effort. A resounding thunder crack sent rival fans into a frenzy of anger and excitement, each equally extreme. Bruno didn't stop to admire the ball as it sailed over the outfield; he ran down the first base line like his life depended upon reaching the bag.

When he looked up, he saw he'd laced the ball back to the wall, then over it. The nearest umpire held up his hand and waved the sign. There was no denying the two-run homer.

Weare slowed his jog to a trot past third base, allowing Bruno a chance to catch up. A step ahead, the rookie crossed home plate first. Bruno, as if watching the younger man's back, crossed quickly behind. When the roar subsided and the Socks had come home, they high-fived, then hugged. It was obvious to the Werewolf something more than team spirit had passed in the manly gesture. It made a chill ripple down his spine.

Bruno and Weare punched knuckles with Bradley and the batboy, Catalano, before returning to the dugout. A testosterone-drenched line of high-fiving and butt spanking ensued around the two victorious batters. Once it reached the Werewolf, Thorne was ready with a butt spank of his own.

"You did it, you big stud," he growled.

Bruno flashed a cocky, happy grin and shook his head in disbelief, spattering a hail of clean sweat. "It's given me a hard-on."

"Yeah, I'll bet," Thorne said. He playfully punched Bruno's flat gut before seeking out Vandercastille in the dugout.

Tuc Vandercastille slept well—damned well, considering all. Celebrating his first major-league victory, not to mention one on opening day against the Socks' all-time enemy, kept the young pitcher up long after the last of the beers were guzzled. A first win, however, was not a sweep, so the team retired early to the hotel. He and Thorne iced up, kicked back, and crashed sometime after 1 in the morning.

Dreams about the game followed the knuckleball pitcher awake. He heard Thorne shuffling around in the bathroom, then the unmistakable music of morning piss splashing against porcelain. Thin shafts of sunlight pierced the window blinds. With an exhausted, appeased sigh, Vandercastille rolled over and stretched, unabashedly displaying his own piss hard-on. He gave it a few firm shakes that snaked his cock to its full eight inches and yawned.

"What a fuckin' great morning," he sighed. He flexed his bare toes atop the covers. Thorne caught him by the foot on his way around the bed and rubbed the sole. Vandercastille growled.

"Feel good?" Thorne asked.

Still groggy in the room's morning light, the rookie yawned and stretched again. "Would feel better if you'd stop playing with my stinkin' feet and take care of my dick."

"We can do that," Thorne sighed under his breath. A second later, two hot lips wrapped around the rookie's straining cock head. The sensation made his sore muscles—which had worked together for a total of 65 pitches in his seven and a half innings in the big game the day before—relax immediately. It was better than any rubdown or massage. Vandercastille—Thorne's 'roadie,' as he'd been called the night before—got so excited and hard, he was ready to shoot his wad in minutes.

"Fuck," the rookie knuckleballer groaned. "What are you doing different?"

Thorne spit out Vandercastille's cock to lick his heavy-hanging sac of nuts. "You got some nice balls on you, guy," the other man growled. He spent a few minutes sucking on the hairy low hangers before stealing a nip at Vandercastille's tight asshole.

"Go ahead," the rookie moaned. "Eat my butt."

A few licks was all he got. "I'm not really into ass, kid, as much as I am cock."

The comment made Vandercastille scoot up to his elbows. "Since when?"

Thorne didn't answer right away, only kept sucking away with his face buried between the rookie's legs. When the veteran looked up, Vandercastille gasped. It wasn't what was familiar about having the Werewolf catcher's mouth on his cock that made him suck in a deep breath but what was different. Thorne had shaved.

"What the fuck did you do to your 'stache and goatee?"

Thorne's only response was a predatory cock-in-mouth grin. His intense blue eyes shimmered in the sparse light filtering through the blinds.

"Fuck, dude," the rookie gasped. "You're the best cocksucker I've ever had—guy or chick. I mean it. You know just how to take care of another man's needs. Shit, I might never go lookin' for pussy again if you keep this up." Vandercastille reached his glove hand down and stroked the veteran catcher's smooth face. "You're so fuckin' handsome, dude."

Thorne spit out Vandercastille's cock and sucked on his fingers with the same intensity. When he'd paid attention to all five, he returned to the rookie's ball sac. "You think so?"

Vandercastille flashed a goofy, excited smile. "Aw, yeah. I never thought I'd be begging another teammate to suck my cock—or to let me suck his. That thing you did last night. Fuck, that was hot!"

The handsome face making love to Vandercastille's fat eight-incher tipped up to one side with a curious expression. "That thing?"

"You know, suckin' on your own cock. I ain't never seen nothing like it before. It was intense, man. Really turned me on."

Thorne wrapped a hand around the rookie pitcher's wet shaft and jacked him closer to shooting his load.

"Sucking his own cock? I didn't know he could still do that."

The strange comment caused Vandercastille to jerk on the bed. He'd worked his way to a seated position that gave him a better view of the face on his cock. Thorne was dressed in a blue polo shirt, black shorts, and a pair of sandals that showed off his perfect feet and hairy legs. Vandercastille didn't recognize the clothes, though he thought he knew everything Thorne had brought with him to the hotel. He realized the guy working his cock wasn't the Werewolf just as the first shudder of an orgasm tensed through his sore muscles.

Vandercastille gasped something unintelligible that made the mouth on his cock work faster. The face between his legs caught the first few blasts of his morning load. For the last he spit out the rookie's bat and let the come dump across his clean-shaven cheek. The Thorne look-alike pumped him until Vandercastille swore both of his balls were empty. The strangely familiar face licked him clean.

"Who the fuck are you?" the rookie eventually grunted, wiping hot sweat off his forehead.

Before the other man could answer, the hotel door opened. Dressed in a very familiar pair of gray sweat shorts, a black T-shirt, and a baseball cap bearing the Socks' trademark insignia and sporting his neat goatee and 'stache, the Werewolf nonchalantly strolled in. The image of his reflection between the rookie's legs made the veteran catcher stop in his tracks. An uncomfortable silence filled the room as both men locked eyes.

"What the fuck is going on?" Vandercastille asked in a confused growl. "Invasion of the cocksuckers? I'm seein' double!"

The man between his legs, licking his still-wet lips, rose from his crouch. The two mirror images faced each other with tense, chest-puffing stares. Just when Vandercastille couldn't stand it another second, the Werewolf's handsome face broke into a wide smile. The two men rushed each other to embrace in a manly bear hug. Once the official greeting ended, both faced the confused rookie.

"Meet my older brother," the veteran said.

"Older?" Vandercastille shrugged. "You two could be twins."

The clean-shaven clone brushed the back of his hand over

his mouth. "We are. I'm only a few minutes older."

Still locked together in their buddy-brother hug, Damon Thorne extended one of his big bear paws toward the bed. "This is my brother Steven. Steven, Tucker, my new roommate." The Werewolf's introduction was cut short when he narrowed eyes on the wet side of Steven Thorne's face. "I see you guys have already met." With that, he leaned closer and licked the stale come off his brother's cheek. He ended by giving his brother a loud, sloppy kiss.

"This is fuckin' wild," Vandercastille said. He watched the brothers as they slowly undressed. Steven gave his own bulging tent a firm squeeze before working his way out of his sandals and shorts. The Werewolf pulled his gray workout sweats to one side, freeing the balls Vandercastille had gotten to know so hungrily the night before. Soon both brothers had stripped down to nothing.

"You were right, bro," Steven Thorne said. "He's a fine-looking cock knocker." Like the Werewolf, his brother's dick was average-sized, a hot little nubber that made the rookie's mouth water for a taste. A flash of gold near Steven Thorne's manhood captured Vandercastille's gaze. The sparkle had come from a wedding ring. The fucker was married.

The rookie's spent cock rapidly hardened. He groped his reawakened eight-incher and jacked it while staring at the double dose of Thornes standing at the edge of the bed, stroking themselves. "You guys share fuck duty often?"

"Whenever Damon gets down to Philly, or when I haul my ass up to Seaside for a game. It's kind of a tradition that goes back a long way."

Damon wrapped an arm around his brother's shoulder and gave him a manly squeeze. "We been tricking our girl-friends—and sometimes our buddies—for as long as I can remember. You want to be shared, dude?"

It was all the invitation Vandercastille needed. "Fuck, yeah!" he exclaimed, rising from the bed with a grip on the handle of his bat. He dove to his knees like he was sliding home as Steven bent over, baring his hard, hairy ass. Without hesitation the rookie started licking the furry ring in front of his face. "Mmm..."

Both Thorne brothers reacted to Vandercastille's rimming. With Steven bent over, clutching at his hairy ankles, Damon urged the rookie on. "That's it, champ. Eat my brother's butt. Do it! Get a finger up his tight hole. Yeah, you're doing a good job, kid. Make him hump that finger just like it was your cock, only smaller—much smaller."

The rookie sucked around Steven's asshole while simultaneously working his fuck finger into the tight knot. As he ate the older twin out, Damon knelt down in front of him. At first he wondered if Damon wanted to join him in eating Steven's butt and just how far the brothers would go. But as Vandercastille watched, the Werewolf positioned himself to eat Vandercastille's butt, sandwiching the rookie between both Thornes. The veteran catcher's mouth rubbed his asshole and low-hanging sac of nuts the same way Steven had at the start of the morning.

It was as if each brother sensed the other's needs and used the rookie between them as a conductor. Damon gorged on the rookie's can. Vandercastille, in turn, plowed deeper into Steven's. Together their motions pumped the older Thorne into such a frenzy, his cock was dripping precome without even being touched. In tune with his brother's rhythm but unwilling to bring him over the edge so soon, Damon spit out Vandercastille's nuts and stood. "Not yet," he growled, pulling back on the rookie's hand. The knuckleballer's fuck finger popped out of Steven's butt.

A moment later the rookie found out what the Werewolf and his brother had in mind.

Vandercastille lay spread-eagle on the hotel bed. As had happened so many times since the team's arrival in Philly, the rookie could hardly believe his good fortune.

"Call me crazy," he growled with a shit-eating grin, "but I'm fallin' in love with both of Daddy Thorne's boys."

Steven and Damon had licked the rookie from head to toe, paying special attention to his armpits and abdomen, his feet, calves, and asshole. The brothers were now poised on either side of his rock-hard eight-incher. A shower of kisses and licks made Vandercastille hump his cock up between their handsome faces. Vandercastille felt Damon handling his balls, while Steven worked a finger up the rookie's asshole.

"If Daddy could see us now," he sighed.

Damon grinned as he ran his mouth up the stiff eight-inch bat in his grip. Once he'd reached the head, the veteran catcher took it between his lips and sucked it down to its hairy root. Steven, meanwhile, choked down his nuts. Vandercastille shifted on the bed and moaned, "That's it, dudes. Suck my cock and balls."

Damon didn't disappoint him. He spit out the bulk of Vandercastille's cock so that just the head was in his mouth, anchored by his tongue and lips, then sucked it all the way back in. The teasing cock job—like his ass work had done to Steven—brought Vandercastille right to the edge of shooting. And just when he thought he'd dump his load in the younger Thorne's mouth, the veteran catcher deep-throated him down to his balls.

"Don't be so greedy," Vandercastille heard Steven say. "You get him all summer."

The brothers switched positions, with Steven's clean-clipped mouth on the rookie's bat while Damon, for a time, contentedly licked the knuckleballer's nuts. After a solid ten minutes of service, Damon lifted his mouth from the pitcher's sac to join him at the head of the bed. The men kissed.

"My turn," Damon said, shifting positions so that he and the rookie were in a comfortable sixty-nine. Vandercastille gave Damon's hard, dripping knob a few sucks before taking it all the way down his throat. The brothers resumed humming on his cock. When it all got to be too much, Vandercastille spit out the Werewolf's bat and begged for a piece of Thorne tail. Steven quickly volunteered.

"You wanna fuck me with that big bat, pal?" Steven growled, going to his back beside Damon on the bed.

"Yeah," enthused the rookie. He ran his tongue over the older brother's hole. It was still wet from his earlier rimming. He lined up his cock. The rookie knuckleballer uttered a long string of breathless swears and pushed in; all the precome oozing out of his dick head helped. Steven Thorne's can was so tight, Vandercastille felt his nuts ready to pop before he'd even finished his first pump.

"That's it, slugger," Damon urged. "Fuck my brother's ass while I fuck yours."

The veteran catcher moved up behind the joined men, assumed the position, and slipped his pole up into the rookie's hole, linking all three men together. Vandercastille rammed his straining eight inches into Steven's can. Damon's much smaller bat followed suit into the rookie's. The older Thorne bucked, taking all of the knuckleball pitcher's cock. The rookie's low-hanging nuts slapped Steven's ass with each thrust. Vandercastille struggled to hold his spunk in, but unlike the ball game from the night before, this was one he wouldn't win. He pushed into Steven one last time before the room went out of focus, catching fire in front of his dazed eyes. The rookie shook, clenched his hands tighter against Steven's hips, and blasted what felt like a gallon of come up the older Thorne's well-stretched asshole.

The sensation pushed Damon over the edge. When the rookie pulled back, he pushed in. Damon heard his brother let out a howl a few seconds before his own cock spurted one, two—six bullets of come up Vandercastille's butt. They held on a second longer as the rush of heat subsided, then, one at a time, they collapsed atop the nearest bed.

The three men lay together, sighing heavily. They'd filled the room with the hot, sour smell of man sex. Vandercastille swore he didn't have a load left in him. Then the Werewolf reminded him there were still two hours left until the mandatory workout at Pilot Field.

☆   ☆   ☆

Steven absently toyed with the rookie's meaty prong until he'd unintentionally hardened it again. "You're fuckin' amazing, kid."

Vandercastille grinned stupidly as he watched his cock swell. "Yeah, it's pretty big, ain't it?"

"I meant out on the field, fuck nuts," Steven growled, though he continued to toy with the rookie's bat. "I mean it. There's jocks, champ, and there's athletes. You're an athlete. It's an honor to watch you go to work."

The comment caused Vandercastille to blush and stretched

his pole back to its full eight inches. "Thanks. Beating the Pi-lots was incredible."

"I hear the Thunderbird's pitching tonight off the disabled list," Steven said matter-of-factly. "That dude's a powerhouse. Bet he's hung like a fuckin' bull too."

Damon nodded. "You'd choke, bro. It hangs halfway down his thigh." Adding his hand to his brother's rough fumblings between the rookie's legs, the veteran catcher locked eyes with his roommate. "And speaking of choking, I've told—and shown you—who it was that got me addicted to sucking my own cock. The least you can do is come clean and tell me who on the Top Socks sucked yours."

SIXTH INNING

Tim Weare knew immediately that going to the bar after losing the rubber game to the Pilots was a big mistake. Two wide-screen TVs on opposite walls of the dark, smoke-filled room flashed highlights of the Pilots' victory and the Socks' defeat. The throng of conversation, mostly from an army of sports enthusiasts, revolved around the Pilots' stellar defense and what in that day's game had been an unbeatable offense.

The Dugout wasn't much different from most of the sports bars Weare had been in before. The sweet smell of beer, the choking mix of odors from guys wearing too much aftershave, and a haze of cigarette smoke hung in the air. Its dark green table lamps kept the brick walls and bar stools barely in focus and set a subdued mood for the usual sports debates.

"I need a fuckin' drink," Bruno swore.

Weare gave the big guy's ass a safe, respectful butt slap. "So do I, dude, but I'll wait till we're back in Seaside."

Bruno growled a snide laugh under his breath. It was the first sign he was coming out of his mood since the game's crushing nine-zip conclusion.

"Thunderbird," some guy chewing on a cigar huffed at the nearest television from his seat at the bar's right. "Looked more like a fuckin' chicken out there!"

Bruno mumbled "Fuckin' asshole" under his breath.

"Guy," the rookie said. "Let's grab us a sixer and chill till the bus leaves. I got a bad feeling about being here."

Bruno stepped up to the bar before turning back. "They won a ball game, not a war," the veteran center fielder said. "Look at you, all dressed up. Why waste that on a six-pack and a hotel room?"

The comment made Weare flush. He glanced down at his clothes: a bone-colored linen jacket over a white T-shirt and old blue jeans. Like Bruno, Weare didn't need much to look sharp. "Thanks," the rookie said. "Since you put it that way—"

Bruno play punched Weare's shoulder. "I mean it, kid. You're a stud tonight."

Weare sized Bruno up. In the open dress shirt that showed the thick hair at the top of his chest, a pair of black slacks, and shiny black dress shoes, the big guy also had put on the dog for a night out at the local sports bar. "Hey, you're the stud. I'd go out in public with you anytime."

The bartender set them both up with frosted mugs of tap beer. Veteran and rookie clinked their glasses together and left the bar for a small table in the corner. As remote as it was, it afforded them an unobstructed view of the game's highlights.

"Like I need to be reminded," Bruno groaned. He took a swig of beer.

Weare shook his head in disgust. The clip showed Phil Jette, one of the Pilots' star pitchers, one-two-threeing Scott Bradley, Damon Thorne, and Hector Valenza. "Arrogant fucker," he sighed under his breath as Jette made a triumphant fist and pumped it through the air on the TV.

"You don't know half of it," Bruno said. "Fuckin' prick. I'd like to shove my size 12 up his ass for lunch, but the fucker would probably thank me. I been hit twice by that asshole, once real hard."

Weare downed the last of his beer and rose. "Next round's on me."

"I accept," Bruno said.

Weare returned a few minutes later, only to find somebody else had taken his seat. It was the one man the rookie never expected to see sitting across from Tom Bruno. Bruno's game face had been restored. He was showing it to Phil Jette.

"That seat's taken, fucker," Bruno growled. Jette flashed a cocky smirk and shook his head. "You got two seconds to vacate."

Weare set both glasses loudly down. Jette turned. The cocky leer on his cold, handsome face softened. "Hey, it's little Timmy Weare. Isn't it past your bed time, boy?"

"It's past time for you to haul ass outta my face," Weare coolly responded. "Or didn't I just hear the gentleman ask you to leave?"

"Gentleman?" Jette said, looking around in a purposeful daze. "You see one?"

Bruno chuckled. "You smell something funny, Tim?"

"Yeah," Jette interjected before the rookie could answer. "It's you guys. You Top Socks really stink."

"And you Pilots are gonna crash," Weare said. He grabbed the back of Jette's seat and gave it a rough shake. Jette finally took the hint and lifted. The Pilots' number 2 starting pitcher faced Weare with a cold, unblinking scrutiny.

Jette was handsome, but his face had a cruel look to it. His blue eyes, unlike Bruno's, were icy. The angle and clench of his jaw and the way he kept his hair major-league perfect was typical of ballplayers and their egos. Jette, dressed casually in a green polo shirt, faded jeans, and black high-tops, no socks, looked good—damn good—and he knew it. Weare recognized that immediately.

"I don't think so, little man," Jette growled, puffing his chest to match Weare's. The two men sized each other up, and neither backed down.

Bruno had seen enough. He pushed out from the table. The chair's loud screech on the tiled floor brought every eye in the bar to their corner. "Lay off the rookie, asshole. You wanna talk trash and bust somebody's balls, take a stab at mine!"

Jette made a sarcastic huff as Weare took a swig of his beer. "Don't sweat it, Bruno," the rookie said, casually wiping his mouth. "I can handle this arrogant sack of shit."

The two men again locked eyes. Only the bartender drove them apart.

"These guys bothering you, Philly?"

Jette's coldly handsome face broke in a sinister leer. "No, Jake. Everything's choice."

Gradually, the sound of conversation around the bar filtered back. As the men gathered in front of the TVs returned to what they'd been discussing, Weare handed Bruno his beer. Bruno chugalugged it in record time. Weare followed suit.

"Come on," Bruno said. "He really does stink."

Weare set his empty glass down and followed. He only got one step when Jette's voice stopped them both in their tracks. "I'd say I'll see you in the playoffs, but the postseason is for professional ballplayers, not Little League."

"Bruno's right, man," Weare sniffed the air loudly. "You stink!" He and the veteran center fielder high-fived, leaving Phil Jette alone at the table of empty glasses.

Jette halted their escape from the Dugout. "Bruno, don't you and your little boyfriend want to know why I decided to crash your party?"

Bruno, his back to the enemy pitcher, sighed a deep, angry growl. "Fucker," he said, just loud enough to be heard.

His face in a casual pout, Jette reached into his back pocket. Bruno revolved in time to see the Pilots' star pitcher pull out a dog-eared photograph. "It's funny you should say that, Tommy boy, 'cause that's just what I did: fuck her. Course, to hear her talk, it was the first time she really liked it. Seems the thought of fucking you used to make her want to puke. I taught her how to handle a real man's dick. Even made her give up that towel. What did she used to call it when you were married? A come-catch towel?"

Jette extended the photograph. The look on Bruno's shocked, suddenly pale face made the diabolical grin on Jette's widen. For one breathless moment neither man spoke. Weare glanced over Bruno's shoulder to see some spread-eagle pussy with Jette's grinning face perched on top of it. "Ronnie," Bruno growled, his mouth open, his eyes wide and disbelieving.

"We set the camera on automatic. I got a whole roll of 'em—her and me fucking. Why don't you take this one," Jette said, waving the photo. "I got plenty."

Weare sensed what was going to happen a moment before Bruno lashed out, punching the photo out of Jette's hand. It might have been their newfound closeness; two buddies didn't do what he and Bruno had without coming to a different kind of understanding. That helped Weare get a step ahead of the game. He quickly stepped between Bruno and Jette, blocking the veteran from taking a swipe with the fist he had aimed at the pitcher's coldly handsome face. "No!" Weare shouted. "He's not worth it! Neither is she!"

"Get out of my way, kid," Bruno shouted. "I'm tearing this fuck head a new asshole!"

"Face it, Bruno," Jette taunted from the other side of Weare. "I'm plugging your ex-wife's pussy 'cause you weren't man enough to."

Weare let go of the veteran center fielder and shoved Jette a step back. "Go screw, Jette!" Before either of the opponents could continue the fight, the rookie grabbed Bruno's arm. "We're out of this toilet." It took all his strength, but he managed to drag Bruno through the bar's front door. When the warm night air hit him, Weare released his grip. Bruno didn't struggle. He was obviously shocked and understandably angry. Fresh beads of sweat covered his face.

"It's not worth it, dude," Weare said. "You get pissed, you're playing right into that cocksucker's hands."

"But Ronnie... He doesn't care about her. He's just fucking her to get at me!"

A wave of nausea squeezed Weare's insides. He didn't know immediately why. A gust of wind cooled the perspiration on his own forehead and cleared his thoughts. "You don't need Ronnie," he said, his voice lowered humbly. "You got me."

As if not hearing, Bruno shook his head. "I don't fuckin' believe this. He's fucking my ex just to piss me off." In the silence that followed, Weare's promise sank in. Bruno clapped the rookie's shoulder before pulling him into a tight, reassuring hug. "Thanks, kid. I would've killed him back there."

"Much as I'd like to see you do it, I wouldn't like to be visiting your ass in jail." Bruno's shoulder grip became a headlock. He playfully pretended to throttle the rookie. Weare eventually struggled free. "I mean it, guy. You don't ever have to worry about looking for someone who wants to be with you again."

The color returned to Bruno's handsome face. He smiled. "I'm not. Not anymore."

The sexy grin and Bruno's admission of something bigger than the sex they shared each night sent an icy-hot chill through the rookie's blood. He playfully clapped Bruno's ass. " 'Sides, I have a plan on how we can get back at that fuckin' prick. It might not happen tonight or even tomorrow. But you just trust me, dude. It's gonna happen."

☆   ☆   ☆

The sound of the rain falling on the bus roof, the endless drone of tires turning on the slick road worked Weare halfway to sleep by the time they reached southwestern Connecticut. Not alone, he heard snorts and snores from most of the team. Some of them snoozed with their headsets on. Others were sprawled across the comfortable double seats. The big loss at Pilot Field seemed to have drained the Socks of the fire they started the road trip with.

Being near Bruno at the back of the bus didn't help. The vibrations from the wheels, the sound of rain whisking past the bus windows worked Weare closer to sleep. Eyes half shut, the tired rookie yawned.

"Wish you wouldn't do that," Bruno mumbled, yawning, too, from the chain reaction Weare had caused.

The rookie forced a grin for Bruno's benefit. "Can't help it," he sighed. "I'm whacked." He turned his head toward the window and rested his cheek against the cool, moist glass.

A shuffle nearby, a man clearing his throat made Weare tip his head back toward the aisle. Hector Valenza, clad in a pair of workout shorts, a black T-shirt, and black high-tops, moved sluggishly toward the tiny bathroom boxed in the corner across from his and Bruno's seats at the back of the bus. He carried a folded-up newspaper that barely concealed his baseball mitt.

Through his half-closed eyes, Weare watched Bruno flash the team's shortstop a cocky grin. Valenza sent back a smirk of his own. The handsome Latino disappeared into the bus's head, locking the door behind him.

Weare liked Valenza. He was outgoing, friendly, and a real joker. Once, in the locker room, he'd grabbed the Cowboy's bare butt in front of the entire team, professing his undying love for Mike Young. Everyone, including Weare, had laughed. Nobody took it seriously; butt play was a given when it came to the locker room, no matter what the sport. Weare knew it was considered as straight and natural as apple pie and baseball.

The rookie was deep in half-asleep thoughts about Hector Valenza when he felt a tug on his right hand. Weare started awake in his seat. "What?" he sputtered.

Bruno leaned in. "Shh. It's only me."

The big guy had him by the wrist and was guiding his hand toward the bulge between the veteran's legs. Bruno was rock-hard. A tiny wet spot crowned the tent of his blue jeans.

"What are you doing?" Weare whispered.

Bruno answered by unzipping his pants and spreading them open, exposing the crisp white cotton of his briefs. "Give me a hand job, kid," the big guy begged, pleaded in a voice meant only for Weare. "I've had this boner for the last 40 miles. I tried to make it go down, but that only got it harder." Bruno rubbed Weare's outstretched fingers over the moist fabric of his underwear. The big cock trapped beneath it thrust up against the palm of Weare's hand.

The rookie wanted to grip it, to free it, to take it in his mouth and suck Bruno's cock more than anything, but the terror of getting found out made him pull back his hand as if he'd just been burned. "Are you fuckin' crazy?" Weare gasped, just loud enough to be heard. Every snore, fart, and crackle of rock music over headphones suddenly sounded twice as loud. "Here, on the team bus?"

Bruno toyed with the hard lump sticking out of his open fly. "Everyone's sleeping," he said. "No one's gonna know. Come on, pal. I really need it."

Weare took a heavy swallow and found that his mouth had gone completely dry. He'd never said no to Bruno, not in the days that had bonded them as the best of buddies, when they took care of each other on the road or at home in Seaside. He glanced into Bruno's blue eyes, then shifted his focus back to the white cotton tent only inches from his grasp. The hunger to lick it, sniff it, suck it, made the rookie swallow again. "What about Hector?" he asked, tipping his head toward the john. "That shit's not gonna take too long?"

"We got plenty of time," Bruno answered with a knowing grin. "Don't worry about Valenza. He didn't go in there to read the sports page. Didn't you see what he had with him?"

Weare shrugged. "The paper?"

"And his mitt. He's in there beating that uncut stick of his."

The last trace of sleep fled Weare's senses. His eyes snapped open. "He's jackin' off using his glove? Aw, fuck. That's sick." In his mind's eye Weare imagined the handsome Latino shortstop working his hairy, uncut cock into his sperm-soaked mitt. The uncomfortable heat between Weare's legs from playing with Bruno's hard-on suddenly grew worse. The rookie shifted in his seat to accommodate his stiffening cock. "Sick—and fuckin' hot."

"Not as hot as me, kid," Bruno growled. Weare glanced down to see the veteran center fielder pull his underwear aside. The head of Bruno's bat snagged in the damp cotton while his low-hanging bull nuts and the shaggy root of his dick dipped into view.

"Here," Weare whispered, giving in. "Let me take care of that."

He reached over and shook the arrow-shaped head of Bruno's cock free. A small pearl of precome zipped through the air, catching the back of the seat. True to his plea, Bruno was as hard as he got and dripping like a leaky faucet. The rookie stroked it a few times for him. Bruno's gummed-up piss slit stretched and winked in Weare's direction.

"Fuck, dude," Weare gasped. He squeezed down on Bruno's cock. The hot, slippery bat throbbed in his hands. "You are hard and hurtin'."

Playing with Bruno's cock and balls made his own rod stretch to full-mast in his shorts. He dropped the big guy's lumber long enough to adjust the pressure in his underwear, but when he returned to the veteran's cock, it wasn't just with his right hand. Gripping Bruno's bat at its root, Weare leaned down to suck the head and the first few inches of shaft down his throat. He went deeper, until his nose brushed the mossy-smelling musk of the hair surrounding Bruno's boner.

Bruno tried his best to remain quiet, but couldn't hold back a muffled growl as Weare sucked his cock all the way in, burying his face between the big guy's legs.

Weare loved Bruno's cock—the way it smelled, its taste, the strange and wonderful way it felt on his tongue, especially how it sweated inside the big guy's jock and uniform. The rookie—who didn't smoke, drink anything harder than beer with the guys, and stayed far and clear of the pro-athlete drug scene—realized he was addicted to something different: Bruno's cock.

He thought about all the times he'd brought the big guy over the top in the weeks since training camp and all the times Bruno had done the same for him. The rookie was so focused on sucking Bruno's cock, he didn't hear the bathroom door unlock until it was halfway open. By that point the veteran center fielder was a handful of heavy sucks shy of shooting his load. Then he heard the bathroom door creak. Both rookie and veteran seized in place. Weare quickly spit out Bruno's cock. The precome painting his lips identified his guilt.

All Bruno could do was try and stuff his dick painfully back into his pants. It was easier to attempt than to actually accomplish. Bruno almost made himself come from fumbling with the spit-shined shaft and the panic of knowing they'd been found out. A hundred imagined scenarios about what would happen now that one of their teammates knew they'd been sucking each other off flashed through his mind. Bruno expected the worst and, for one terrifying instant, held his breath. He'd built himself up so much, when he dared look over his right shoulder in the bathroom's direction, his first thought was, *What a letdown.*

Valenza was still seated on the bus toilet, shorts down around his hairy, muscled ankles, his dark brown eyes narrowed on Bruno and Weare. Bruno knew that Valenza knew. It wasn't so much the shit-eating smirk on the shortstop's handsome face as much as what Bruno saw him doing into his baseball mitt. The wet, purple-red knob of Valenza's uncut cock bobbed in and out of his glove. The second baseman was getting off on watching Number 31 and Number 13 in action at the back of the bus.

Bruno wordlessly returned Valenza's horny smile. If it was a show the shortstop wanted, they'd give him one. He released the hard cock barely covered by his underwear and grabbed Weare by the back of the neck. Any protest the rookie might have made was silenced by a mouthful of veteran dick.

Valenza let out a deep growl, just loud enough for them both to hear. The sound drew Weare's eyes back to the bathroom door, to the sight that convinced him to complete what he and Bruno had started. He watched Valenza watching him make love to Bruno's cock, sucking the big guy closer to the bounty of ball snot he planned on swallowing. To show the shortstop just how good he was at servicing Bruno's needs, Weare spit out the dick in his mouth and passed his tongue over the hairy nuts hanging beneath it. Weare sniffed and licked at Bruno's balls while conspicuously stroking his own bat.

Valenza flexed his hand inside the baseball glove. The speed with which he was jacking his uncut lumber increased. The fleshy purple head blurred at the edge of the worn leather. Valenza, with his tongue hanging out of his mouth, narrowed his eyes on the back seat action. Like Bruno, Weare knew the handsome Latino was getting close. He spit out Bruno's nuts and returned to the cock in his mouth. Being watched turned him on more than he thought. It fueled his hunger for the center fielder's load. Taking the head of Bruno's bat between his lips, Weare jacked the shaft faster and faster.

Bruno kicked back in the bus seat as best as he was able. He wanted nothing to block Valenza's view of the final moment, when he squirted what promised to be a bucket of come down the rookie's throat. Weare sucked harder. Valenza's glove-hand squeezed down.

The Latino shortstop shot first. Bruno saw the jet of nut juice spray over the edge of Valenza's glove. Watching Valenza shoot and knowing how turned on they'd made him sent Bruno beyond his limits. He planted his feet down hard and strangled the growl in his throat as the first wave of come raged up his rod and into the rookie's mouth. Weare gulped and swallowed, which only prolonged the sensation. But as good as he felt, to his own surprise, he wanted Valenza to see it.

He yanked his cock out of Weare's mouth and dumped the last of his juice on the handsome rookie's lips. Not being able to grunt and howl caused Bruno to slowly come down from the electric sensation that had pinned him to his seat. He rubbed the back of Weare's head and exhaled deeply. Only the sound of Valenza's shorts being hiked up snapped Bruno's spell. Both he and the rookie looked in time to see Valenza close the door behind him. The handsome Latino fumbled once with the bulge in his well-packed shorts, then with a performance that could have won him an award, pretended to drop his glove and the newspaper he'd hidden it in. Going down to his knees to retrieve it put Valenza face-to-face with the rookie between Bruno's legs, with only the big guy's spent cock separating them.

"Don't worry, guys," Valenza whispered with a grin. "I ain't tellin' nobody." As if to cement his promise, he passed his tongue over Bruno's still-hard cock. Though Weare didn't respond to Valenza's words, he didn't fight it when the handsome shortstop brushed his tongue across the rookie's lips, mopping up Bruno's come. The two men kissed between Bruno's legs, sharing the veteran's musk.

Bruno exhaled deeply when Valenza rose and seesawed his way up the aisle back to his seat. He and the rookie played it safe the rest of the drive home to Seaside, though once the door closed behind Bruno at the house they now shared, the big guy decided it was only fair to return the favor—and the hum job.

Curly Ellis seemed pretty cool with the Socks taking only one of the three games in their home stand against the Florida Fins. Considering Ellis had the third highest batting average in the league, Weare couldn't understand how losing 0–4 in the Sunday day game wouldn't piss the giant off. Weare, however, was not so easy with what would have been a sweep for the Fins, who led the Eastern Division by five games, had Scott Bradley not laced one over the wall in the bottom of the ninth with two men on. The Socks avoided total humiliation with one swing of the bat.

Weare stripped down to his midlengths. Ricky Catalano passed towels around to the men. Most of the guys had finished with the press and were either naked or pretty close to it. They were all still talking about the game—all except Ellis, who peeled off his jockstrap and tossed it into the pile of dirty clothes on the floor near his locker. Trying to be casual about it, Weare tipped his head slightly in the first baseman's direction. Ellis's soft, dark cock slumped over his two huge shaved balls. *Maybe that's why he's so cool about things*, Weare thought. *If my prick was that huge, I'd be pretty fuckin' laid-back too.*

With a disgusted sigh, he followed the Socks' hung first baseman into the showers. The smell of soap, shampoo, and old sweat being washed away by hot water and the echo of deep masculine voices dulled by the steamy spray gushing out of the wall nozzles greeted him.

The showers were crammed, especially with the bull pen having been put to full use in the final two innings. Vandercastille, who'd started the game, braced the wall and let the hot water unknot his ripped body. Bruno and the Cowboy stood close to the same showerhead, sharing it. The slightest pang of jealousy surged through Weare at seeing them soap up side by side, though he just as quickly admitted to himself what a stupid concept that was. Curly Ellis sidled between the Werewolf and Aaron Sweeney. Weare glanced down in time to see Ellis's tight-looking pink asshole wink as he walked into the spray.

Only the anger and depression of being five games behind the Fins and four behind the Pilots kept Weare's cock soft. Given what had happened with Hector Valenza on the bus, the rookie's journeys to the shower—a trip he'd always taken in stride—were getting harder, usually thanks to his cock. Once, during their first West Coast swing, he'd stood with his back to the others and had gotten so stiff, he'd soaped himself into shooting a load across the wall. Now his only options were standing beside the Cowboy and Bruno and the cock he loved to suck so much, thereby risking a hard-on for all to see, or squeezing in beside Tucker. He took his chances with the other rookie. It wasn't a much better choice; memories of a drunken night in Cincinnati came flooding back when Weare slapped Vandercastille's wet, soaped-up ass.

"Tuck it in, Tucker," Weare said. "Buck over, dude."

Vandercastille stuck his face under the water, straightened, then shuffled his spread legs to one side. "Hey, pal," he grinned.

Weare ran the soap through his mossy cock shag and soaped his nuts, then his can. "I'm fuckin' whacked, dude. Today really knocked me out."

Vandercastille agreed. "No shit, dude. Fightin' off the Fins was like pulling teeth. Took everything we had to take a win away from 'em."

Weare hunched down and washed the sweat from between his toes, rubbing his tired feet under the steam before lathering his legs. "All I want to do is go home and crash for about 12 hours. Thank Christ we got tomorrow off. I need it big time." He glanced over his shoulder, hoping to catch sight of

Bruno under the spray, but the big guy had already finished showering and was gone.

The rookie found him ten minutes later combing his hair in front of his locker, dressed only in a white towel. The smell of Bruno's deodorant filled Weare's senses with a reassuring, masculine scent. "Hey, guy," Weare said innocently enough, even though he felt his bat begin to toughen at the sight of Bruno.

The handsome veteran, his wet hair combed neatly, flashed a cocky grin. "Hey yourself, pal. Good game out there today."

The comment made Weare's Cheshire-cat grin widen. "Yeah?"

"Better than a loss," Bruno stated matter-of-factly. He peeled off the towel, exposing the rest of his perfect body. The veteran's thick, soft cock and low-hanging bull nuts—loosened and made meatier, no doubt, by the hot shower—spilled down the side of Bruno's hairy leg.

Weare sighed. It had been unintentional, but he couldn't help it. Seeing Bruno naked each time was like the first. From his handsome face down to his just-as-handsome feet, Weare studied the image of the center fielder as he splashed cologne on his chest and face, and even applied a dab to his nuts. "You want to go for a drink after?" Bruno asked, as if oblivious that his body was being worshiped by the rookie.

The question snapped Weare's focus. He turned toward his locker and shrugged. "I don't know. I'm kinda tired. I was hoping to catch an early night tonight."

"Whatever you want, pal," Bruno conceded.

Weare reached for his stick of deodorant. "No, guy. You go out with the club. I'm crashing tonight."

"No, really," Bruno said. Before Weare could continue the conversation, Curly Ellis breezed by the bench the way he always did, like an angry thundercloud, a force of nature.

"What's this, a lover's spat?" Ellis said with a chuckle that wasn't altogether good-natured. A sarcastic laugh followed.

"Yeah," Bruno said. "You jealous?"

While Weare was proud of the big guy's comeback, it didn't shut Ellis up. Instead it spurred him on. "It sounds like the two of you were asking your wives for permission to go out with the boys for drinks."

"I was asking my roommate if he wanted to join us," Bruno growled. All friendliness had fled his voice. "You got a problem with that, Curly Joe?"

Ellis didn't answer right away. For seconds that felt like hours, Weare occupied himself pulling on fresh briefs and socks, watching as the other two men sized each other up. Ellis was the first to look away. "I just meant that you two are inseparable lately, like the Bobsy Twins."

Bruno teased his thick, soft cock. It was unabashedly half hard when Ellis glanced down for a look at it. Bruno released his grip and took hold of his low-hangers. "We're the Ballsy Twins, Curly Joe. Biggest nuts in the league."

"Biggest?" Ellis chuckled in a threatening tone. Weare knew instantly it was a challenge to the big first baseman. Rising to meet it, Ellis undid his towel. It fell to his feet, leaving him as naked as Bruno. "I don't think so."

Bruno studied Ellis's big black cock and shaved nuts. "I didn't say cock, Curly Joe. You got the whole team outclassed with that log of yours. I said balls."

Weare suddenly piped up. "Yeah, dude, sac. Nobody's got bigger balls than Bruno's," he said proudly.

Bruno released his clean-smelling bag and high-fived the rookie. Ellis didn't appear impressed.

"You may have stones, Bruno, but so do I, and I got the best control over 'em." Ellis toyed with his thick black cock, rolling the foreskin over its moist, pink knob. "But unlike you, I ain't ruled by my prick."

"I can control my nuts," Bruno countered. "I tell it when to sit up and when to jump."

"Yeah, right." Ellis leaned down and picked up his towel. His half turn made his tight, puckered hole wink again at Weare. "And you two ain't bangin' each other when the rest of us aren't looking. Shit…"

He started to walk away but only got a few steps. Bruno's roar stopped him where he stood. "Curly Joe, you'd better watch that crap, son. Teammate or not, I'll tan your fuckin' hide."

Ellis slowly revolved. The pink head of his uncut cock was fully exposed now. Despite the surge of adrenaline and rising panic in his blood, Weare watched the first baseman get hard with silent fascination. Ellis, true to Bruno's claim, had to have the biggest cock on the whole team. Weare swore the fucking thing hung halfway down his leg, and it wasn't even completely stiff. "You're gonna tan my hide?" Ellis growled. "I don't think so. Not some white boy with nuts smaller than mine who can't control 'em."

"I got sac," Bruno said. "Dollars to the size of your dick that they're bigger than anything you got hanging under that gorilla cock of yours."

By that point some of the guys dressing at the other benches had taken notice of the growing debate. The Werewolf, wearing a fresh pair of white briefs and matching ankle socks, added his vote. "My cash is on Bruno," Thorne said. "I ain't never seen such big nuts."

"Yeah," Hector Valenza agreed. "Bruno's got the *cajones*."

Aaron Sweeney's vote didn't come as any shock. "You're all fuckin' blind. Curly's got Bruno's baby-nuts by the sac. I'll put $20 on it."

A round of bets began, and wallets opened around the lock-er room. While things seemed to be getting out of control when it came to the subject of who had the biggest nuts, Weare was relieved; it deflected any attention concerning his and Bruno's closeness. Adding to that was a sense of pride, since the overall team consensus pointed to Bruno's come-filled low-hangers as the hands-down winners in the Socks locker room.

Lesser men might have given in but not the team's first baseman. "You don't get off that easy," he said to Bruno. "Not until it's proven."

Bruno gave his famous bag of nuts a scratch. "How you gonna prove it, Curly Joe? You gonna weigh my balls?"

"No," Ellis said. Not to be outdone, he shook his inflated prong and ogled his shaved sac. "Not weigh them, measure 'em."

"Yeah," Bruno said with his best game face. "I bet you'd like that."

"Oh, no," Ellis said coolly. "I ain't doing the measuring. Cat!"

The batboy nearly tripped over his big feet stumbling front and center.

"Yeah, Curly?"

"You got a ruler or, better yet, a yardstick hanging around somewhere?"

"I think there's a tape measure in the toolbox," Catalano shrugged. "Why?"

"Get it," Ellis ordered. "We got a little bet going, and we need you to take some measurements."

A look of barely contained panic flashed through the bat-boy's eyes. His Adam's apple moved under the influence of a heavy swallow.

When Cat returned a few minutes later, a small mob had gathered around Bruno's locker. Weare, Thorne, the Cowboy, and Valenza flanked the center fielder. Sweeney, Bradley, and Tuc Vandercastille formed a half circle around Ellis. Several of the utility players and the bull pen, while occupied with getting dressed, were watching the huddle intently.

"H-here, Curly," Cat said, extending the tape measure.

Ellis shook his head. "No, kid. We need someone impartial. You got to take the measurements."

The horror in Cat's eyes intensified. For one brief moment he glanced down—first at Ellis's half-hard black monster with its moist pink head poking out of its skin sock, then at Bruno, whose perfect, cut column of dick pointed up at him. "Guys, I can't!"

"Sure you can, Cat," Weare said. "All you gotta do is measure Bruno's and Curly's nuts—sac and all—to see who has the bigger bag."

To reassure Cat, Bruno patted the trembling batboy's shoulder. "Don't worry, son. It's gonna be a short contest."

"For you," Ellis said, indicating Bruno. He stepped up to the bench and put a leg up on it. His heavy black nuts and unsheathed bat hung proudly for all to see. "Start at my root and make sure you warm up the end of that fuckin' thing. I don't want my sac shriveling up 'cause it's cold." Slowly, nervously, Cat blew on the metal tip of the tape measure. He rubbed it between his fingers, avoiding everyone's eyes when he'd finished. "Come on, guy!" Ellis demanded.

Cat reached between the first baseman's legs. He set the metal tip against the bare, shaved skin at the root of Ellis's cock.

"Make sure you get it right," Aaron Sweeney demanded from over Ellis' shoulder. "Every inch. Roll his nuts so you get all of it!"

The first few inches were easy to measure, but as Cat ran the tape into the dip between Ellis's nuts, he had to lean closer—closer to the unsheathed monster bobbing below the first baseman's flat, shaved abdomen.

Cat couldn't help but stare at Ellis's cock. It was hard not to. The big black bat stretched to within inches of his face. He could smell the moist, musky skin of its uncut head, the clean scent of soap in the sparse hair ringing it. To the bat-boy's embarrassment and horror, Cat realized he too was getting stiff just from breathing in the odor of Curly Ellis's cock. The whole locker room—the smells of sweat, cologne, deodorant, and clean skin—pressed in on him.

"Go on," Sweeney huffed.

Cat extended the tape measure. He hadn't meant to touch Ellis's cock, but the back of his hand rubbed against the trigger of nerves under the first baseman's dick head. The black skin sock and pink knob slid over Cat's knuckles and seemed to double in size. Ellis groaned. The lump in Cat's uniform grew painful. Before he could stop himself, he hefted the big black cock in one hand and squeezed it, pulling it out of the way. With his other hand he took the final measurement. The big black nut bag came in just over the seven-inch mark, from one tip to the other.

"What's it say?" Weare asked excitedly.

Ellis didn't urge Cat on. By now his rock-hard ten-incher, clamped in the batboy's hand, was leaking syrup.

"Seven inches," Cat said in a breathless whisper. "Root to root." He released the first baseman's straining cock and silky, shaved pouch. Cat sensed things could only get worse because now it was Bruno's turn. Bruno, who Cat got off on each time he jacked his own bat at night. Bruno, whose sweat-soaked socks and underwear he kept stealing just long enough to bury his face in them before dropping them into the washing machine.

Bruno stepped up to the bench, putting a leg up to allow Cat easy access to his manhood. The veteran center fielder's clean smell again sent the locker room spinning around Cat's head. Time seemed to slow. For one heart-stopping moment, the batboy could only stare at the half-hard cock hanging over Bruno's nuts.

He'd seen Bruno's dick before but never so close, never as touchable. All it would take was a bold, openmouthed lean forward, and he'd have his sports hero where he'd always dreamed of taking him. The hairy band of hard muscles surrounding the center fielder's hard cock were so hypnotic, smelled so manly, Cat sucked in an unintentional lungful of air and held his breath. Time came rushing sharply back when he reached out and placed the metal tip of the tape measure at the hairy root of Bruno's cock. The hot skin under his fingers made Cat's face flush worse than when he'd touched Ellis.

"Mmm," the batboy sighed, exhaling. The tape measure's numbers went out of focus as a line of sweat dripped into his eyes. He rapidly wiped the arm of his uniform over his face. Touching Bruno—first the sac of hairy nuts, then the cock his thumb pressed the measuring tape's tip against—convinced Cat he was either going to pass out, die of a heart attack, or blow some serious come into the front of his uniform. Bruno's dick, thick-veined, hairy, and rock-hard, strained up to stare at him with its one, unblinking eye.

It was all Cat could think about, Bruno's cock and how much he wanted it. He was jealous of anyone who'd ever had it. He both hated and admired Tim Weare, the Socks' hotshot rookie, Bruno's new roommate and best buddy. Cat wanted—needed—Bruno's cock. He at least had to feel it.

Cat brought the tape measure around the circumference of

Bruno's bag. Faking that the veteran's cock was in the way, the batboy grabbed it by the head and moved it to one side. It was an obvious motion, but Cat couldn't stop himself, and Bruno didn't complain. Like Ellis, he growled a deep, masculine sigh at the feel of being roughly fumbled by the batboy. His hard cock pulsed in Catalano's hand as the batboy squeezed down hard. Cat felt something hot and sticky slip between his fingers. With a rising sense of horror and excitement, he realized Bruno had oozed a trickle of jizz onto his hand.

Cat pulled back with Bruno's prize between his fingertips. His other hand released the tape measure. Cat held it up for all to see. "Seven inches," he announced.

"No fuckin' way," Weare argued. "Bruno's got to have bigger stones than that."

"It's an even match," Cat said. All he wanted to do was get away from them so he could lick the musk off his fingers.

"You're both studs," Mike Young drawled. He clapped Bruno's hard, bare ass and continued on to his own locker. The Cowboy flashed Cat a shit-eating grin. Before the batboy could take a guess at the true implications behind the gesture, Ellis drew all eyes back to where he stood at the bench.

"We may both be giants in the nut department," the first baseman huffed. "But I still got the most control over mine. I bet you by the end of the regular season, mine'll be twice the size of yours."

Bruno chuckled loudly. "You? You'll be pumping so much cream out of that log of yours between now and late September, they'll be half as big as mine."

"I don't think so, pillow humper," said Ellis.

Bruno extended his hand for the first baseman to shake. "Deal. Put your money where your meat is."

While Ellis shook Bruno's hand, cash wasn't the kind of

stakes he had in mind. "Not money, Bruno. Respect. Loser has to kiss the winner's ass. Literally."

The confident grin on Bruno's face flattened. "OK, but why not keep it as respectful as possible: Instead of kissin' ass, the loser has to lick the winner's nuts like the dog he is."

Bruno's intention had been to make Ellis back humbly down. Instead, the plan backfired. "You're on," he said. The two men shook again. It was a done deal.

Weare was about to argue the spoils of winning such a bet when Mitch Hudson broke up the show. "What the fuck's going on in here?" the coach snapped. All eyes turned. Cat quickly swiped his hand over his lips for a stolen taste of Bruno's come.

"Nothing, coach," Ellis said. "Just a little team meeting."

"Yeah?" Hudson asked. "About what?"

As casual as he'd been all day, Ellis took the whole thing in stride. "A little bet to make the season interesting."

"Interesting?" The pissed-off scowl on Hudson's hard, handsome face sagged into a crass grin. "Yeah, well when you guys are done whacking each other off, why don't you try and find some other interesting reasons to prove yourselves like you did out there today? I'm not happy, gentlemen." The last word was stressed purposefully. "You cockroaches better not scatter just 'cause I turned on some lights," he spat in the direction of the bull pen pitchers. "You looked sloppy out there. You want to win games, then I expect you to throw strikes. The rest of you," he now indicated the men assembled near Bruno's locker, "you either bunt it down the baseline or drop it in the gap when I tell you to, or you'd better slug it over the wall. These are your options. This is the big time, not some neighborhood sandlot. I see mistakes in defense again like I saw today, and I'll snap you down to the minors faster than you can blow a fart. I mean it. You dudes think I'm being hard-assed? Well, pals, let me also remind you that we got a few ball clubs coming in here after the midseason break who aren't letting bloop singles win games." Hudson drew in a deep breath and passed his angry eyes from one of them to the next. "The Minnesota Monarchs, gentlemen. They own the Central Division. We got the Seattle Stirrups a week after that if you think it ain't already hard enough. And then it's back to our old friends in the Eastern Division, those fabulous Fins. I shouldn't even need to remind you who's coming in on their heels 'cause, guys, that one's a kick in the balls. Yep, the Pilots."

Somebody grunted. Bruno tipped his focus to the guilty looks on the faces of his teammates, then addressed Hudson. "Point taken, Mitch. We got a slump. We need to play better if we plan on clinching our division."

Hudson's anger softened—but only slightly. "Good. That's all I'm gonna say on the subject. I'll leave the rest of you to discuss what pro baseball means to you, if you want to keep playing on this team." Hudson's didn't stop there. His bad mood shifted suddenly to Catalano. "You," he growled. "My office, now!"

The salty musk on Cat's lip soured. "S-sure, coach," he stammered as he followed Hudson out of the locker room.

☆   ☆   ☆

Hudson slammed the door hard, shaking its drawn metal blinds. Cat jumped in place. "What is it, coach?" he asked. "Ain't I been doing a good job?"

"I'll ask the questions, come stain," Hudson bellowed. He muttered a pissed-off swear, then moved beside the batboy and did his best drill instructor's study of him, from Cat's big feet to the goofy grin under his baseball cap. "But to set your skinny ass at ease, yeah, you've been doing a damned good job. You're probably the best batboy this team's ever had. The guys love you, and I know you love the guys."

The stupid smile on Cat's face got two shades dumber. "Well—"

"I mean, you really love 'em. I seen the way you look at them when they hit the showers and the bulge in your uniform whenever you're near Bruno or the Werewolf." The hard scowl on Hudson's face broke in a swarthy grin. "I even seen you sniffing their ripe jocks and sweat socks, kid."

Cat's jaw dropped down. "N-no way," he said, his voice rising an octave. "It's just—"

"That you like sucking cock. Don't deny it. What did I just walk into out there? I caught you red-handed, with your hand around Bruno's prick."

"I can explain, coach!" Cat started to argue.

Hudson gave the batboy one final up-and-down inspection, then unexpectedly grabbed the bulge between the younger man's legs. Cat jumped again, this time gasping in disbelief. "How do you explain this?" Hudson demanded. He fumbled with the tent in the front of Cat's uniform pants. The batboy went rigid, too shocked to move. Without asking, Hudson hauled down the batboy's zipper and reached in. After a few deft tugs, Catalano's skinny, hairy Italian cock with its pink head and dark shaft spilled out along with two meaty nuts. Hudson stroked the batboy's cock a few times, until it had hardened fully. That done, he toyed with Cat's nuts. "Yeah, don't even try to deny it, cocksucker," Hudson growled in a threatening voice. "I know all about you horny pups who get off on other guys."

The words shook Cat out of his stupor. "It just feels so good...."

Hudson released the batboy's balls and took a step back, admiring his handiwork. "Strip," he ordered.

Cat's wide, stunned eyes widened more. "What?"

"If you want to stay in that uniform, you'd better get out of it—and fast. We got a cocksucker on our team, and his punishment has to fit the crime."

In a daze Catalano began stripping, sneakers first, then cap, pants, stirrups, and socks. The last things to go were his shirt, T-shirt, and underwear. Once the briefs were down and Cat stood totally naked and stiff in front of the coach, he looked down to see Hudson's hard, hairy cock sticking from his open uniform pants. A shudder rippled down the batboy's bare spine.

"You know what to do," Hudson growled. "Get that sweet mouth of yours on it—quickly. I don't care if you pretend it's Bruno's wang, but you'd better do a good job, or I'll kick your ass harder than the Pilots have kicked mine."

Cat wasted no time and was quickly on his knees. In a flash he had Coach Hudson's cock down his throat and was sucking on it as fast as he could. Cat imagined that the hot, sweaty taste of Hudson's bat belonged to Bruno. The coach's cock was smaller than Bruno's, the hair on the sides of its shaft and the two fat nuts a shade lighter. Cat hummed on it with his eyes shut. That made it easier to suck on, believing it was Bruno's.

"That's it, boy," Hudson growled. He passed a hand through Cat's thick, dark hair and pressed the other against the back of the batboy's neck, forcing him to take his cock to its hilt. "Cocksucker. Show me how much you love sucking dick."

Cat massaged the sweaty sac of nuts, then rolled the musky

bag over his nose. He took deep breaths of Hudson's mossy aroma before spitting the cock out of his mouth and sucking on the coach's balls. Hudson groaned at the sensation of having his nuts swallowed.

"Not that hard, kid," Hudson moaned. "Those are my nuts, not marbles." He pulled his bag out of Cat's mouth with a savage yank. "You wanna suck something hard, then suck this."

Suck it, Cat did. He slurped the coach's hard-on back into his mouth, taking all of it. In the breathless minutes that followed, he worked Hudson right to the edge. When the batboy reached down to tug on the coach's nuts, it was the final push Hudson needed.

"Here it comes," he groaned through clenched teeth. Hudson pulled back so that just the head of his cock was pressed against Cat's glistening lips. The first blast shot into the batboy's mouth. The second exploded across his cheek. His need to see the humiliation of his load satisfied, Hudson shoved his dick in Cat's mouth again and dumped the rest of his juice down the batboy's throat. "That's it, son," he growled. "Swallow my scum."

Once the coach had stopped squirting, Catalano licked him clean. The mean look on Hudson's face loosened. "You done a great job, Cat. As always." Hudson's grin widened. "But you ain't done yet."

"I'm not?" Cat gasped.

A moment later Hudson's motives became clear. He reached between Cat's spread legs and gripped the straining Italian bat. Kneeling down, the coach ran his tongue over the batboy's balls. From there he moved up to Cat's skinny prong, sucking it all the way down. In a total turnaround Hudson swallowed Catalano to his root. After just a few sucks, the batboy was leaking precome.

Hudson pulled back and polished the gooey piss slit with his tongue. Cat's juice was sweeter than other men's but just as addictive. He jacked Catalano's cock and licked the pink arrow-shaped head crowning its shaft. It wasn't easy administering the punishment he'd planned with Cat's come tasting so sweet—and him being so hungry for it. But he had to see if what he'd been told was true, if the batboy was capable of doing it. Placing his hand on the back of Catalano's head, Hudson gripped the batboy's cock by the root and forced the two together.

"What are you doing?" Cat sputtered.

Hudson smiled. "Seeing if you can really suck your own cock, kid."

"Who told you I could suck my own cock?"

Hudson's smile vanished. "Who do you think? Do it, cocksucker. Get your lips around your own prick and show me how you do it!"

Cat reluctantly did as ordered. He slurped the head of his own cock and the first inch. It was already wet with Hudson's spit and was dripping faster the longer he hummed on it. As the batboy sucked himself, Hudson forced another inch into his mouth.

"This is fuckin' hot," the coach grunted. He leaned in and licked Cat's shaft, tasting his own stale come when he licked his way up to the batboy's lips. Together they worked the cock in Catalano's mouth to the point of shooting, though Hudson had other plans and was far from finished.

With Cat going down on himself, the coach dipped between the batboy's legs for a taste of his hole. Hudson loved eating ass, and Catalano's didn't disappoint him. It was just sweaty and hairy enough to make him want more.

Cat sensed what was coming and spit his own cock out of

his mouth. A frightened look swept over his sweat-soaked face. "What are you gonna do?"

"I thought you already knew, cocksucker." Hudson took one last lick of the batboy's asshole and moved into position, his own cock back to its full six inches.

Cat swore and shook his head, but Hudson's aim was right on target. Though his cock was smaller and not as thick as Aaron Sweeney's, the first bullet of pain made Cat seize in place. "Shit," he moaned.

Hudson thrust all the way up into Cat's asshole. "You can take it, son. I know you can." Cat didn't argue, and soon the searing pain from getting fucked by the coach turned to pleasure that was just as intense.

"If there's one thing you'll learn to do being one of the Socks, it's to take it like a man."

And take it, Cat did. His own cock seemed to double in size with the coach's lodged up his asshole. Without being asked he moved back into the fetal hunch and sucked on his own bat. Hudson watched the action for a few moments, shaking his head, smiling, before he too planted his lips on the dripping pink head in Cat's mouth. The coach thrust in harder, faster. The movements of both men reached a fevered pitch.

Cat shot first. The geyser of come flashed between his lips. Hudson took his share of the batboy's milk as he pushed in one last time. A shower of hot ball snot flooded the inside of Cat's hole. Through the haze and stink of sweat, the coach and the batboy locked eyes. Cat untwisted, but Hudson matched his moves so that his spent, still-stiff cock remained lodged in the hot slime of the younger man's ass. To the batboy's surprise, Hudson locked lips with him again, and they shared the combined taste of their come in a kiss.

"Don't worry, kid," the coach said once they parted. "Like

I said, everyone thinks you're doing a hell of a job, including me. In fact, you should find a nice surprise in this week's paycheck."

"A raise?" Cat sputtered.

Hudson smiled and stole another kiss. "You deserve it. 'Sides, there's talk about the guy who told me you could suck your own cock. Think we might trade him. Don't like his attitude. He's not a team player." Hudson pulled out. He spread Cat's legs and started licking his own load out of the batboy's asshole. "If there's one thing I hate, it's a stoolie."

SEVENTH INNING STRETCH

Tim Weare collapsed onto the bed. He was tired. Damned tired. He hadn't waited for Bruno to join him in the bed they shared together at the house in Seaside. They'd exchanged little more than a tip of the head back in the locker room following that day's victory against New York. The time for sex— for one night at least—would have to wait until morning. Weare never denied the big guy a little relief, but as if sensing how truly exhausted his roommate was, Bruno bugged off returning home early to join the Werewolf for a drink at the local sports bar. Weare climbed into bed dressed only in a clean jockstrap and in minutes was snoring contentedly.

Thoughts about the team meeting followed Weare into sleep. Coach Hudson had left the possibility of pulling together and advancing to the top of the Eastern Division on the shoulders of the men. What had followed was an intense but fratlike meeting of the minds. The end result was a promise not just to do better—like they had that afternoon against New York—but a hell of a lot better, aiming toward a run at the postseason.

Weare thought he felt Bruno shift on the bed sometime just shy of dusk, after the sound of footsteps and a door closing brought him back from his dreams to the half-lit shadows.

A rough fumbling of hands between his legs and into his jock-strap woke the rested rookie. A shaft of final sunlight streamed through the open windows, blinding him. Weare pinched his eyes and looked away. Once the stars had cleared, he could see that the digital numbers of the alarm clock read just shy of 8 P.M. With a low growl, Weare stretched out, allowing the hand attentively pulling on his rock-hard cock easier access. Weare closed his eyes again and spread his legs as a second hand released his balls from the fabric of his jock.

"That feels good, dude," the rookie sighed. In his mind he was already happy that sex didn't wait till morning. The fingers around his bat slid into the tangle of cock shag inside the elastic of his jock, then returned to stroking him from root to head. A moment later a hot, wet set of lips wrapped around the tip of his knob, sucking down until most of his cock was swallowed. A horny, muffled groan whistled up from the foot of the bed.

Something about that sigh shocked the last trace of sleep from the rookie's mind. It wasn't the feel of the lips on Weare's cock that told him something wasn't right but what was unfamiliar about the groan. Weare reached down with his right hand, into the thick, neat hair of the head bobbing up and down on his cock. The head of hair was too long to be Bruno's neat military buzz cut.

"What the fuck?" he gasped, scrambling up on the bed to his elbows, then a seated position. His dick popped out of the hot, sucking mouth.

The young man straddling the middle of the bed wiped his mouth and grinned. "Sure, dude, if you want."

At first Weare was so shocked at the stranger's bold handling of his private parts, the rookie could only stare. He gawked at the youthful, handsome face, the muscled body,

ripped from playing varsity sports the way Weare's had been
made hard, dressed in an emerald-colored T-shirt and denim
shorts. Some unaffected part of Weare's scattered senses noticed the young dude—who stood at an easy six feet and had
to have been just over the 20-year-old mark—had strong,
hairy calves, white socks bunched down on the tops of his
black high-tops, and big feet. Another part recognized the
slightest resemblance in his chiseled face and thunderhead-
blue eyes.

The young dude's smile widened. A shudder traced the
sweaty column of Weare's spine in spite of the warm summer
breeze billowing through the windows.

"Who the fuck are you?" he demanded, though he'd figured
it out by then.

Shaking his head in a cocky, sexy gesture, the handsome
dude reached back between Weare's legs and groped his spit-
shined bat by its hairy root. "Even though I'm only a few years
younger than you, guess you could say I'm your stepson."

The young man again went down. The mouth on the rookie's cock sucked harder and deeper.

"Aw, fuck," Weare moaned. "Tom Jr.…."

The handsome face making love to Weare's bat pulled
back, but the hand continued to stroke the rookie's boner,
coaxing out a drop of precome. "Hope you don't mind," he
coolly stated, looking up to meet Weare's eyes with his heavy
blue-grays. "You know—me just dropping by without calling
first." Tom Jr. leaned down to give Weare's cock a slow, sloppy kiss. "Hope you don't mind me getting a taste."

Temporarily shocked, Weare whistled out a sigh. "Don't
mention it, kid." There was a moment of silence between
them, tense and uncertain, when Weare didn't quite know
what to do. But the strangely taboo concept of being hummed

on by Bruno's jock of a son was making his dick so hard it itched, and the fact Tom Jr. seemed to know exactly what he was doing made it even harder.

The handsome young man slid off the bed to stand straight, showcasing the prominent lump in the front of his denim shorts.

Like father, like son, Weare thought, gripping his own cock, pumping the taught skin of the shaft around the itchy edges of his dick head. He aimed his free hand toward the packed pouch of the younger Bruno's shorts, gave it a firm knock the way ballplayers did their cups. Tom Jr. smiled.

"So," he said. "You want me to finish?"

Weare answered by reaching around, groping the hard-as-nails can of the young college jock's butt. "On your knees, slugger."

Tom Jr. did as he was told and soon had reassumed his stance at the side of the bed. Weare put his hand on the back of the younger Bruno's head, played with the longer-than-military mop of dark brown hair as the warm mouth again took hold of his cock head.

"Suck it, dude," Weare growled, bucking up to meet the downward motion of Tom Jr.'s throat. "Aw, yeah, suck my fuckin' cock."

The younger dude's rough right hand took hold of Weare's balls, rolling the fat egg-shaped nuts in their hairy, meaty sac. Weare leaned back against the hedge of pillows at his back, spread his legs apart, and eased his other hand down, taking Tom Jr.'s T-shirt by the shoulders. He managed to pull it over the younger Bruno's head without either one of them missing a beat; Tom Jr. kept sucking, and Weare slid a hand over the college jock's chest to find that it was peppered with a good dose of hair, just like Bruno's ripped torso. A few sucks later,

Tom Jr. spit out Weare's cock.

"You're sure you want me to do this?" he asked, his voice a sexy growl.

For a moment Weare was taken aback by the question. Then it sank in, what they were doing, what the consequences could be if they followed through with it.

Weare playfully tousled Tom Jr.'s mop of hair. "You've done this before, haven't you, dude?"

"I'm playing college baseball. What do you think?"

Weare let out a deep sigh, half closed his eyes, and muttered, "Fuck..."

"So, tell me—you want me to continue?"

Weare's eyes opened fully to look at the handsome, young face with the sexy grin and Bruno's blue-gray eyes. "I'd be lying if I said this didn't turn me on."

"You turned on, dude?"

"Fuck, yeah," the rookie sighed. He took hold of his cock by the root with his free hand, pulled the jock dude's head down with his other, and was soon in his mouth again, being sucked by an expert dick lover. Tom Jr. continued to toy with his nuts, until at last he spit out Weare's cock to give the rookie's meaty low-hangers some attention. The younger Bruno ran his hot tongue over Weare's sac, pressing his nose into the coarse patch of shag surrounding them for a smell of clean man sweat. "That's it, buddy. Hot little fucker..."

Weare gripped Tom Jr.'s face and raised it to his own. Both men kissed automatically, lips crushing together. The rookie tasted the tang of his own precome and the sweat of his nuts on Tom Jr.'s mouth. After their tongues had further mingled those tastes together, Tom Jr. eased down, raising Weare's arms so that he was able to lick at the rookie's shaggy, damp pits. After he'd brushed his tongue over the dark hair under both arms, Tom Jr. kissed his way to each of Weare's nipples, gently biting and sucking each dime-sized cap. From there he moved lower, down the rookie's chest to his sculpted six-pack of abs, where he licked a circle around Weare's taught belly button. As the younger Bruno eased Weare's jock all the way down, exposing the crisp upside-down triangle of pelt surrounding the rookie's bat, Weare again took hold of the high, hard ass on the handsome college jock.

"You've got a hot can, son," Weare growled.

Tom Jr. stood up straight and undid the button on his jeans. "You wanna see it?"

For a second Weare hesitated, but they both knew there was no going back. He loved Tommy Bruno, and in a strange, sick way, having sex with his college-aged son was like being with Bruno too. Before he could talk himself out of it, he took Tom Jr.'s hands off the fly of his shorts, replaced them with his own, and eased down the zipper. Hauling down Tom Jr.'s shorts bared a pair of clean white boxer briefs, tented in front.

"Holy fuck..." Weare sighed, groping the bulge. Tom Jr. moaned and pressed against Weare's touch. Soon a tiny ring of wetness had appeared on the bulge in Tom Jr.'s underwear. Rising to his toes, he kicked off his sneakers. A line of fresh sweat seeped down from his brow, onto Weare's forehead. The rookie glanced up. Tom Jr. nodded. It was all the invitation Weare needed.

Gripping the elastic waistband of the boxer briefs, Weare pulled them down. A gust of musky-smelling man sweat billowed into the rookie's face. Weare inhaled it, drunk on the heaviness of college cock and nuts.

Tom Jr.'s bat stood stiff and straight, an even match for his dad's. Weare stopped tugging down his underwear once they reached the younger Bruno's knees. Taking the hard eight-

inch cock by the shaft, Weare gave it a few stiff jacks, notic-
ing in the poor light that a trickle of spunk seeped out to coat
his fingers. Growling out a muffled "Fuck," Weare moved in,
lapped the wetness on his knuckles. From there he took Tom
Jr.'s bat head between his lips and sucked on it with the same
hunger he showed Bruno. Tom Jr. bucked, going to the tops
of his toes as he pushed another inch of cock down Weare's
throat. Both men moaned their approval—Weare at the salty
taste of college precome, Tom Jr. from the incredible feel of
the rookie's experienced mouth on his lumber.

"Suck it, dude," Tom Jr. grunted. "Suck my fuckin' cock."

Suck it, Weare did. Soon he had Tom Jr. on the verge of
shooting his load. Weare was no stranger to buddy sex, the secret coming together of two guys getting each other off, and
since becoming Bruno's best pal, he'd gotten good at sucking
cock. A few deep thrusts followed by concentrated sucks on
Tom Jr.'s straining dick head quickly had the younger Bruno
squirming to blast his tar.

But Weare wasn't ready for that yet—not until he had gotten some more of Tom Jr.'s technique on his own stick. Spitting out the younger Bruno's cock, Weare went lower, burying his nose in the crisp smelling musk of Tom Jr.'s fat, furry
nut sac. After a few hungry licks, he settled back on the bed
and wordlessly invited Tom Jr. to join him by spreading his
hairy jock legs. The younger Bruno smiled, licked his lips, and
assumed the position. Soon both men were settled into a perfect sixty-nine, each sucking on the other with loud, wet
slurps.

Weare knew the sound well, the noise of men dripping precome, ready to unload. Weare moved so that each time the
younger Bruno thrust or pulled back, just the straining head
of each man's bat was perched on the other's lips. A ribbon of

milky goo slipped out of Tom Jr.'s mouth and splashed the side of his cheek. A second after that, Weare unloaded, shooting six steady spurts into the other man's willing mouth.

On the third blast Weare's own mouth filled with something hot, bitter, and familiar: the taste of Bruno come.

☆   ☆   ☆

They lay together, kissing deeply, exchanging the taste of each other. Summer darkness had settled over the house, and still there was no sound of Bruno's car in the drive or the front door opening. Each time Weare felt a stab of guilt for what he'd done with the big guy's son, Tom Jr. would kiss him again, and it was so like being with Bruno, he'd forget the danger of what had been shared that night in the veteran center fielder's bed.

"You should get dressed," the rookie said. "Just in case. You know…"

Tom Jr. shook his head. "I called Dad earlier. Said he planned on being out late tonight and not to disturb you 'cause you were tired. Told me to stow my gear and help myself to anything in the house."

Weare chuckled. "Yeah, like my fuckin' cock?"

"Couldn't help it," Tom Jr. grinned, reaching down to toy with Weare's bat, which had softened but not completely.

"Well, it's good to make your acquaintance. I think."

"You think?" Tom Jr. growled in a sexy deep voice. "I'll give you 'think.'"

Without asking, Tom Jr. slid down the sweaty front of Weare's hairy chest until at last reaching the rookie's cock.

"Son, you are a cock hound."

Tom Jr. spit out Weare's cock. "You complaining?"

Weare moaned after the first few sucks on his knob brought it back to its full thickness. "Not a bit. You've got a hot mouth. I just think this time there's a better place to bury my cock than your mouth, slugger."

At first Tom Jr.'s only response was a throaty grunt from around the bat between his lips. Pulling himself off the younger Bruno, Weare eased out of the bed. In the light filtering in from the streetlights outside and in the glow of the alarm clock beside the bed, he noticed that Tom Jr. was up again, hard and ready for anything—and Weare planned on giving it to him.

Kneeling by the edge of the bed, Weare took his second taste of the younger Bruno's cock, inhaling the clean, mossy smell of his flat, hairy abdomen. Weare moved from cock to nuts, licking, sniffing, and toying with every inch of the college jock's skin on his way to the real target: Tom Jr.'s asshole. Finally, Weare zeroed in on it, and Tom Jr.'s tight, fuzzy shit hole puckered under his lips. The younger Bruno moaned out a string of barely audible swears as Weare ate his ass. But each time the rookie tried to ease a finger up the young slugger's can, Tom Jr. lurched off the bed. Weare soon realized that Bruno's son was a virgin when it came to his butt. This caused the rookie to lick and toy with it more fiercely.

"Come on, dude." He growled the hot, sexy words into Tom Jr.'s crack. "Give up a piece of that tight ass." Weare closed his eyes and tasted the tangy, nervous sweat from the younger Bruno's asshole.

"Feels so good," Tom Jr. spat through clenched teeth.

Weare knew he had him hooked. "I'm gonna make it feel even better."

He pushed his finger in all the way to the last knuckle. Tom Jr. tensed beneath him, and his already hard cock bounced up off his hard-as-concrete abdomen. Weare began to finger-fuck Tom Jr.'s asshole with the same finesse Bruno had used on his own during spring training.

"Yeah, you're gonna like this, son."

"Do it," Tom Jr. grunted. He knew he was going to get fucked. To silence any protest, Weare gulped Tom Jr.'s straining rod back into his mouth. The younger Bruno groaned. Weare knew he was ready. The wait was over.

Rising, wagging his cock at Tom Jr.'s spit-shined hole, Weare hawked a wad of spit into his glove hand and gave his bat a final stroke. He assumed the classic fuck stance Bruno had used on him and lined his cock head up with the target in Tom Jr.'s ass crack. He pushed in.

The first bullet of pain made fresh sweat appear across Tom Jr.'s forehead. He seized under Weare's weight, his asshole coughing out the rookie's stick.

"No, dude," Junior groaned. "I want to, but I can't take it. It's too fuckin' big!"

Weare reached down and gripped his cock by the ring of taught skin beneath the head. "You can do it, fucker. You can take it."

Tom Jr.'s body jolted under Weare again, but this time he didn't fight it. The rookie leaned down, ran his tongue over the younger Bruno's lips, which still tasted like his last load. They started to kiss. As Weare's cock head eased in, Tom Jr. puffed out a hot, heavy breath. Weare pushed in the next inch, then another.

Tom Jr.'s cock felt like a lump of freshly forged steel against his stomach. And soon the pain in his guts turned strangely pleasurable, as he'd hoped it would.

Weare eased the last few inches in, his patch grinding against the base of Junior's balls while his own low-hangers slapped the college jock's ass. "Fuck, son!" Weare hooted, pulling back a few inches so he could shove in again, the incredible pressure of Tom Jr.'s unfucked asshole squeezing his cock tighter than any pussy—even Barbara's. Weare's dick moved in and out of the young stud like a piston. The alternating pressure of the rookie's dick filling him up, then withdrawing began to slowly, steadily loosen Tom Jr. up and turned the grimace on his handsome face into a grin. "That's it, dude."

To signal his approval Tom Jr. lip-locked Weare's mouth again. Each man's tongue stabbed against the other's, two sweaty baseball jocks who had found the best kind of sex any man could hope to get off on.

"I'm gonna come," Tom Jr. moaned as they kissed.

Weare humped faster, cutting off the college boy's grunts. For one moment that was totally disturbing and equally exciting, it was as if he was fucking Bruno. Thinking of the big guy drove him over the edge. A split second before Tom Jr. blew across his stomach, Weare shot his second load that afternoon, this time into the younger Bruno's asshole. Not totally satisfied, with his cock still spurting, Weare pulled free of the tightness and aimed his cock into Tom Jr.'s face. Junior caught the last few sprays between his lips, then began to clean the tang off of Weare's bat. Weare let the younger Bruno have at it, until the itch of coming turned to a sting. Then, like his dick, he collapsed limp onto the bed beside Tom Jr. Both men stretched across the nasty sheets.

They lay together in silence. Neither talked nor broke the huddle until Weare woke to the sound of footsteps, unaware he'd fallen asleep. Standing at the door to the bedroom was Bruno. A moment after the light snapped on and Weare realized he was cuddled up beside Tom Jr., the light snapped off, and Bruno's shadowy silhouette vanished back into the house, leaving Weare alone, weighing the consequences of what had happened.

A hundred times that morning, he thought about going out to the living room where the telltale ghost of the TV cast haunting reminders of what Bruno had seen in the bed he shared with the Socks' rookie third baseman. Every time he tried, Weare retreated back into the sweat-soaked huddle on his side of the covers. When he woke to the sunlight the following day, feeling sick, feeling like he'd been punched in the gut, he was alone on the bed, and Tom Jr.'s clothes, shed in haste the previous night, were gone.

Weare pulled on a fresh pair of workout shorts and staggered out into the kitchen, where the sound of muffled, happy voices could be heard. The 12 steps there seemed like a thousand, but to his surprise he was greeted by the smell of fresh coffee, eggs, bacon, and hot buttered toast.

"You coming to the game today?" he heard Bruno ask as he rounded the corner.

"Of course, dude," Tom Jr. said. "Who you playing?"

Weare jumped in to be greeted by the three-alarm grin on Tom Jr.'s chiseled face. "The Monarchs."

"For another chance to see Timmy and you trash the competition," Tom Jr. said, "you betcha!" Toast in one hand, the younger Bruno extended his other for a high-five. Weare gave it a hard jock spank and took the bar stool beside him. Bruno, bare-chested, looking magnificent in the sunlight streaming into the kitchen, went suddenly silent with his cup of coffee.

Later that afternoon at McKinsey Field, the flood of guilt

hit home squarely. From the on-deck circle Weare glanced up behind him into the seats on the other side of the dugout. Bruno had introduced Tom Jr. to Cat in the clubhouse before the game. When Bruno fouled the first pitch, the batboy smiled, then chucked the ball up into the stands for Tom Jr. to catch, which he did effortlessly. The image of Tom Jr. rooting his father on, holding the prized ball, did it. Bruno made it onto base with a walk, only to have Weare hit into a double play.

He couldn't help but wonder, with all the guilt punching at his guts, if it was somehow an omen of things to come.

The losing streak broke on the road, at a point when the Fins led the Eastern Division by eight games. After sweeping the Oakland Hombres in a four game away stand, something happened to the team as a whole. The slugging average rose while pitching ERAs lowered. Tuc Vandercastille assumed Aaron Sweeney's place in the rotation after Number 44 was traded to Philadephia for cash, two minor-league prospects, and a player to be named later. Vandercastille went two-zero on the road, bringing his record to nine wins, three losses.

The Socks robbed the Sluggers in a five-to-one victory the first night in Seattle. No big celebrations were planned, and most of the team crashed early in anticipation of the daynight doubleheader scheduled to follow.

Unlike in other cities, in Seattle the players were put up in individual luxury rooms with king-size beds, one of the perks of a new franchise that boasted its own convention center. Weare planned to meet Bruno later in his room, but Bruno hadn't said much since they'd left Seaside after four awkward days he'd spent on the couch, away from their bed. The big guy claimed his knees were killing him. Bruno iced up and kicked back with a beer and a little room service. He and Weare met in the lobby the next morning on their way to the dome and a crushing sweep of the doubleheader that went to the Socks. The celebrations started ten minutes after the team shuttle dropped the players off at the hotel, most of them still streaked with sweat and baseball-diamond dirt, all proudly wearing the trademark insignia of the Seaside Top Socks.

☆　　☆　　☆

Weare met Hector Valenza outside the Cowboy's room. Mike Young appeared a moment later with a brown shopping bag tucked under one arm.

"Where's Bruno?" he twanged in his gravelly southern accent.

Weare shrugged. "Crashing and icing," he said.

The news made the Cowboy scowl. "Son, you just got tell that bad boy I got cold beer and blue movies!"

It was a concept Weare found hopeful, but after calling Bruno's room from Young's, the desk informed them they'd been instructed not to disturb the veteran center fielder.

"Well, shucks," the Cowboy crooned. "Ain't gonna seem the same with Mitch doin' team business and Bruno actin' like a lost puppy." Despite the letdown, Young tipped the bill of his baseball cap and flashed a swarthy smile ringed by day-old stubble. "We still got us some celebrating to do. Drink up, boys!"

Each man yanked a can free of the six-pack's plastic ring. They popped them, then toasted.

"To us," Valenza said. "And the streak!"

The three cold cans met in a chiming of aluminum. It could have been $100 champagne for all they cared. The elation of winning and inching closer to the Fins in the standings had grown infectious, even if some of the perks hadn't been as cool as the beer.

Weare aimed his nose into the damp stink of his uniform shirt's armpits. "Whose idea was it not to hit the showers?"

"Mine," Valenza said, clapping a hand to Weare's shoulder. "Old baseball winning streak ritual, like lucky socks."

"Lucky jocks?" Weare chuckled. He took another deep swig of the cold, foamy beer.

"Careful, son," the Cowboy said. "Too much of that'll put hair on your chest."

Weare laughed again, this time raising his shirt. "In case you ain't seen it in the locker room, that's hair on my pecs, dude."

Young boldly reached out and ran his big, rough hand, cold from holding the can of beer, over Weare's chest. The chill in his fingertips instantly hardened the tight, dark-pink nipples capping Weare's pecs. "Looks more like peach fuzz to me, pal."

Weare responded with a good-natured "Fuck you."

The swarthy grin on Young's face turned serious. He now openly rubbed Weare's chest. Stunned, the rookie shuddered as his nipples were pinched and rolled between the Cowboy's forefinger and thumb. The room suddenly felt ten degrees hotter, the sweat soaking their uniforms fresher, more powerful.

Just as quickly as it started, Young's exploration of the rookie's chest ended. The Cowboy chugged another mouthful of suds, and with the can still in his hand, collapsed on the bed. He sailed an exhausted sigh, spread his legs, then rumbled out a deep, guttural burp.

"Fuckin' pig," Valenza chuckled. "I never *b-u-u-urp!*"

The three men broke in a round of hearty laughter. When Valenza moved to join the Cowboy on the bed, Young sprang up, catching the team's shortstop in a headlock. Valenza struggled and grunted, spilling beer on the bed.

"Cut the shit!"

"Stop pissing on my bed, you macho hombre!"

"Yeah," Valenza grinned. "Why not? It'll cover up your stink."

Weare watched the two men play on the bed, first fascinated, then with a sense of rising panic—not because he felt threatened by their safe buddy antics, but because he realized that seeing the two other ballplayers groping each other was making him hard in his dirty jock. He rubbed the bulge in his sweaty nut holder while Young and Valenza wrestled, convinced they were too distracted to notice. Touching himself helped the rookie shift his lumber into a more comfortable position. What Weare didn't realize was that Bruno's coldness since catching him in bed with Tom Jr. was keeping him stiff all the time now. His tool, just from watching a little innocent buddy play, had gotten harder than he could remember. Weare glanced down to see a stain of what could only be pre-come on the tent in his uniform mixed with all the dirt and grass stains he'd gotten from sliding into home plate in the second game of the doubleheader. "Fuck," he huffed. Biting down on his sense of guilt, Weare finished his beer, crushed the can, and did a perfect slam dunk into the barrel near the dresser. "You two gonna get married, or are we gonna get this party going?"

The comment drove Valenza and Young apart. His swarthy smile restored, the handsome left fielder aimed a hand at the brown bag on the dresser. "Well, shit, son," Young drawled. "Put in a tape and jump-start this celebration!"

Weare flashed his own Cheshire-cat grin. *Fuck Bruno*, he thought. *If he's mad at me for what happened, it's his hang-up, not mine.* He reached into the bag and pulled out a video tape. The only identifying mark on the hard plastic case was a rental number.

Flipping on the room's big-screen TV, Weare plunked the tape into the VCR without bothering to read the title. It began to play automatically. Weare jabbed the fast-forward button through the copyright warning and was halfway into the opening scene when it hit him. Weare slowed the tape to see a man with a mustache sucking on a hairy sac of low-hangers: It was two guys having sex!

"What the fuck?" Weare sputtered. At first he was so shocked, he didn't hear the bedsprings shift or the sound of sneakers padding up behind him. A moment after he smelled the beer breath whistling by his ear, a hand wrapped around Weare's waist. The rookie glanced down as five rough fingers groped the straining tent in the front of his uniform. Weare swore the question again.

It was Valenza's hand. The handsome Latino pressed his beer-cold lips against Weare's ear. "Party's just starting, amigo."

Weare turned around. The Cowboy was still sprawled across his bed, had one hand tucked beneath his undone belt, and was scratching away at the coarse shag under his belly button. An even more swarthy smile curled on his lips. "And we're gonna party till we drop—some loads, that is."

"Wait a minute," Weare started to protest, though he got no further. Valenza pulled down the rookie's zipper, opening the tent of his sweat-soaked uniform pants. The quick-footed shortstop then reached into Weare's jockstrap. A rush of overwhelming pressure the second Valenza's hand touched his cock sent the room spinning around Weare.

"Wait nothing," the Cowboy drawled. "Hector told me everything 'bout you and Lug Nuts. How long you been swiggin' juice outta his cock?"

Weare shook his head and sighed. His eyes shifted between Mike Young on the bed, Valenza who'd freed his bat and was now stroking it, and the hot cock-sucking action taking place on the TV screen. "No, dudes, you got it all wrong...."

"Yeah, right, amigo," Valenza said. "That time on the bus wasn't no first for you guys. I seen the way you look at each other. That's more than just being buddies. You guys are taking care of each other, going down on each other." The Latino's fingers slipped down, taking Weare's nuts, giving them a solid groping. "Fuckin' beautiful, buddy."

"Aw, shit," Weare grinned. He tipped his head in the TV's direction. The guy with the mustache was now eating out the other man's hole. Images of Bruno came back to Weare so clearly; he had to have it, the taste of sex with another man. "Yeah," he finally admitted. "I've been giving it to Bruno. Been sucking his fuckin' cock since spring training."

"You lick the sweat off his nuts?" the Cowboy asked with a hungry sigh.

Weare nodded. "Those big fuckers smell and taste so fuckin' hot, I can't get enough of them. I haven't eaten pussy since."

"Pussy's OK, son," the Cowboy reminded him. "But sometimes there's a hunger only another guy can understand." Young let out another beer burp. "I'm feeling pretty hungry, men. Timmy boy, why don't you feed me some of that lumber of yours."

Before Weare could argue or agree, the handsome Latino shortstop shoved him onto the bed. "Wha—?" Weare gasped.

He landed ass down, his stroked-stiff dick flopping with his balls immediately into the Cowboy's hands. A second later, the Cowboy lowered his head, wrapping his swarthy smile around the rookie's cock. Weare swore again, only this time it was from the shock of Young's mouth feeling so good on him. He pushed in, shoved his bat down the Cowboy's throat. The Cowboy matched his every move. The first thing Weare thought was how good it felt to have his cock sucked; the second, how good Young was at sucking it. Mikey Young had done this before.

Valenza went to his knees at the side of the bed, and soon Weare had a hot mouth on either side of his manhood. Both teammates took turns running their tongues over his lumber. While Young stroked the shaft between his lips, Valenza took a stab with his taste buds on Weare's hairy, sweaty sac of nuts. As hungry as the veterans were for the rookie, they weren't greedy now that they'd finally gotten him. They took turns on the head of his cock, sometimes kissing each other over the precome oozing out of it.

"This is what I call a celebration," Weare growled, running his hands through the short, clipped hair of both men after knocking off their team ball caps.

Young, who'd been sucking on Weare's knob when the rookie had spoken, spit out the young jock's dick. "Son," he drawled. "The party is just beginning."

That said, the Cowboy reclined back to the head of the bed, leaving the servicing of Weare's cock solely to the handsome shortstop. Young pulled the rookie into a tight bear hug. Their lips met roughly, filling Weare's mouth with the taste of beer and cock. The next kiss was deeper, harder, wetter and ended with tongues against lips. "Yeah, son. Lap the juice of your own dick off my mouth," Young growled.

Weare did. He cast one last glance toward the TV. The dude with the mustache was still eating ass, and with Valenza doing such a stand-up job from his crouch at the side of the bed, he knew it wouldn't take long to shoot. Weare was focused on dumping some come down the shortstop's throat when the Cowboy grabbed his hand, guiding it onto the sweaty, dirty bulge in the left fielder's soiled uniform. Weare took hold of the veteran's meat and gave it a gentle shake. "Fair's fair."

Young threw both hands behind his head and relaxed. Weare shifted on the bed into a better position. As he fumbled with the Cowboy's jockstrap, his cock slipped out of Valenza's eager mouth. Weare wanted Young's cock. He'd seen it soft and soapy enough times, and though it wasn't as big as Bruno's—certainly not as thick as Tuc Vandercastille's big, hard bat, the very first cock he'd ever swallowed—it was just as sexy to think about sucking it. Jutting out of the Cowboy's pulled-aside jock, the veteran's prong pointed up from his egg-shaped, hairy nuts. It demanded attention. It demanded to be sucked.

Timmy Weare was just the Top Socks player to do it.

The taste of Young's cock was incredible—guy sweat and musk, the clean stink of manhood inside a baseball player's uniform pants. While licking the head, Weare gave the Cowboy's cock shaft a few playful strokes, bringing it up to its full six inches. Then he took it fully into his mouth. The Cowboy grunted a long line of breathless, half-mumbled swears. "That's it, son," he groaned. "Choke down my fuckin' cock."

Suck it, Weare did. He alternated between deep-throating the ample-sized cock and working just the head, tonguing the piss slit, which rewarded him with the bitter taste of the Cowboy's precome. After a few minutes of sucking, Weare spit out the Cowboy's cock to lap the mossy-smelling balls in their hairy sac. He gave the left fielder's nuts a thorough bathing, then returned to his cock, swallowing it to the root.

"Fuck," the Cowboy growled. "I'd love to have Bruno watching you do this, sucking my cock. I wish he and Mitch were here, then we'd really have a team party."

Weare coughed up the Cowboy's bat. "Coach Hudson? You don't mean—"

The Cowboy flashed his cool, sexy smile; this time his lips still glistening from having tasted Weare's precome. "You don't think you and Bruno invented buddy sex on this team, do you?"

A wave of fresh, horny heat flashed through Weare's insides. "You and the coach?" Young nodded. "That's fuckin' hot, pal!" The rookie leaned down and licked the knob of the cock in his hand. He was about to resume making love to it when Young yanked it out of his mouth. "I'll show you hot. Hector, get your ass on the bed."

"Si, amigo," Valenza said. "'Bout fuckin' time. I'm gonna come in my jock."

Weare and the Cowboy both eased off the bed, clearing a path for their teammate. Valenza kicked off his sneakers, then scooted between them. The handsome shortstop's sweaty toes had soaked the damp cotton of his white socks and filled the already ripe air above the bed with the stink of a locker room.

Without asking, the rookie went to Valenza's big jock feet. He rubbed and toyed with the handsome Latino's sweat-soaked toes, then took a deep whiff from each foot, sighing with a smile when he was done. "Nice," Weare whispered.

"You do that to Bruno's big feet?" the Cowboy asked. Weare grinned his answer. "Fuckin' A, buddy. You play with Hector's feet while I take care of this."

As Weare watched, Young fumbled in the front of the shortstop's well-stuffed uniform pants. He hauled Valenza's zipper down and spread the hair-filled fly, giving the shortstop's jock and midlengths a good tug. A quick pull unsheathed Valenza's uncut cock. Another tug spilled out two balls covered with black shag.

Weare had seen Valenza's cock stiff once before, on the bus, but here it was now, not blocked by the bathroom door or the shortstop's baseball glove. Fascinated by the sight of it close up, at first Weare could only gawk at the sight of Mike Young dipping his tongue into the handsome Latino's tight foreskin. The Cowboy licked, then gave Valenza's bat a firm squeeze. The thick, pink head, already moistened with natural juices, popped out of the taught brown skin sock. Young deep-throated their uncut teammate, groaning as he rolled the foreskin up and down. It was too wild not to be a part of, so Weare joined in, going down on the gamy pink knob, tasting not only the musk of the the shortstop's cock but also Mike Young's spit. As had happened to the rookie himself, both teammates moved to either side of Valenza's drooling cock. They worked in unison, each man intent on only one thing. The handsome shortstop rewarded them with it a few minutes later.

Weare knew Valenza was coming; he'd swallowed Bruno enough times that summer to recognize the shudder deep in the shortstop's nuts even before Valenza's cock expanded between their lips. The rookie pulled back as the first gush of salty jism flew out of the shortstop's juicy cock. Valenza's load geysered up into the Cowboy's face.

"Do it, hombre!" Young shouted with a deep hoot. "Shoot that white gold!"

Valenza grunted, bucked off the bed, and dumped the rest

of his load into Young's mouth. The toast—this one with come instead of beer—made it a real celebration.

☆   ☆   ☆

Weare thought about sucking the Cowboy's six-inch lumber, but the earlier hunger he'd been at the mercy of took hold again. He yanked down Young's funky uniform pants and dove between the left fielder's hairy legs. Thinking that the rookie had wanted to milk his cock to the point of shooting, Young urged Weare on.

"Suck it, Timmy," he drawled. "Suck it like you suck Bruno's."

Weare lifted the veteran's heavy sac. Young's hairy asshole became visible. "That's a firm ass," he growled, licking his way down to the left fielder's shitter.

Weare groaned an appeased sigh. Satisfying his hunger with a generous taste of the other man's asshole pushed them both closer to the moment. Using his tongue, Weare stabbed in and out of the Cowboy's tight, hairy knot.

Even thought it was the taste of the Cowboy's ass that pushed Weare over the edge, the rookie thought of Bruno and the secret jock sex they'd shared—sex that was no longer secret. The rookie rose from between Young's legs. Valenza was waiting for the fountain of come. Weare doused the shortstop's mouth while howling Bruno's name.

Young wasn't far behind. Beating his meat frantically, he blasted his load across the dirty shirt of his uniform. Weare and Valenza took care of the mess.

Shortly after that, the tape in the VCR ran out. The party was over.

In their stinky, sweaty baseball uniforms, each feeling good and satisfied, the three sluggers collapsed onto the bed. It wasn't Weare's intention to fall asleep in Young's hotel room, but he woke two hours later, sandwiched between the others, protected on either side by his teammates.

☆   ☆   ☆

Aaron Sweeney didn't have a plan after being pulled in the top of the fifth. With the Socks, his former team, up four runs and that arrogant pup Tuc Vandercastille knuckling a shutout against his new team, the Socks' greatest rival, the Pilots, this double humiliation made him go on automatic.

The score had swollen to a six-zero drumming when Mitch Hudson yanked the knuckleballer who'd assumed Sweeney's place in the starting rotation. Knuckleballs being unpredictable worked both ways; Vandercastille loaded the bases on walks with no outs in the seventh, and one stroke of the bat could cut their lead to almost nothing. When relief pitching for the Socks came on to strike out the next batter, and the Pilots hit into a double play, ending the threat, Sweeney snapped. He stormed out of the Pilots' dugout, trashing a cooler of sports drink on the way. One thing was clear to him: He had to make Tuc Vandercastille pay, no matter the cost.

Getting into the Socks' clubhouse was easier than he'd expected. Then again, he knew all the ways around the old ballpark, and by that point an army of dicks wouldn't have stopped him. He stormed through the equipment-room door, picked his way through the dark tunnel to the back of the clubhouse, and past a towel boy and a housekeeper, neither of whom spoke English. Determined to have his revenge, Sweeney continued on, into the locker room. The stink of fresh sweat hit him immediately.

Vandercastille was already down to his midlengths and socks. The rest of his uniform—shirt, pants, spikes, and stirrups—lay in a neat, perspiration-soaked pile on the bench. The sight of the rookie pitcher who'd usurped his place in the Socks' rotation—his bare muscles glistening, his handsome game face, and the perfect goatee and mustache ringing his smile—suddenly gave Sweeney the plan that had, until that moment, eluded him.

"Aaron!" Vandercastille sputtered. "What're you doing here?"

Sweeney rushed the rookie, screaming "Mother fucker!" as he charged. The two men connected hard—damned hard—though Tuc Vandercastille wasn't the easy pushover Sweeney had anticipated.

They flipped each other onto the locker-room floor. Sweeney's nose crunched into the tiles. The first things he smelled were bleach, sweat, and lemon-scented floor cleaner; next was the coppery stink of his own blood. He swore again and lashed out, clipping Vandercastille with the his elbow. Sweeney whipped around. This put him back on top, face-to-face with the fucker his team of five years had chosen over him.

"What the fuck?" Vandercastille bellowed. "You fuckin' crazy?' He pushed both of his hands against the Pilots' pitcher's solid chest. Sweeney wrestled the rookie's arms back down. He had to lock his knees on both sides of Vandercastille's to prevent himself from getting flipped off. Vandercastille bucked and growled, but Sweeney finally had him pinned. The two men, one pressing against the other, faced off.

"You little fuck!" Sweeney huffed down onto Vandercastille. "They give you my old locker too? What about my number?"

Vandercastille's face went red. A wave of fresh, clean-smelling sweat beaded his face. "I got my own number,

Sweeney," the rookie said. "And as far as that crab-infested locker of your goes, no one'll even go near it. It ain't my fault they cut your strings. It's yours."

"Yeah?" Sweeney growled. He flashed a sinister smile. Their heavy breathing scattered hot air through the sudden, angry silence. "You just think you're some hot-assed shit, don't you? Fuckin' knuckleballer, taking over the Socks. Big tough guy. You a tough guy?"

"Get off my ass for one second, and I'll show you how tough," Vandercastille grunted threateningly.

Sweeney's sarcastic grin widened. "Oh, yeah, we got us a tough guy?" While Sweeney wasn't instantly aware of it, the hard, squeezed lump between his legs stiffened to its full size. He'd been unconsciously pressing it, rubbing it against the meaty bulge protruding from the front of the rookie pitcher's baseball shorts.

Sweeney's cock took over, as it usually did in confrontations. Using his chest and one arm to secure Vandercastille, Sweeney snaked the other between their legs, rubbing his own cup-covered bulge. He managed to get his zipper down and to pull the first few inches of his cock out of his fly. The hot air kicked up by Vandercastille's bare skin gusted across the trigger of nerves lining the underside of Sweeney's boner.

"Oh, yeah," Sweeney growled. "You got to pay, Tucker. Nobody fucks with Aaron...."

Sweeney groped the lump in Vandercastille's underwear, rolling the cock and balls in the sweaty material. The rookie pitcher froze beneath him. "What the fuck're you doing?" Vandercastille demanded. "Guy, you're touching my dick!"

The veteran's response came in the form of a swift yank that ripped down Vandercastille's underwear. The smell of hot, sweat-drenched balls billowed up from between the rookie's legs. Sweeney shifted, just enough so he could gauge his accuracy. He wasn't disappointed. He'd pinned the rookie's shorts below his nuts. Vandercastille's hairy, half-hard bat lay halfway up his flat, hairy abdomen.

"Fuck," Sweeney groaned. "I knew you were big, fucker, but that's a fuckin' donkey dick."

Sweeney gripped Vandercastille's cock and gave it a hard squeeze. The rookie lurched beneath him, howling both in anger and shock. It was all Sweeney needed.

"You like that?" he huffed in an intense, disgusted voice. "Like having another guy play with your cock? Cocksucker!" Sweeney gave the rookie knuckleballer a few stiff strokes. When Vandercastille seemed to end his struggle against the veteran's body slam, Sweeney let go of his cock for a good feel of the bull nuts dangling below it. "Big fuckin' balls, mother fucker! You like me playing with those too?" Again the rookie's only answer was a grunt.

Sweeney toyed and played with Vandercastille's manhood, sputtering insults as the rookie squirmed and moaned, seeming to enjoy it more and more the longer Sweeney kept at it. In the breathless seconds since taking the rookie down, Sweeney had gotten him so hard, Vandercastille's dick began to drool the first trace of clear precome. Sweeney teased the tip of Vandercastille's cock head, forcing the rookie to drip more between his fingertips, then brought the spoils of his conquest to his lips. Vandercastille's come tasted sweet and musky.

"Fuckin' cocksucker," Sweeney said again, resuming his masturbation of the knuckleballer pinned below his own straining cock. He jacked Vandercastille until the rookie was humping his hand. Once it had sunk in that he'd crossed the line and there truly was no going back, Sweeney shifted on top of the handsome pitcher, lining their cocks up perfectly so the unmistakable heat being generated by both bone-hard bats worked in sync. Vandercastille's cock ground into Sweeney's. Both men pumped the sensitive undersides of their dicks against each other. Sweeney growled another string of locker-room words. "Fuck," he moaned. "You got a hot cock, cocksucker. Fuckin' feels great."

The precome of Sweeney's veteran bat lubed up the rookie's fat, hard cock. It felt so good, Sweeney half shut his eyes and groaned out an appeased sigh. It was the distraction Vandercastille had been waiting for and all he needed. In a blur of muscles in action, predator became prey, as the rookie knuckleballer knocked Sweeney aside. The ex-Socks pitcher landed cock down on the floor, howling from the pain, blinded by the stars that filled his eyes.

"Shit!" Sweeney howled. He'd hit the tiles knob first—and hard.

Vandercastille was on top of him in a flash. Sweeney's unbelted uniform pants, baseball shorts, and cupless jock came down in a swift yank that exposed the veteran's ass and cinched his legs together. Sweeney's tight, hairy asshole winked out from the dark pink center, a bull's-eye Vandercastille intended to spear.

"Fuck you," the rookie growled defiantly. He mounted Sweeney's solid, sweating ass before the veteran could argue. Gripping his cock, using Sweeney's own precome for lube, he pushed in. Sweeney's cries from having his previously unfucked butt penetrated drowned all else in the locker room. It also urged the rookie on. He shoved in all the way, felt Sweeney's unwilling shitter unknot around his cock head. Had the seal not been such a tight fit, Sweeney's buck would have knocked Vandercastille off. Somehow, with his hands around the veteran pitcher's waist and chest in a doggy-style death grip, Vandercastille held on. He pulled out a few inches of his cock before lunging in again. Aaron Sweeney's hole was, without argument, the tightest he'd ever popped off in.

Sweeney swore again, this time from the position of the conquered, not the conqueror. "You're fuckin' dead, cocksucker! Nobody fucks my asshole!"

Vandercastille's grip on the veteran's abdomen lowered. Holding Sweeney's rock-hard eight-incher upped the stakes. "Shut up, fucker," Vandercastille huffed in Sweeney's ear. "I'll rip your fuckin' cock off if you even try to stop me from riding your pussy hole." He jacked the veteran's manhood with one hand and grabbed his balls in the other. "Try to fuck with me in my own locker room, you arrogant fuck! Calling me a cocksucker when I catch you playing inside my fucking underwear! You're the one who's a cocksucker, playing with my dick like a pro!" Vandercastille slammed in again. The harshness of his fuck thrusts coupled with the verbal abuse he shouted into Sweeney's ears through clenched teeth made the load in the balls slapping against the veteran's butt cheeks build. The thought of having turned the tables and maybe capturing a piece of what Sweeney accused him of taking made the veteran's tail feel all the sweeter around his cock. Unable to stop his rhythm now, Vandercastille jabbed in hard. At the same time, something hot and wet gushed over his fingertips. Sweeney was close—damned close—and Tuc wasn't that far behind, ready to unload up the veteran's ass.

"You got a hot, tight cunt, fucker," Vandercastille moaned. "You like being my cunt?"

Sweeney struggled against Vandercastille's knob and the hand jacking him helplessly toward shooting some serious wad. "I ain't no man's cunt. I eat cunts like you for breakfast and fuck it till it's hamburger. You better hope you never run into my prick in a locker room again 'cause next time my dick's gonna do you some permanent damage!"

They were big words, and though Vandercastille hadn't given much thought to what would happen once he'd dumped his load up Sweeney's can, the false bravado and frustration in the veteran's voice was enough to send him over the edge. Vandercastille rammed in again, tormenting Sweeney's prostrate beyond control. A geyser of hot, sticky foam squirted into Vandercastille's hand. With Sweeney still coming, Vandercastille brought his fingers up, smearing the veteran's own load across his open mouth.

Sweeney sputtered a sperm-choked "You're fuckin' dead for that!"

Vandercastille grunted out a laugh. "Eat your own nut juice, you boy cunt," he answered, at that moment launching what felt like a gallon of hot sperm up into the veteran's asshole. He kept fucking Aaron Sweeney's angry ass long after he'd pumped all seven blasts of come inside it. When the pumps turned painful, sending shivers down Vandercastille's spent cock head, he quickly whipped it out of Sweeney's can. The stink of men and sex billowed up around him as Vandercastille returned to his feet, ready to fight.

Sweeney spun around fast, his reddened face coated with his own spunk, his long, thick cock still rock-hard and dripping. That was when both men, ready to take on the other, noticed they'd been joined by a third. Sweeney's jaw, like his pants, dropped.

"Aw, shit," he growled in defeat.

Vandercastille took a heavy swallow as he attempted to stuff his bat back into his baseball shorts. But he was still too hard, too sore, and the pressure made him wince. When the locker room stopped spinning, Ricky Catalano was still standing at the door, a fresh stack of towels in hand, a smug grin on his handsome, youthful face.

"I'd pay a million bucks to have gotten that on tape," Catalano said before he chuckled out a high-pitched laugh. He dropped the towels where he stood and started clapping. The echo sounded off the locker room's walls. "'Bout time some dude fucked you for a change, Sweens. Good work, Tuc."

"You little fuck," Sweeney spat. He took one step, fist clenched, but got no further. Vandercastille's sweat-soaked foot to the veteran pitcher's ass sent him back down to the floor. Sweeney shouted a breathless "Fuck!"

Vandercastille moved to Cat's side, protecting him with his new status in the major-league food chain. "Get that sorry butt of yours out of here, Aaron." The rookie and batboy exchanged a knowing smirk. "It's leaking my load all over the floor."

Sweeney hiked up his pants, and with a leer of total hatred for them both, slowly plodded toward the locker-room door. It might have been the sound of approaching laughter and footsteps that clinched the victory, his old team returning after the spoils of their shutout against the Pilots on home turf. Whatever the cause, sensing his defeat, the veteran pitcher left.

Two days later Aaron Sweeney was sent down to the Pilot's Triple-A farm team. He'd played his last major-league game in either uniform, Pilots or Socks. By that point the Socks were two games back in the Eastern Division, closing in on the pennant.

Bradley lined the ball down the third base line, over the head of the Fins' MVP contender. Bruno glanced up from second. The third-base coach's signal forced an extra burst of speed around third. Bruno was sure he'd score, and that would put them on top of the Fins.

Dan Murray in left field recovered the ball quickly, fired it to the cutoff man at third base, who got it home a step ahead of Bruno. The veteran center fielder went into a slam dive into the Fins catcher, a boulder hitting a brick wall. Both men went down. The first base ump called Bruno out. Bruno jumped up, put his red, pissed-off face into the umpire's, and the argument began.

Mitch Hudson flew out of the dugout. Both got ejected after Bruno told the umpire where he could shove home plate.

Weare had never seen Bruno so mad. The big guy stormed into the dugout, kicking his helmet in a punt that would have done the Seaside Soldiers major-league football team proud. A long string of "Fuckin' assholes" and "Son of a bitches" trailed him down the steps and into the tunnel to the clubhouse.

Weare's heart drummed loudly in his ears. He didn't know if it was the right time to act on it, but with a man on base and two more outs to spare, he knew he didn't have much of a choice. Bruno's continual silence on and off the field had grown unbearable. Before he could talk himself out of it, the rookie took off after Bruno, with just two guys ahead of his place in the lineup if Valenza and the Cowboy kept the inning alive. Each step down the dugout stairs felt like five.

He found Bruno at the urinals, standing in a classic piss stance, his zipper down, his fat, soft cock and both nuts hanging out of the sweat-soaked side of his jockstrap. The big guy's handsome face was frozen in an angry scowl. Beads of clear, clean perspiration dotted his brow and neck.

"What an asshole," Weare said in his best diplomatic voice. "'Sides, he knows he'd enjoy you shoving the plate—or any-thing—up his ass. Then again," he said moving right up to Bruno's side at the urinal for an unobstructed view of the handsome veteran's tense, unpissing cock. "Who wouldn't?"

Bruno shook his head. "This ain't a good time, pal," the big guy warned.

"No time's been a good time for you since Tom Jr. was here." Bruno shook his head. "Shut the fuck up, Tim. I'm in no mood for this."

"You haven't been in the mood since I fucked your son. I've got news for you, dude. Me, Tom Jr.—we're both adults. What happened happened. Both of us did something we wanted to do, including your boy, who's a man now."

"How the fuck would you know?" Bruno growled threaten-ingly.

Weare glanced down. Bruno's cock bounced under the ob-vious strain of a nervous bladder being forced. The first squirt of hot gold came out, but that was all. Bruno strained again.

"How would I know? Shit, guy," the rookie said. "You're feeling weird about what you saw? Damn, Bruno, that kid of yours is a man, whether you want to admit it or not, and he didn't do anything different from what you've been doing all summer. The kid really loves you. I know..." Just then, Bruno's piss flared out. The big center fielder groaned. "I know 'cause I love you too, you big dumb jock. I love you more than anyone in the world."

Bruno sprayed the urinal. A small trace of a hopeful, happy smile played out on his stubbled lips. "You love me?"

"Of course, you stupid shit. I'll prove it if I have to."

It happened so fast, neither man fully prepared for the

other's reaction. There, alone at the Top Socks' urinals, Weare went quickly to his knees. He gulped Bruno's pissing cock into his mouth and down his throat.

Bruno swore as Weare choked on the first blast of liquid gold. He started to gulp faster on the raunchy, sour piss; it was Tommy Bruno's, and that alone made it vintage.

By the time he'd drunk the last of it, Bruno was hard in his mouth. The veteran center fielder pushed in, though Weare, contrary to the earlier love he'd shown to Bruno's cock, spit the rock-hard bat out. His mouth slick, his face blanched in disbelief at what he'd just done, Weare rose from the bath-room floor. He let out a loud, vulgar burp that tasted like what he had just swallowed.

"No guy, not now. I got a ball to hit. Later, at home. I miss sucking your cock and you sucking mine."

Bruno nodded. "Yeah, pal, later."

As Weare crossed back to the exit, Bruno hauled up his zip-per. "I look forward to it, buddy," the rookie said. He was halfway out into the tunnel when Bruno's words temporarily stopped him in his tracks.

"Spank that one over the wall for me."

Weare grinned and gave his cup a knock. When he looked back Bruno was smiling. Light streaming through the tall ven-tilation windows lit his grin, making him glow. Without reservation, Weare knew he loved Tom Bruno.

With Bradley advanced to third base on a sacrifice bunt and the cowboy onboard at first, Weare stepped up to the plate. He took a sliding curve ball, and with one swing of the bat, it was a whole new ball game. In Bruno's honor he spanked it over the wall. As he raced around the bases with his hands held high, he knew the big guy would be proud of him.

EIGHTH INNING

When August slipped into September and the dog days gave way to brisk nights, Scott Bradley always experienced the same bittersweet malaise. The baseball season reached its most exciting point when the pennant chases became mad dashes, but with that excitement came the sad reality that the summer was winding down into a fall classic that came and went too quickly and a winter that seemed way too long.

The Socks were up four games on the Fins and three on the Pilots. Any of the top three teams could run away with the division. On the road, with a two-day break between games and close enough to his off-season house in St. Louis, Bradley went home feeling both sad and elated at the same time. He knew the Top Socks were just that: the tops. There'd been a different chemistry to this year's team, something between the rookies and veterans, something the addition of Tim Weare and Tucker Vandercastille had only made better. The team was a true team, bigger than the individual players. Bradley knew teams like that season's Socks only came around once in a while. The next year's team might not have the same magic.

So, happier than he could recall and feeling sadder than it was sane to be at the top of your game, Bradley dropped his bags inside the door, kicked off his deck shoes, and stripped to his briefs, flexing his bare toes on the plush carpet. He pulled the framed team photo from his suitcase and promptly gave in to it all, a tear running down his cheek.

"I fuckin' love you guys," he said out loud. Bruno and Weare, the Werewolf and Cowboy, knuckleballs Tuc and the Thunderbird, Valenza—all of them.

Bradley hadn't been home in almost two months, though the caretaker he employed kept the house clean, took in the mail, maintained the yard, and kept things in order. The bedroom, its white comforter and sheets smelling fresh and clean, welcomed him back to his home away from Seaside, Mass. This was the place he would go to when the season wound down, when winter kept the game dormant until early spring and Bradley was given some time to reflect on the previous year.

He stretched out on the bed, absently tugging on his cotton-covered sac of nuts and his soft, thick cock. Before Bradley realized it, he had stroked his cock to its full size and thickness. He was so intent on studying the photograph of his hard-hitting, handsome team of fellow sluggers, the shudder racing up his cock was twice as intense. The eruption inside his underwear musked up his clean white briefs and turned the cotton over his cock opaque. Bradley swore in disbelief. He'd jacked himself off without even trying.

"There's so much shit on my mind," he whispered to himself. "I can't even keep my dick under control."

He peeled the wet briefs off and brought them up to his face. The juice from his nuts was still warm and runny. Bradley always ate his own come after jacking off, and this was no exception, left in his shorts or not. He sucked on the moist cotton, then, with an exhausted, sad sigh, tossed them on the floor and stretched out. The bed felt comfortable, and

despite the early hour, sleep overwhelmed him almost instantly. Maybe, he thought right before passing out, a nap
would clear his head and remind him there was still a lot of
baseball to be played in September—and quite possibly October, if the Socks stayed on top. His dreams were filled with
images of his teammates, his friends, the men he respected-
and even—hell, yes—loved: the Top Socks.

Tommy Bruno, his solid, perfect body and four-alarm smile
on a face that put other men to shame. The Cowboy and his
jocular Southern twang, easygoing attitude, and undeniable
handsomeness. Tim Weare and Tucker Vandercastille's raw
energy. Then there was the Thunderbird, who he'd come to
know and respect in every way, over every inch of his
pumped, hard body. Bradley remembered what it had been
like that long-ago day with Twain in the doc's office, how
he'd tasted, smelled, felt.

"Roger," Bradley groaned. He started awake from a dream
about sucking the big guy's cock. The phantom taste of Twain
still lingered on his tongue. The feel of the Thunderbird's
married-man lips wrapped around Bradley's bat persisted.

The first thing Bradley noticed was the sun, lower behind
the trees outside his window but still bathing the room in
hypnotic mosaics of late-summer light; the next was the wetness of a mouth on his cock. Bradley wasn't dreaming, and the
blow job wasn't only in his thoughts.

He froze on his back and scrambled to his elbows, pulling
his cock from the expert set of lips sucking away on it. "What
the hell?" he sputtered, but then it hit him, just how familiar
those lips felt.

Bradley saw the baseball cap a moment before he recognized the handsome face under its bill. Jeff Brunson's pale
blue eyes and perfect white teeth sparkled in the sun's broken

glow. The man had sucked Scott Bradley's dick until it was as big as the sluggers cock had ever been.

"Fuck," the Top Socks' second baseman growled in a sleepy voice. "It's good to see you, Jeff. 'Bout time you fuckin' got here."

Brunson spit out the erect cock head in his mouth and scooted up the bed until both men were face-to-face. The press of Jeff's body—clothed in a white dress shirt and un-knotted tie, comfortable-looking faded blue jeans, and deck shoes—against Bradley's nakedness felt wonderfully electric. Bradley cupped the other man's jeans-clad butt as they kissed. He knew right away that Jeff was as hard as he was. The full, tented crotch of his pants hobnobbed up and down against Bradley's straining bat. The kiss, deep and hungry, tasted like the second baseman's erection.

"I mean it, Jeff," Bradley said once the kiss ended. "Damn good to see you."

Brunson reached a hand down and started playing with Bradley's cock. Bradley spread his legs below his ex-team-mate. For the brief moment of silence, he gazed into Brunson's pale blue eyes. Jeff, with his shaved head, neat goatee and major-league 'stache, and corn-fed Midwestern muscles, flashed another innocent, boyish smile. "Same here, bro. Checked the schedule. Saw you guys would be in the neigh-borhood for a few days. Figured you'd be home for at least a night." Brunson glanced to the right of Bradley, at the framed team photo on the empty pillow. "It's a good-looking team you guys put together this time around."

Despite the incredible feel of Brunson's glove-hand grip on his cock, Bradley had to force a smile. "It'd be even better looking if you were part of it."

The Socks' former first baseman turned his head slightly,

focusing on a peripheral target in the wan glow streaming through the bedroom windows. Arcs of light embossed Jeff's pale eyes, giving them a heaviness. "Wish I could be there with you, playing for a pennant instead of playing just for pride. You got the late-season blues again, don't ya?"

Bradley nodded, then reached up. In one deft motion he flipped Jeff onto his back. Their lips met again. The kiss lasted longer this time. Lips crushed together, Bradley slowly unknotted Brunson's tie, then, one at a time, he popped the buttons of his dress shirt until the St. Louis Steam's all-star first baseman's hairy, solid chest glowed in the afternoon sun. Brunson's dark-pink nipples, each ringed by reddish-blond hair, captured the light fully.

Bradley worked lower, toward Brunson's belt. He gave it a tug. When Bradley undid the snap on his former teammate's pants, their lips still holding, Brunson kicked off his deck shoes. All that separated them from equal footing was Brunson's zipper, and Bradley quickly took care of that.

"It's just like the old days," Brunson said. "You and me, the Socks all over again."

"Yeah?" Bradley groaned. "This bring back memories?" He leaned in, sliding both strong hands down Brunson's flat, hairy abdomen, until they slipped under the elastic of his white briefs into crisp, rough shag.

Bradley dove in, pulling Brunson's blue jeans and briefs down. The action sent a wave of smells—soap and sweat—into his face. The heaviness of the first baseman's tight, hairy nuts and the carpet of shag surrounding them and his thick, stubby cock called to mind a hundred memories of baseball, summer, and the night on the road they'd crossed the line. Sex with Jeff Brunson was a routine Scott Bradley knew well, something he had never tired of—certainly not in the last

year after Brunson had been traded to St. Louis for Curly Ellis.
The taste of his old pal's erection sent shivers through
Bradley's entire body.

He started first by licking just the head. Brunson's bat came
in at a decent, average six inches and was already leaking the
clear syrup he'd end up dumping buckets of once Bradley finished with him. Wasting no time, the Top Socks second
baseman licked up Brunson's precome. A few sucks were all it
took for Brunson to respond; he pulled Bradley's legs into position over his face so that his shaved head was between the
other man's hairy knees. Bradley's fat low-hangers vanished
into Brunson's mouth.

Bradley answered by swallowing the hard cock he'd been
polishing with his tongue. Brunson's rod was a perfect fit. He
didn't choke on it the way he had Roger Twain's horse cock.
Again in familiar territory, Bradley also toyed with Brunson's
tight, full sac of nuts. The first baseman spread his legs wider
to accommodate Bradley's touch.

Both men settled into a comfortable sixty-nine on the bed,
yin and yang, man to man, buddies who knew the ways, small
and big, of pleasing each other. There was no place they
weren't allowed to explore, and in the minutes that followed,
no region of bare, masculine ballplayer skin went neglected.

Bradley stripped Brunson of the last of his clothes. That
done, he began at his buddy's feet, touching, rubbing his way
up the handsome slugger's hairy calves. His hands reached the
first baseman's inner thighs and from there moved to the familiar, tight, furry knot winking underneath Brunson's nut
bag. Brunson's asshole tasted clean and sweet. Bradley licked
it without hesitating, his tongue extended, his nose aimed
straight at the puckered hole.

"Shit, Scott," Brunson groaned. "I ain't been eaten so good

since the last time I was in Seaside."

Bradley chuckled a gust of hot air into Brunson's shitter. "You're in for a great time, dude. I've had some practice this season."

"Yeah?" Brunson asked. "With who?"

Doing his best imitation of a crackling lightening strike, Bradley resumed licking his ex-teammate's asshole. It didn't sink in right away, but after a glance at the team photo, a shit-eating smirk momentarily replaced the look on Brunson's face.

"Son of a bitch," he growled. "Roger Twain? You dorked the Thunderbird?"

Bradley answered with a tight lip seal on the other man's asshole. He sucked the tight clean-tasting knot until he'd lubed and loosened it enough to insert a finger. Brunson pushed back against the finger as Bradley shoved in. His finger vanished up into the steaming hole.

"Shit," Bradley swore. "You've really forgotten what it's like to have me in there."

Fighting the unease, his forehead streaked in fresh sweat, Brunson nodded. "That's 'cause I didn't have Twain's donkey dick up it, you lucky fucker."

Bradley lifted into position. He pulled out his finger, licked the tang off, and worked the hard, ready head of his cock into the first baseman's hole. The first rush of heat and pain caused Brunson to seize in place beneath his former teammate. "Roger's fuckin' huge, dude. But he's my buddy and team-mate. I only got him off. You...you're a lot more than that to me. It's an honor to be here on top of you." Bradley pushed the first few inches slowly up into Brunson.

Through clenched teeth, the one-time Top Socks first base-man drew in a deep breath, then held it painfully. "It's all coming back to me, buddy," he said, finally exhaling with a sigh.

Bradley went in slowly, until his cock head was teasing Brunson's prostate. The blond shag lining the second baseman's bat brushed up against Brunson's nuts. Reaching down, Bradley gave the other man's tight balls a playful tug. "You ready, pal?"

Brunson nodded. His stubby, rock-hard cock was up and really dripping now. Brunson took himself in his right hand and pumped a rivulet of milky juice out of his piss slit.

This time Scott Bradley didn't come so fast. He lowered and clamped his lips over Brunson's major-league mouth, loving the feel of the neatly clipped goatee and 'stache. Slowly, he pumped in and out of Brunson's well-eaten asshole, teasing them both to the point of unloading but not over the edge. Bradley had waited a hell of a long time to get back in his ex-teammate's can, and feeling the way he did—the late-season blues, as Brunson called it—he didn't want to rush it. Both men remained locked together, kissing as only men could, tormented by the need to come but more by the need not to just yet.

The sun had slipped far from sight behind the wall of trees outside of the house's windows when Bradley lost control, and the floodgates opened. The room, robbed of all light, felt for one brief instant as if it was on fire.

"Shit! Here it comes!" Bradley proclaimed.

Brunson huffed, "I know!"

Bradley pulled out after dumping half his load in the other man's ass. The rest got deposited on Brunson's bat. The St. Louis first baseman jacked his monster nonstop in an effort to join in his buddy's excitement. The added lubrication of Bradley's come did it. Brunson shot a steady geyser of foam into the air, down onto the sweat-soaked white sheets. At the last moment, Bradley tugged on his pal's balls, adding to the blast a sensation he knew Brunson loved.

"Yeah, dude," Brunson gasped, a second blast spurting up and over his stomach and across the bed. "Pull on my fuckin' bag. Squeeze those balls."

Brunson's pleasure quickly turned to pain as the orgasm subsided. The room that had felt so warm seconds before fell cold under the influence of a breeze that felt like autumn, even winter. The sticky drops of spent come coating the pillows and sheets cooled too.

"Aw, man," Brunson apologized, wiping the now clammy sweat off his forehead. "I'm sorry. I really messed up your sheets. I'll get something to clean 'em up."

Brunson kicked his legs over the edge of Bradley's bed but got no further. The Socks' second baseman pulled him back into a pig pile on top of the load-soaked sheets. "It's OK, buddy. Leave it. I think I'd like to have you all over my sheets when I come home after winning the pennant. It'll make winter go a little easier." A bittersweet smile broke on Bradley's handsome, youthful face, making him seem much older.

Brunson was a true friend in every way. He knew he had to remove the sad look off Bradley's face, no matter how or at what cost. "What makes you fuck nuts think you're getting away with a pennant?"

"Fuck you," Bradley said, taking his pal into a headlock. "I was on top of you, that's how!"

Naked and wet, sweating and smelling like a pair of baseball players after the game, they wrestled on the bed until collapsing in a silent heap, face-to-face on the sperm-soaked pillows. A large drop of come had sprayed the glass of the framed photograph of the Socks. Bradley tried to wipe it off, only to smear a dose of whitewash across the faces of his teammates. The sad, somber look Brunson had seen twice that afternoon returned to Bradley's face. This time it would be even harder to remove.

"Scott," he whispered, his voice a deep growl. "You guys do have the better team this year. You've proven it, and you deserve to go all the way to the top. Try and enjoy it—the friendships, the games, the summer. The unmistakable rush in your nuts and guts that'll come when you clinch the division. And when it ends, come home for the winter knowing that baseball, like the spring, will be back when the snow melts."

Bradley nodded and pulled Brunson into a strong bear hug. "For tonight I just want to be with you."

"No prob, bro," Brunson said. He reached down, freeing the comforter cinched around their ankles. He pulled the blanket over them as a strange silence settled over the house.

They loved on and off all night, until dawn broke, sending them back to their respective teams. As Brunson had said, there was still a lot of baseball to be played.

A wind over the right-field wall played havoc with Vandercastille's knuckleball. Three wild pitches and a passed ball put the Philadelphia Pilots on the scoreboard in the first inning. After two more, Coach Hudson pulled Vandercastille for one of the late-season insurance call-ups that would hopefully carry his weight if the Socks made the postseason. Vandercastille left the mound pissed off and full of rage, which he took out first on a cooler of sports drink, then on himself, punching the bench until Hudson and Valenza reminded him they'd need that hand the next time.

Winning over the Pilots on their own turf was one thing, but losing to them on Top Socks soil when McKinsey Field was packed and the team was a game away from clinching the division was too much to handle. Vandercastille, game face and all, left with a trace of tears in his eyes.

Hudson followed him out of the dugout, sure his star knuckleballer was going to do something stupid. He put the bench coach temporarily in charge and pursued the hot-tempered ballplayer knowing he had to cool him down.

"Tuc," he said in a deep shout that left no room for argument. "My office, pronto."

The rookie knuckleballer gave his locker one more size-12 kick and screamed, "Fuck!" The lone word echoed through the empty locker room.

Reluctantly, Vandercastille entered the small office with its shuttered windows and blinds. "Close the door," Hudson growled from the corner of his desk. Vandercastille did. The stone scowl on Hudson's face quickly deflated the rookie pitcher's anger. "Cool your fuckin' nuts off, boy. The last thing I need—specially with Roger just off the DL and doing his job better than best—is to have my other star fuck up the team's chances in the playoffs by punching walls!"

"But, coach!"

"I'm not finished," Hudson interjected, cutting Vandercastille off mid speech. "I'm telling you like it is. I'm proud of you, kid. Real proud. But let your steam off without breaking any bones. We got 24 bottles of champagne being chilled, just waiting for us to clinch. You won't be able to pop a cork in a cast. Now you get to speak."

Hudson's words crushed most of Vandercastille's anguish. He shrugged and shook his head, an action that rained sweat drops across the room. "I sucked out there, coach. I really let all of you down."

"It's one game," Hudson growled.

"Yeah—but the one that counted. We coulda clinched tonight if I hadn't thrown like shit out there."

Hudson sighed, rose from the edge of the desk, and stepped closer—enough to reach out and put both hands squarely on Vandercastille's shoulders. "You're a baseball player, kid. You're tough. My guys don't get phased when they're down four runs in the first. 'Sides," he said, softening. "You've always looked real good out there."

A single tear slipped out of Vandercastille's eye. Hudson wiped it clear.

"Real good. Let it go, kid—now, while it's just you and me."

Vandercastille toughened up again, but it was obvious how upset he still was. Sensing it, Hudson pulled him close into a tight bear hug that soaked the upper chest of his jacket with the rookie's sweat. Hudson had seen it all before at the end of the baseball season, when emotions were running high, and the guys, especially the rookies, were feeling the pressure to perform.

"Sh-h-h," Hudson soothed. He patted Vandercastille's back gently. To his surprise the rookie pitcher held on just as hard, his face against the side of Hudson's. It wasn't intentional, but at one point, in trying to console the handsome knuckleballer, Hudson realized he'd gotten stiff. He shifted uncomfortably against the rookie. All it did was press his hard cock into Vandercastille's packed jockstrap.

Hudson had wanted Vandercastille from the moment he saw him pitch on the farm-system team. Given what he knew in confidence through Catalano about the confrontation between Vandercastille and that prick Aaron Sweeney, whom he'd replaced in the rotation, Hudson threw caution to the wind. This might be his one and only chance—all or nothing, sink or swim. Win or lose, Coach Hudson reached down and gripped the soft, manly fullness his own erection was pressing against.

"Coach?" Vandercastille asked in a dumb, disbelieving voice between sniffles.

"Like I said, Tucker," Hudson soothed. "Let it go. Let it go. You look real good out there...." With that and no further permission or resistance, Hudson dropped to his knees. He slowly unzipped the rookie's pants and fumbled inside Vandercastille's sweat-dampened jock. The knuckleballer's meaty, soft cock and come-packed sac of low-hanging nuts felt hot and heavy in his hand. "And kid," Hudson growled. "You ain't looking bad from where I'm kneeling now." Leaning in, Hudson ran his nose over Vandercastille's balls while loosening the rookie's belt. "Let's give these hot nuts of yours some air to cool off."

"Aw, coach, what are you doing to me?"

Hudson answered by lowering the rookie's uniform off his hard, high ass. Vandercastille's jockstrap followed. With the rookie's cock in his face, Hudson reached around and explored the knuckleballer's hairy crack, searching for the tight knot at the center of his concrete butt cheeks. Vandercastille jumped in his spikes when Hudson's fuck finger pressed against his tight knot.

"Coach!" the rookie pleaded.

"Loosen up, kid," Hudson huffed. "You need to learn how to deal with pressure this time of year. You know how to handle yourself. I heard what happened between you and that prick Sweeney."

Vandercastille held up a restraining hand. "I can explain that, coach."

"No need to," Hudson said. "Loosen up, buddy. Take it." He forced the resisted finger deep into the rookie's asshole.

Vandercastille moaned but didn't fight it much more than that. The cock dangling an inch from Hudson's mouth jerked.

Wasting no time, with the rookie now grinding against his fuck finger, Hudson wrapped his lips around the soft, fleshy, arrow-shaped head of Vandercastille's slugger. The knuckle-baller's shaft toughened instantly, and in seconds he was pushing eight bone-hard inches down the coach's throat.

"Shit, coach," Vandercastille grunted. "You got my bat all big and wet. Fuck, that feels good."

Hudson growled a full-mouthed reply as he concentrated on sucking the rookie's cock head and the first few inches of his shaft. If there was one thing besides baseball Hudson knew, it was how to service a hot-dog jock. Vandercastille's cock, so thick at the head, sported a trigger of nerves the coach wasted no time before focusing his attention on. The finger he'd worked up the rookie's shit hole helped his cause. Soon Hudson caught the first dribble of the young pitcher's precome on his tongue.

Vandercastille reacted well to being fingered. He pushed forward each time Hudson sucked in. In turn, his cock worked deeper and further down the coach's throat.

Hudson sensed the rookie was getting close. The dribble of spunk turned into a mouthful that painted the corners of his lips. He groped Vandercastille's meaty low-hangers and rolled his hairy, musky nuts over his nose. Vandercastille quickly responded to having his nuts tugged on. After a few firm yanks, the first blast of hot, sour spunk hit the roof of Coach Hudson's mouth.

Vandercastille bucked back against Hudson's finger as he fucked the other man's face. Hudson continued to rub his star pitcher's prostate raw, which sent the rookie knuckleballer into overdrive. Hudson sucked harder, faster, all the time squeezing Vandercastille's big bag of nuts forcefully. His reward was a second shot of come, a gigantic third volley, and the trickles of a fourth and fifth.

Hudson didn't swallow the mouthful of come right away; he rolled the thick, pungent fluid over his tongue to savor Vandercastille's taste before gulping it down. That done, he spit out the rookie's cock and cleaned it off with slow, full laps.

"Fuck, boy," Hudson huffed. "I've been wanting to do that from the moment I saw you in action back in March. Good things do come to those who wait."

Hudson rose from his crouch. Vandercastille, a pained, sweaty look on his disbelieving face, groped the bulge in the coach's uniform pants. To his surprise Hudson denied him. "No, kid."

Vandercastille, his spent cock still hanging half hard, out in the open, shrugged. "Don't you want me to take care of yours?"

Hudson flashed a cocky grin before pressing his lips against the rookie's. Vandercastille drank the taste of his own come. "Yeah, kid, but let's make a deal. You get me into the post-season; I give you what I got down there. Deal?"

"Deal," Vandercastille said. The two men shook hands. "But I feel kinda guilty. You sure?"

Hudson ogled the knuckleballer's spent monster one last time, shook his head, and headed for the door. "Not now, kid. I got a game to see to the end out there. But I promise, this was just the first, not the last.'

Hudson left Vandercastille in his office, big baseball player's dick and balls exposed, uniform pants around his ankles. He emerged in the dugout in time to see his second baseman knock in Bruno on a sacrifice fly. In his absence Weare had also gone yard. Somehow Hudson knew this game was far from lost.

Four innings later, champagne flowed like the sweat and semen that were the Top Socks' signature that year, as the boys of summer from Seaside clinched the Eastern Division.

☆   ☆   ☆

A mix-up plunked Damon Thorne in with Bruno at the hotel on the Socks' last road trip of the regular season. The Werewolf seemed more disturbed by it than the big center fielder.

"I didn't mean to split up the Ballsy Twins," Thorne apologized. "I know you guys like to hang together on the road."

Weare clapped the Werewolf's shoulder. "I don't mind, Wolfie," the rookie teased in a jocular voice. "I'm sure Roger's farts can't be half as bad as Bruno's." Both men chuckled heartily.

Bruno wasn't so happy. "Hey," he growled. "You've let some silent-but-violents loose!"

Weare flashed a cocksure Cheshire-cat grin. "Hope you brought your gas mask. You'll be a bald werewolf if he gets anywhere near the salsa and nachos. That green cloud'll burn off your pelt." The rookie slapped Thorne's solid butt and exited the hotel room.

"Asshole," Bruno said with a good-natured laugh, aiming both middle fingers at the closed door. "I hope the Thunderbird's snoring keeps him up all night."

Thorne's good mood followed him into and out of the shower. With a weekend day game scheduled for the final showdown of the year between the Top Socks and Pilots, he retired early. Bruno wasn't far behind him. They both crashed, clad only in their underwear, on the room's two double beds, with the TV on and cable sports droning updated scores.

Bruno was half asleep when he heard the knock at the door. He started, fully awake. The knock sounded again. Thorne's deep breaths became snorts. As the third repetition of knuckles on the door sounded, Bruno tore the covers aside. He wiped his eyes and crossed to the door to answer it. Weare waited on the other side, dressed in a pair of sweats, fresh white socks, and a new pair of sneakers.

"Dude," Weare whispered excitedly.

Bruno scratched at the meaty bulge in his crisp white briefs and shook his head. "Quiet. My roomie's snoozin'."

Weare slipped his head beneath the veteran center fielder's armpit. The Werewolf snored on cue. "Fuckin' perfect," the rookie sighed. He did a London Bridge beneath Bruno's arm, into the room. "He's out like a light."

The handsome veteran spun around. "What're you, fuckin' crazy?"

"No, horny," Weare whispered. "I gotta have some of what I'd be getting if they'd put us in the same room." He reached a hand and groped the heavy, meaty bulge in Bruno's underwear. The rookie's fingertips slid beyond the elastic into Bruno's coarse man hair. Bruno let out a moan, then reached down. He pulled Weare's hand out of the hairy warmth.

"I don't fuckin' believe you," Bruno growled in a whisper. "Playing with my cock when there's a teammate of ours in the room."

A shit-eating grin twisted the rookie's mouth into a sexy smile. "I'm gonna do more than play with it, big guy." Before Bruno could protest, Weare slipped to his knees, pulling the veteran's underwear with him. Weare took Bruno's meaty, soft cock in his mouth and greedily sucked away while massaging the come-packed bull nuts hanging low beneath it.

Bruno grunted his approval but let out a breathless "No,

fuck, no," urging the rookie to stop. He put his hands on Weare's shoulders, tried to pry away the hot mouth making love to his cock, but it was hard to fight. The itch in Bruno's nuts, which made him want Weare to continue, made his dick stiff in record time. Only the danger of being discovered if the Werewolf snorted or farted himself awake finally drove them apart.

"No," Bruno huffed. He whipped his manhood out of Weare's wet mouth. To his own surprise he was already dripping precome. It painted the handsome rookie's lips with a milk mustache. "Not here. Not with the Wolf over there."

As forceful as Bruno's denial of Weare's hunger was, it only seemed to spur the rookie on. He continued to massage Bruno's nuts and leaned in to kiss the dribbling tip of the rock-hard boner he'd brought to its full size. "Damon?" Weare said. The cocky smirk on Weare's face widened. "You worried about him finding out and disapproving?"

Bruno scowled. He gave his rod a few stiff strokes, one eye narrowed on the man kneeling in front of him. "You fuckin' high or something?"

Weare stood. "No, I already told you—horny." The smirk on the rookie's handsome face sagged into a pout. Before Bruno could question him further, Weare sidestepped to the still-occupied double bed where Damon Thorne lay sprawled on his back, snoring and oblivious to the heated debate that had taken place a yard away. Weare gave the comforter covering Thorne a casual tug. "I never told you this," Weare continued, exposing Thorne's flat, hairy stomach and the perfect white of his underwear. "Back in the minors, Tuc Vandercastille and me got pretty close. Not like you and me, but enough that we got to know each other real good. You notice how tight he and the Werewolf are?"

Bruno stood motionless, his arms folded, his mouth agape, silent, as if the words he might have wanted to say had clogged halfway up his throat. The veteran center fielder's only reaction came from his rock-hard cock, which continued to pulse and drip in anticipation of the rookie's next move.

"Tuc told me something about the Werewolf," Weare went on to whisper. With that and no more, he went back to his knees, this time at the side of Thorne's bed. Bruno watched, horrified, as his best buddy gently folded the bedclothes down off the bulge of the Werewolf's slumbering knob and balls. He groped the package with one hand and pulled the elastic around the leg of the Werewolf's underwear aside with the other. Thorne's soft, meaty balls spilled out. His limp cock followed.

"I don't fuckin believe you," Bruno stammered. "Timmy, no."

Weare took his first taste of the Werewolf's hairy cock, licking the soft, fleshy head and the furry shaft, sniffing the tangle of mossy-smelling shag surrounding it. In the breathless minute that followed, he bathed all of Thorne's exposed manhood until it glistened in the light from the TV. Glancing back, he noticed that, despite his protests, Bruno was stroking his own bat, more turned on by what he had seen than terrified of getting caught.

Weare toyed with Thorne's soft cock and rolled the fleshy skin up and down, making sure to pay the most attention to the trigger of nerves lining the area under its head. The ploy worked. Several more strokes into it, Thorne's bat began to toughen up. It's lone eye stretched out, straining against the rookie's fingertips. To help it along, Weare leaned down for a lick. Thorne hardened fully. The rookie's teasing licks became solid, all-out sucks.

The Werewolf's cock pushed against Weare's tongue, and

soon the first trickle of precome oozed out. Weare pulled back, taking Thorne's lumber between his forefinger and thumb. Two more strokes did it: Thorne, who'd started to unconsciously hump Weare's hand, started awake. Bruno swore, shocked to be standing there with his dick hanging hard and in the open. Weare returned to sucking Thorne's cock. The Werewolf grunted and stretched.

"Fuck," he growled in a sleepy, cracked voice. "What the fuck are you doing?" Weare answered with a muffled groan, his mouth full of hard, wet cock.

Bruno held up his hands, shook his head. "Sorry, man," he started to say.

But a smooth, sexy smile replaced the confused scowl on the Werewolf's face. Thorne spread his legs and took a deep breath. Going up to his elbows, the Werewolf tipped his head at Bruno. "You have anything to do with this?"

"Werewolf," Bruno sighed. "Like I said..."

The Socks' star catcher flashed a bright, toothy smile. "I could fuckin' smell it all the way back in spring training, you big dumb stud." Through the dim light of the TV, Thorne focused on Bruno's hard, hanging cock. "No more fucking around, Bruno—unless it's with that."

The veteran center fielder got the point. With Weare still engaged between the Werewolf's legs, Bruno moved to the top of the bed and straddled the catcher's face. Thorne took him into his mouth without hesitation, sucking the center fielder's already rock-hard wood to its hairy root. Bruno sighed and gripped the back of Thorne's head, burying the most of his shaft down the catcher's throat. Instantly he knew it wasn't Thorne's first taste of another man's dick. The Werewolf sucked cock too well; he knew his way around a boner.

"Aw, fuck, Wolfie," Bruno sputtered. "I never thought you and me would end up doing this."

Thorne spit out Bruno's cock. "Yeah, it's kinda nice, you and me and the rookie," he said between licks of the center fielder's nuts. "I've been thinkin' about this for a long time. You know, we've been teammates for a few summers, buddy. Always wanted to see that wang of yours hard."

Bruno smiled and stroked the side of Thorne's hairy face. "Well, now, son, you got the chance. That's it, Werewolf. Suck my fuckin' nuts like a dog. Swallow those sweaty fuckin' balls of mine."

Thorne did as Bruno commanded. He sucked the veteran's meaty low-hangers down his throat and stroked the big guy's bat at the same time. Bruno smiled, partly because he realized that, like his namesake, the team's catcher really was an animal and gave head like one—hungry, wet, insatiable. What shocked Bruno too was the Werewolf's hunger for his ass; Thorne let go of Bruno's nuts only to plant his lips on the big guy's hairy asshole. Thorne licked and sucked on it until Bruno's tight knot was slick with spit.

Still straddling Thorne's face, Bruno pivoted into a sixty-nine position on top of the Werewolf that put him face-to-face with the rookie. He and Weare kissed over the Werewolf's dribbling cock. If Bruno had any doubts minutes before about the decision to come clean with his oldest buddy in the ball club, having his balls licked and the image of Weare, his handsome face full of Thorne's manhood, removed them. They braced both sides of the Werewolf's cock with their lips, going up and down, masturbating Thorne with their mouths.

Getting the catcher off came quicker than Weare or Bruno expected. While playing with the Werewolf's balls, Bruno felt the tongue up his ass pull back. Thorne groaned a hot, loud breath into Bruno's crack. A second later a bullet of sweet-tasting juice gushed between their mouths; together rookie and veteran licked it up, though the party was far from over.

☆   ☆   ☆

The Werewolf took hold of Weare on one side, Bruno grabbed him on the other. They tossed the rookie onto Thorne's hotel bed, and after Bruno rid Weare of his sneakers and socks, the two veteran ballplayers savagely yanked off the rookie's sweats, first his shirt over his head, then his pants from his waist. Though he'd just shot his load, Thorne went down on the rookie with the same hunger he'd shown Bruno's ass. He had Weare's cock—the fattest of the bunch—in his mouth before Bruno could even show him how the rookie liked it.

Bruno got off on watching his oldest friend working between the legs of his best—two buddies intent on taking care of each other's cocks. Bruno moved in and pressed his bare chest against the Werewolf's back for an unobstructed view. He was so into watching Thorne suck the rookie's cock, Bruno was humping the catcher's ass before he realized it. He knew he had to follow through. Whether Thorne liked it or not, he was about to get his ass fucked but good.

Bruno moved down to Thorne's tight, hairy hole and licked it out of respect for their long-standing friendship. Once he'd tongued it full of spit, Bruno lined up. Thorne didn't fight being penetrated, though the tight ring of muscles that circled the Werewolf's shitter made it hard for Bruno to get in.

"That's it, Werewolf," Bruno growled. "Take my dick. Suck Timmy's cock while I fuck you."

The three men worked together once more, forming a pig

pile on the bed, headed by Weare. Watching the Werewolf suck the rookie's cock caused Bruno to buck harder, pushing him farther up Thorne's ass, grunting and growling as the heat of their sweat filled the room with the musky stink of athletes.

"This is fuckin' great," Weare yowled, his hairy legs spread on both side of the Werewolf's face. "Just three guys from a team sitting at the top of the division getting off before a game with a team that's only playing for pride. Fuckin' A!" He focused on Bruno, who pushed in hard again. "Fuck his butt, dude," Weare urged. "Hammer that fuckin' hole!"

The elation the rookie felt watching his other half bone Thorne worked him into overdrive. He grabbed the catcher by the back of his head and shoved his cock deeper into Thorne's wet mouth. The Werewolf moaned loudly, his grunts muffled around the rookie's bat.

Bruno pushed into Thorne's ass harder. "You like that?" he asked in a deep, mean voice. "Both of you, you like it?"

Thorne again answered with a guttural affirmation.

Weare's answer was clearer. "Shit," he huffed. "Here it comes!"

The next time Bruno pumped into Thorne's can, Weare unloaded into the catcher's mouth. A river of foamy semen leaked from the corners of Thorne's tightly sealed lips and trickled down the catcher's goatee, coating Weare's already sweat-drenched nuts.

Bruno pushed in one final time, then injected his spunk deep in Thorne's asshole. He was still coming when he pulled out, spritzing the Werewolf's back. The veteran center fielder aimed his head between Weare's legs and cleaned up what Thorne had missed. The veterans kissed.

The moment their lips parted, the Werewolf let out a loud howl. Weare joined in. With Bruno's deep, masculine bellow added, the sound bonded them together like a pack of wild animals from that moment forward.

☆   ☆   ☆

The night continued with a little oral relief—Bruno sucking Weare's cock, the Werewolf's mouth on Bruno's, Weare sucking on the team's star catcher. It wasn't like the contest running between Bruno and Curly Ellis; the game became to see who could get who off first.

Bruno's come was the saltiest and the first to flow. He was also the first one ready for round 3, but Weare gave the center fielders half-hard cock a good-natured shake and slipped off the bed.

"I gotta take a piss," he said.

Thorne grabbed Weare's retreating ass by the hairy left cheek and pulled him back. "Where do you think you're going?"

"I told ya," the rookie sighed. "Gotta piss."

A cocky grin broke on Thorne's handsome face. "So, like I asked you: Where the fuck do you think you're going?"

Weare finally got the hint. Standing at the edge of the bed, he assumed the classic piss stance: one hand on his hip, the other holding his tube by its hairy root. The Werewolf stroked the rookie's flat, hairy stomach, massaging Weare's abs to relax him. A blast of piss flew into the catcher's mouth, first as a spurt, then a stream. Thorne got most of it.

Bruno, a little curious after what had happened in the urinal with Weare a few weeks earlier, joined the catcher on his knees. Weare cut off the flow in mid stream, put his cock into Bruno's mouth, then finished off. To Bruno's surprise the bitter liquid tasted a little like beer and a lot like the rookie's come.

The two veterans, spurred on by Weare's sour-tasting gold, settled back on the bed in a sixty-nine, while Weare ordered the real thing from room service—a six-pack of cold ones. They drafted Bruno to get the ice. He argued, saying he was close to shooting his third load in as many hours, but was out-voted. By the time he'd pulled on his underwear and wrapped a big bath towel around his waist, Weare had replaced him on the bed with Thorne. The image stopped Bruno in his tracks at the hotel-room door.

As much as he loved watching them suck on each other, Bruno couldn't shake the smallest pang of jealousy. With a shrug he told himself the quicker he returned with the ice, the sooner he could rejoin their private party—but the one-minute walk to the ice machine turned into ten.

Luckily the ice machine was located in a small room two doors down from their suite. Bruno thought he might bump into some of the other players. The team had the whole floor, so if he got caught in just a towel, it would have been business as usual, but he made it to the ice chest unseen. He filled the bucket, closed the ice machine's cover, and turned around, nearly tripping over Ricky Catalano.

"Fuck!" Bruno gasped, dropping the ice—and his towel— while trying to recover. A dozen cubes rolled across the carpet. Bruno and Cat braced each other for support. The batboy moved automatically to recover the spilled ice. The angle put him at eye level with the bulge in Bruno's underwear.

"S-sorry," Cat apologized. "I didn't mean—" He tried to hand Bruno the towel, but the veteran held up a restraining hand.

"It's OK, guy," Bruno said. He grinned and shook his head. "I'm the one that's sorry, Cat. Shit, boy, the name fits. I didn't hear you walk in here. You walk like a fuckin' cat."

The batboy flashed a goofy smile up at Bruno before looking away. Cat's cheeks flushed with an embarrassed rosiness. "Not with these big feet of mine."

Bruno glanced at the batboy's feet, covered in fresh white socks, then higher, to his dark-gray shorts and black T-shirt. The center fielder realized that the batboy was in turn studying him. Bruno's cock unintentionally flexed inside his briefs. In trying to hide it, Bruno covered his bulge with the bunched towel. "I seen you help my boy out when he was in Seaside last month," Bruno said matter-of-factly.

Cat glanced away. The corners of his mouth curled the slightest bit wider, as if the smile was involuntary. "Yeah, Tom Jr.'s pretty cool."

Bruno took a heavy swallow, only to find his mouth had gone completely dry. "He's a hotshot, my Tommy."

"He's real proud to be your son," Cat went on to say. The statement brought him back from the floor, where he'd gathered the last of the ice cubes into a little pile. "Real honored."

Bruno then knew the truth behind the smile on Catalano's face. He'd seen it on Weare and on Thorne. The revelation, to his surprise, didn't hit Bruno the way he thought it might, didn't pierce him the way it had when he saw Weare and his own son lying naked and asleep in his bed, their mouths half cocked in smiles like the one Cat had let slip at the mention of Tom Jr. "Hey," he finally conceded. "Like father, like son."

No longer worried, Bruno let the towel drop. He hooked his now well-worn underwear to one side. Cat looked up, an expression of total shock and undeniable hunger written across his handsome face. The small smile widened. "Bruno?" he gasped.

"It's cool, Cat. Go ahead."

Cat didn't need much more. His hand was on the big center fielder's hairy, muscled leg in a flash. From there, the veteran ballplayer didn't have to explain it to the batboy.

On the ice room floor Catalano moved between Bruno's thighs. He wordlessly sucked the big guy's rock-hard cock between his lips. Bruno closed his eyes and thought about how good it had been to be inside the team's star catcher a few minutes earlier and how good it felt now to put that same cock down the 19-year-old's throat. Bruno savored every moment of Cat's hero worship of him and his cock, the feel of the batboy's tongue and hands, which groped up to fondle the center fielder's hairy balls. Even the heat of the heavy gusts of Cat's desperate breathing turned him on.

Bruno quickly shot off in Cat's mouth. It wasn't just the fact he'd been sucked almost to the point of unloading back in the hotel room, in the Werewolf's hotter-than-fuck mouth, or the possible danger of being found out by other late-night visitors to the ice room. With his eyes still shut, he thought about Cat and Tom Jr., close the way he and Weare had gotten close that summer. Bruno groaned, pushed his bone down the batboy's throat, and crushed his shag into Cat's nostrils. It wasn't a huge shot of pine tar—two steady, solid squirts—but the sensation continued long after he shot.

Cat reluctantly spit out Bruno's spent, musky-smelling cock and shuffled quickly to his feet atop the melting ice that stained his shorts and socks. "I'm real sorry, Bruno," the batboy attempted.

Bruno grabbed Cat by the back of the head and stroked his neat buzz cut. "It's OK, buddy. Who you bunking with?"

Cat glanced nervously away. "Tuc," he said. The lone word cracked.

Bruno smiled. Coming in the batboy's mouth went too fast. Part of him would have liked to have taken it slower, to have prolonged it. But with a sigh Bruno felt up the front of Cat's shorts. The batboy's cock—long and wiry from what he could tell through the loose cotton material—was as stiff as the good wood they'd both made careers out of. He considered sucking the batboy's dick, but the others were waiting, and that was his most important obligation. Besides, with what Weare had told him before the start of the private party, the batboy was probably already taken care of that night.

"I'll do it for you," Bruno said, pumping Cat harder through his shorts. "Trust me; I want to. Only problem is, I'll bet Tucker wants you all to himself."

Bruno released Cat's cock after he got no argument. He playfully punched the batboy's solid chest, then picked up the ice bucket and headed back. A six-pack, Damon Thorne, and the rookie—his rookie—were waiting.

NINTH INNING

"The Dugout Sports Bar?" Weare huffed. "What are you, suicidal? The last place we should be is on the Pilots' home turf, specially since we swept their butts an hour ago!"

Bruno grinned and took another suck off the cigar he'd smoked halfway down to celebrate the last game of the regular season. The Socks had taken it from Pennsylvania in a three-two victory that had sent the other team packing for the last time that summer and left the guys from Seaside with one more night to spend in an enemy city before heading home to the fanfare of baseball's second season.

"I think it's the first place we should be," Bruno said, a shit-eating grin on his handsome face. "Can you think of a better place to raise a glass of cold, cheap piss beer and toast us beating those pricks?"

The big guy's enthusiasm proved infectious—that and the fact that he looked so good in the pair of faded blue jeans and the crisp white pocket T-shirt he'd dressed in following the postgame press call. The T-shirt perfectly showcased the muscles of the veteran center fielder's hairy chest underneath. A smile like Bruno's slowly replaced Weare's scowl. "Yeah, there's something poetic about sipping bad piss beer in the favorite hangout of the Pilots. Guess you know what you're talking about."

Both men high-fived. Bruno handed Weare the well-chewed, spit-wet cigar. Weare took it without reservation and dragged a deep victory hit. Bruno's smiling, handsome face greeted him through the veil of gray-white smoke. "It's been one hell of a regular season," the veteran center fielder said in a matter-of-fact growl. There was a nostalgic tone in the big guy's statement, something rare the rookie recognized.

Weare shrugged. "Yeah, I gotta say, even though I know we're headed to the first round of the playoffs, the World Series if we get lucky..." Weare's voice trailed to a whisper. He puffed on Bruno's cigar again before handing it back. "Anyway, I mean, I'm gonna be kinda sad to see it all end."

"Hey, Mr. Rookie of the Year," Bruno grinned.

"Cut it out, dude," Weare said, making a playful fist and punching Bruno's gut. "I ain't thinking about that till after the postseason! You're one to talk, Mr. MVP candidate!"

"Hey," Bruno grinned. He blew three steady smoke rings in Weare's direction. "The Socks made it this far. Everything after today is gravy, but you and me, we're gonna keep 'em on top until we bring a world championship home to Seaside."

"I know," Weare sighed. Twenty feet from the sports bar's front door, he stopped in place. "It's just—well, shit, dude," the rookie sighed.

Bruno met him eye to eye with his blue-grays. "What is it, pal?"

"I wanted you to know—Barbara..." Bruno's eyes widened at Weare's mention of her name. "I broke up with her this morning."

"What?" Bruno growled in disbelief.

Weare glanced away. "She had her thing, I had mine."

"You broke up with Barbara?" Bruno asked again, as if needing to hear it twice to believe it.

Weare nodded. "Yep. You mad?"

"You broke up with that tight pussy?" Bruno's deep baritone had a tone of disgust that brought them closer outside the sports bar door.

"Yeah," Weare said. "Don't think I'm gonna go back to Cincy for the off-season. I was kinda thinking about staying in Seaside for the winter."

Suddenly the cigar-chewing veteran pulled him into a happy, buddy bear hug. Bruno messed up Weare's hair with his free hand. "Mad? Me and little Bruno are fuckin' honored!"

Weare made a disgusted sigh and shook Bruno off. "Cut it out, you big goof!"

The two men, their spirits higher than ever, approached the Dugout's door.

Weare's revelation seemed to set the course for the rest of the night. Through the hazy smoke-filled room, the legion of disgusted Pilots fans who'd watched their team crash and burn at the end of the regular season, the sweet aroma of cheep beer welcomed them into the sports bar. Though he couldn't exactly explain why at first, Bruno knew it was going to be one hell of a night.

Bruno had barely finished paying for the first round when Weare's elbow alerted him to Phil Jette's presence. The Pilots' star starting pitcher sat all by himself in a shadowy corner beneath one of the two big-screen televisions. Two empty shot glasses framed a half-empty beer glass like two nuts at the base of a big dick. It was obvious by the sour, drunken scowl on Jette's mean, handsome face how the Pilots' go-to guy was dealing with the end of what had started as a promising season for Pennsylvania.

"What goes around, comes around," Bruno growled under his breath. "Fuckin' prick."

"Yeah," Weare chuckled into Bruno's ear. "I bet that fuckin' two-incher of his is shriveled up smaller than the cocktail weenies the barmaid's passing round."

"You think so?" Bruno asked, scratching the meaty bulge in his faded denim jeans.

The action wasn't lost on Weare. "Shit, yeah, I bet Ronnie's feeling pretty empty with that pencil dick after having your big bat in her."

Bruno set his glass down and burped. "Yeah, bet Barbara thinks the same thing the next time she goes on a date."

The two men exchanged a hearty chuckle, then high-fived again. When their hands met, it took their focus; their eyes locked in a breathless gaze. Veteran and rookie, man to man—the cocky jock smiles vanished from their faces.

Bruno swallowed heavily and nodded. "Tim," he said. It was a rare moment when he didn't use buddy, pal, dude, or any number of safe pet names for another guy. "I mean it. This past season with you has been something fan-fuckin'-tastic. I think if you'd gone back to Cincy and Barbara when everything's said and done, I'd have killed her with my bare hands and dragged you back to Seaside by your balls." They both laughed. "I've really gotten used to having you around."

"Is that an invitation to move in full-time for the off-season?" Weare gulped a swig of beer.

Bruno stared into the rookie's puppy-dog eyes. "Buddy," he said in a serious growl. "As long as I got a house in Seaside, you got a home." Then he grinned wickedly. "And as long as I got a face, you got somewhere to sit!"

The mouthful of beer in the rookie's mouth spewed out with an uncontrolled burst of laughter. The barmaid swore in disgust and passed a rag over the counter. Bruno joined in with the rookie, laughing with Weare all the way. When they'd regained their composure enough to talk again, they sealed the arrangement in a toast.

"Deal?" Bruno asked.

"My ass and your face—what a match," Weare chuckled. "Two conditions: First, we fuck till we're senseless all winter long. Just you and me. No Barbara. No Werewolf. Nobody else."

"Damn straight," Bruno agreed. "Number 2?"

"Ball and chain, you and me, from tomorrow on—31 and 13. A team inside a team. No trades. No drafts. The only time we get naked with anybody else is when we hit the showers with the rest of the team. Bruno and Weare. Tom and Tim. The Ballsy Twins, joined together at the nuts. Balls and chains, you and me."

"Sounds like a marriage," Bruno said, grinning ear to ear.

"You proposing?"

Bruno wordlessly reached over the bar. In the moments that followed, he twisted two red stirrers into circles. He handed one to the rookie. "Will this do till we win our World Series rings."

Weare drew in a deep breath. "Damn straight, lug nuts."

Bruno pressed in close, blocking anyone else from seeing him slip the plastic ring on Weare's right ring finger. Weare followed by doing the same to Bruno. It had been one hell of a year.

"You're gonna have to do a few things around the house," the veteran center fielder said, narrowing his eyes. "Help out with the yard work, the laundry."

"Laundry? You mean I gotta wash your stinkin' socks and boxers?"

"You're going to have to rub my tired feet and help me out with this real bad case of jock itch I get in the nuts that makes little Bruno hard all the time."

"I think I can handle it," Weare replied.

Bruno swigged the last of his beer. "Come on. I'm ready to get started now, back at the hotel."

Weare glanced between the big guy's legs. Bruno's erection stretched the faded denim, making it taut over his crotch. The rookie wanted nothing more than to begin things right away, but there were others matters to attend to first. "No," Weare whispered. "Not yet. Marriage officially begins tomorrow, when we're back in Seaside. Tonight you and me's gonna have us one more taste of what it's like to be stags." He tipped his head in Phil Jette's direction. "You up for a little revenge first?"

"We kicked the Pilots clear to the end of their season, buddy," Bruno sighed. "That was pretty vengeful."

"Yeah, well, not enough. Philly boy fucked with you. Nobody does that and gets away with it."

Bruno leaned closer to the rookie. "What did you have in mind?"

Weare pulled out his wallet. The plan took root quickly. A moment after discussing it with the veteran center fielder, they both put it in motion.

☆   ☆   ☆

Bruno plunked the bottle and shot glasses down on the table. Jette sluggishly jumped in his chair, his eyes cloudy, his hard mouth slurring out a "Fuck!" Then, with recognition, he swore again. "What the fuck're you doing here?"

Feigning ignorance to Weare's presence at the bar, Bruno

poured them both a heavy dose of vodka. "Me? I'm just trying to be a good sportsman." He handed the fullest shot to the Pilot's already-juiced star pitcher. "This is baseball, Phil, not some game of capture the flag. You and Ronnie...hey, if it works for you both, I'm glad. I got no claim to what the two of you are doing behind closed doors."

A petty smirk twisted Jette's coldly handsome face. "Yeah, right, fuck wad. Like you don't get hard thinking about me and your wife."

"Ex-wife," Bruno said. "I been doing my share of dorkin' this season myself. It's helped me to forget about Ronnie. You and me," he sighed gruffly, "we're about baseball. Good-natured rivalry. The Pilots put up one hell of a fight. We've played some fun ball this year. I just want to know that we'll do the same next year."

"You burying the hatchet?" Jette slurred.

Yeah, asshole, Bruno thought. *In your fuckin' head—or should I say hole....*

The ploy worked. Jette accepted the shot. He smiled at Bruno and clapped an arm to his shoulder. "Sorry if I've been a dick to you man. You're really a very nice man. Hope I'm as tough as you are when I'm your age, buddy." Two shots later, Bruno was feeling pretty buzzed, while Jette swam deeper into oblivion. With the Pilots pitcher's head start, the two Socks sluggers had him sauced for the plan before the bottle was empty.

Just shy of 10 o'clock, Weare left the bar, and together he and Bruno helped Jette stumble out to his rental car.

"This is gonna be fuckin' cool," Weare said in a giddy, secretive whisper. They found Jette's keys, fished his driver's license out of his wallet, and after a quick assessment of the street map, were on their way back to the drunken pitcher's Philadelphia loft.

☆   ☆   ☆

Weare fumbled with the front door to the loft. Bruno, who'd had one too many and was feeling a decent buzz, swayed under the full burden of Jette's staggering weight.

"Hurry up," the veteran center fielder grunted. Weare threw open the door, reached in, and found a light switch. The first try turned on the outside spotlights. A galaxy of stars blinded Bruno and the dazed opposing pitcher.

"Shit!" Bruno said, stunned back into clarity.

"Whathafuck?" Jette slurred. "Bruno?"

"Yeah, pal, I'm right here."

Weare scrambled inside the door until he found the right switch. His next effort turned on the main room's lights. He shut off the outside spots and helped Bruno stumble in with their drunken prey.

"This is gonna be fuckin' great," Weare said again. He took in the living room quickly: simple and elegant and expensive, white sofas and carpet, brass-and-glass tables, everything matching Jette's cold good looks perfectly. The loft bedroom was no different. As they crossed to the big bed with the white-and-gold laminated headboard, Bruno thought of Jette plugging Ronnie, eating her cunt, forcing his cock up the same hole he'd once stretched on rare occasions. But to his surprise it didn't hurt to imagine them together. He had the rookie, and Number 13, his lucky number, was all he needed.

They slung Jette facedown onto the bed and exchanged horny grins.

"You take the dresser," Bruno said. "I got the closet."

"Better you than me," Weare joked, giving Bruno's ass a typical jock slap.

Bruno flashed Weare his middle finger, then took off.

Weare found a wad of $100 bills in the dresser as thick as Bruno's bat. Bruno came across an instant camera that still had six exposures in it.

"Six is enough," the rookie said, unzipping his blue jeans. "When we're done it's gonna feel like a hell of a lot more."

The last of the haze clouding Bruno's senses fled as he watched Weare undress. His shirt came off, exposing his hairy chest, then his sneakers and socks, revealing his big sexy feet. By the time Weare pulled down his midlengths in one savage push, making his hard-as-wood cock and low-hanging sac of nuts bounce up and down, Bruno's cock was up and itching in his pants.

Weare gave his slugger a few stiff strokes, then shouted an angry whisper across the bed. "What the fuck're you waiting for?"

"I'm just admiring the view."

Bruno pulled his tight white T-shirt over his head. He kicked off his sneakers, left his socks on, and in record time had his jeans and briefs in a pile beside the rookie's. Now there remained just one thing to do.

The two Socks men worked well together, communicating with primitive grunts instead of words. Each peeled off one of Jette's black high-tops and took turns sniffing the damp, sweaty cotton of his white socks before peeling them down, exposing the man's handsome feet and sexy straight-boy toes.

"You turned me into a foot pig," Weare growled between licks of Jette's sweaty toes.

Bruno rubbed the foot in his hand over his boner and itchy nuts. "You were already one before I shoved one of my stinky size 12s under that nose of yours."

Weare smirked and dropped the spit-soaked foot in his hand and joined Bruno on his knees near the one the center fielder held. The rookie licked Jette's toes and the sculpted cock they were being rubbed against. Lovingly, he sucked on Bruno's arrow-shaped dick head and the meaty sac of bull nuts dangling near Jette's ankle. He would have continued, but Bruno stopped him.

"Honeymoon's not until morning, pal," the veteran slugger said. "We're still bachelors."

Together they undid Jette's blue jeans while the Pilots' ace pitcher snored, unaware he was about to be paid back in the ultimate way by Bruno. Bruno slipped the jeans down off Jette's ass, and Weare finished by tugging them off past the pitcher's feet. In several seconds Jette was down to his unbuttoned dress shirt and a pair of white briefs. Weare wasted no time and scooted to the opposite side of the bed until his face was even with Jette's groin. He gave the meaty bulge a good feel. A confused look replaced Weare's grin.

"What the fuck?" Jette gasped. "That you Bruno?"

"I'm still here, pal," Bruno growled, grinning.

"Good," Jette purred. "I'm so glad you're here, guy."

Bruno hauled down Jette's briefs with a forceful yank. Jette's eyes snapped open, and Bruno's went wide. The Socks' center fielder gawked at the small, hairy prong in disbelief. "Is that it? Where's the rest of it?"

Jette muttered a long line of drunken cusses as he tried to raise his head. Bruno gave Jette's cock a firm squeeze, while Weare tugged on the tight, hairy nuts below it. Neither man could believe their eyes at the sight of the much smaller than average size of Jette's manhood; the rest of the package was so big and mean. "You gotta be fuckin' kiddin' me!" Bruno said.

Bruno's bellow of laughter brought Jette closer to the reality of his situation. His head heavy, he tried to focus on the naked men swimming in and out of focus on either side of his prick. "Mmm, that feels good. What're you doin', Bruno?"

Jette slurred. "You playin' with my dick?"

"That's right, cock knocker," Bruno growled. "Though I wouldn't call what you got a cock. This," he said, bringing his bat into clear view by taking a step toward Jette's handsome, drunken face, "is a cock."

Bruno slapped Jette across the mouth, spraying a trickle of precome across the drunk man's lips.

"Hey!" Jette protested. "That's a fuckin' big one."

Bruno grabbed Jette by the back of the head and rammed his rod into the star pitcher's mouth. "Yeah, it's fucking big all right," Bruno grunted. "Suck my fuckin' monster, shit head."

Weare grabbed the camera and quickly spun around. He got the first picture perfectly, showing Bruno only from his abs down, his thick cock crammed inside Jette's mouth. The bright flash made Jette blink. He coughed up Bruno's thickness, but to both their surprise, tried to keep sucking. "He fucking likes it," chuckled Bruno, pulling out and slapping the pitcher with his dick again. The second exposure was just as precise and showed Bruno's hard, hairy manhood dribbling precome on Jette's lips. By this point Weare was so hard, he put the camera down. He had to get a piece of it too before he came without even touching himself.

"My turn," the rookie said. He dove between Jette's legs and spread open his hairy thighs. "I gotta suck this dude's tiny cock, man, soft or not."

"Go ahead, buddy," Bruno said. "You've earned this little dick of his."

The veteran Socks slugger held Jette down and watched as the rookie gulped his cock, doing his best to toughen it up. Weare licked on Jette's beefy nuts, then shoved a tongue up his hard, tight ass. Bruno watched, Jette moaned, and Weare ate.

"How's his puss, buddy?"

Weare groaned a gust of hot air up into Jette's shitter. "Not as good as the piece I usually get," he said, toying with Jette's soft cock and loosening sac of nuts. "And look at how small his prick is. Shit, mine was bigger when I was 10."

Bruno chuckled, and Jette bucked up off the bed, making his limp dick flop ineffectually in the jungle of shag surrounding it. "Cut it out!" he bellowed. A resounding "Fuck!" echoed through the loft bedroom when Weare stuffed a finger up the star pitcher's tight asshole.

"Aw, man," the rookie said, as if he hadn't heard Jette's protest. "You gotta come down here and have a go at him. Fucker's tighter than a tube of toothpaste."

Bruno smacked Jette in the face with his bat one last time before following through on the rookie's offer. True to his promise, Weare had been right about the Pilots' finest. The knot of his unwilling asshole clamped down like a vise on Bruno's finger by the time he was in to the first knuckle. "Shit, dude," the veteran slugger growled. "You're one hot fuckin' jock. I gotta get me a piece of what my ex has been going down on."

Bruno lowered his handsome face onto Jette's ass and mixed his spit with the juice of the hot tongue-lapping Weare had already injected. Jette suddenly bucked his ass up off the bed, spreading his hairy legs. "Do it, Bruno. Do it, buddy."

The action sent both Socks players into overdrive. Weare grabbed Jette's arms as Bruno dealt with his legs, pinning them under his own.

"Get the camera," Bruno said. The rookie let go. Jette tried to move, but the sudden overwhelming press of Bruno's solid muscles ended any resistance the Pilots' pitcher might have attempted. There wasn't any question as to whether Phil Jette would take his cock, willingly or not. The itch in Bruno's nuts—an itch that forced a river of precome out of the slit of his bat's head—was the only lube he planned on giving the asshole beneath him. Spreading his legs forcibly, Bruno shoved in.

"Holy fuck!" Jette bellowed as Bruno rammed in again and again. "No more, dude. I can't take it."

The challenge only spurred Bruno on. He stuffed Jette's can harder with each thrust. "Yeah," Bruno growled into the pitcher's handsome, pained face. "This is the hottest fuck of your life. You're gonna take it. Take it all. Right to the hilt, you fuckin' cocksucker. You're gonna get my big cock up your butt. You're gonna take my seed like a cunt. You ever eat any of it outta my wife's pussy when you fucked her? Huh? You get off licking my spunk outta her wet pussy before you fucked her?"

"Fuck you, fucker!" Jette howled, all softness gone from his voice. He was once again the same punk Bruno knew and despised.

Bruno shoved in. A cascade of sweat poured down his forehead, over his hairy chest, and with each thrust he rained his perspiration down on Jette.

Weare took the third snapshot, and got Bruno pumping into Jette's asshole, catching all but the big guy's face and every detail of the dude getting plugged. The fourth photo was identical to the third.

With the evidence mounting, Weare took time out to join in on the furious fucking taking place on Phil Jette's bed. He started with his tongue on Bruno's feet, then licked his way up Jette's hairy calves, until he'd reached the double dose of balls banging together. The heady odor from Bruno's butt drew his face between the big guy's concrete can, and he cleaned the

sweat off of it with his tongue. He was still eating out Bruno's
ass when the big guy decided on Jette's final humiliation.

☆   ☆   ☆

"That's it," Bruno urged. The big guy held Jette on top of
him in a tight bear hug. Bruno's big arms wrapped around
Jette from behind, pinning the pitcher's back to the veteran
center fielder's chest. Angled in at just the right position,
Bruno's cock, stuffed firmly up Jette's asshole from behind,
was soon joined by another as Weare climbed into the twosome, making it a threesome. Jette, in a burst of fear mixed
with rage, bucked wildly, but the arm around his chest and
the big bat lodged in his shitter kept him firmly locked in
place.

Weare lined up his cock with Bruno's. The veteran slugger's juice made it easier, though Jette's asshole put up a good
fight.

"Go in him," Bruno growled. "Come on, let's give this fucker the fuck of his life!"

The rookie pressed in. Jette, his asshole being stretched
wide open by two cocks, let out a loud moan as Weare's bat
forced it into accommodating six more inches.

"Aw, fuck," Weare groaned. "His cunt's harder to plug than
Barbara's."

"You fuckin' fucks!" Jette screamed, pushing back, spearing
himself on their two dicks.

"Yeah," Bruno grunted. "But for a change, we're doing the
fucking to you, fucker. Come on, pal," he said to Weare. "Get
me off with your cock."

Weare pumped in and out slowly. The incredible tightness
of Bruno's cock beneath his own rubbed the sensitive under-

sides of their dick heads together and sent an icy-hot shudder down the rookie's spine.

"That feels fuckin' great," Bruno howled. "That's it, pal. Fuck my cock with yours, just like that first night in Florida!"

The memory sent Weare into a steady fuck rhythm on top of both men. He leaned down and pressed the brunt of his weight onto Jette, trapping the Pilots pitcher in the center of a Top Socks sandwich. From his position at the bottom of it all, Bruno could do little more than grind his hips into Jette's, wiggling his slugger in the pitcher's ass. But Weare's skill proved enough for both men.

It may have been the excitement of putting Phil Jette in the best, most humiliating place or the way Bruno and Weare had learned to get each other off. The veteran's cock rumbled with the first itchy-sore sign that he was about to blast his load at the same the moment Weare muttered a breathless, "Shit, here it fuckin' comes."

Bruno grunted a response, burying his mouth in the short, clipped hair near Jette's ear. "I'm gonna shoot it, man, right up your cunt—your hairy guy cunt, fucker!" The sensation was so intense, anything Bruno said after that was a gnashed, incoherent groan. As tight as Jette's shit hole was, Bruno's cock felt like it doubled in size inside it. A blast of Weare's juice squirted over his own shooting prong, triggering the nerves in his dick head, heightening the sensation.

Bruno growled a long line of swears as the pleasure in his cock turned to agony and a blinding wash of stars filled his eyes. When they cleared, he realized the rookie had taken the fifth photo by aiming the camera behind him. It developed fully to show both their cocks lodged in Jette's can.

"This one's for us to keep," the rookie said, wiping the sweat off his forehead. When Weare pulled out, a gust of cool air turned the layer of stale spunk coating Bruno's cock and Jette's well-fucked asshole clammy. Slowly, spent all the way through, Bruno eased his spike from the pitcher's knot. He flipped Jette onto his back. The Pilots' pitcher slumped ass-up on the pillows and moaned. A few seconds later he was snoring.

Bruno took the last photo, with Weare's assistance. The rookie spread Jette's butt cheeks and bared the stretched pink hole at the center of its ring of black hair. Their combined loads ran out of Jette's asshole, down the insides of his thighs and over his balls. Once Bruno had the exposure, the rookie ate their spunk out of Jette's knot. It would have been a shame to waste it.

"You sleep things off, Philly," Bruno said. He hauled up his jeans, then pulled on his T-shirt. By the time he and the rookie were dressed again, the clock read half past midnight.

"Stag party's over," the rookie said.

Bruno kissed him once they'd shut the front door to Jette's loft. Outside, Weare handed him the wad of $100 bills. "What the hell's this?"

"About five grand," the rookie grinned. "Charity, thanks to our friend in there." Weare tipped his head in the loft's direction. "Doesn't Philadelphia have an inner-city Little League that could use some help?"

Bruno flipped through the wad. "Five grand's a good start." He shook a hand through the rookie's neat, sweaty hair. "Course, being charitable ain't the only surprise Phil Jette's gonna be greeted by come tomorrow when he wakes up with the worst headache of his life."

The thought made Bruno's aching, satisfied cock toughen up in his underwear. Of the six snapshots they'd taken using Jette's camera, he and Weare had left three propped up on the pillow. Bruno patted the chest pocked of his T-shirt; the remaining three fit perfectly there.

"Let's go home," Weare said.

They walked away together, into the warm October night.

The divisional series went to the Socks against Oakland. From there, only the Fishercats stood in their way. Two fine back-to-back performances by Twain and Vandercastille sealed their victory. The Socks returned to Seaside, headed for the World Series.

The team's winning record had earned them home-field advantage in the first two games of the Fall Classic. They took game 1 at McKinsey Field from the California Cougars, then, to the shock of their fans, were rocked in a shutout in game 2.

The series shifted to the West Coast, and games 3 and 4 went to California. The Socks were faced with the possibility of elimination by the Cougars if they didn't pull together.

In game 5, Curly Ellis's lead-off homer in the first inning set the game's tone. Bruno followed with a stand-up double and was driven home by Scott Bradley, who stole second and was sac-flied to third by a tailor-made Timmy Weare bunt down the first base line. The Socks put two insurance runs on the board in the eighth, from which California never recovered. The Socks victory in game 5 forced a sixth game in Seaside.

Game 6 in Seaside began on a sobering note. They would either win and stay alive or lose the World Series to their rivals in the opposing league on home soil. The Socks pulled out a victory and forced a deciding game 7.

Events leading to the postseason had dulled the earlier furor of the contest to see which man, Ellis or Bruno, had the biggest balls and the most control over them. An hour before

the on-field festivities for game 7 were about to begin, however, Ellis reminded everyone present at Bruno's locker.

"Hey, tough guy," Ellis said. Bare-chested, his jeans unzipped, Bruno was changing into his fresh home whites.
"Today is it. Win or lose. End of season."

"Tell me something none of us ain't already aware of,"
Bruno answered. He nonchalantly scratched at the bulge in
his underwear.

"Well, son, you and me got a contest to decide. The rules
said at the end of the season. This is it."

Bruno huffed sarcastically. He pushed down his jeans and
peeled them off along with his socks, then exchanged a
chuckle with Weare, who had already dressed in his spankin'
clean uniform. "You kidding, Curly Joe? I thought the whole
thing was a joke. I'd hate to think of you down there, licking
my bag."

Ellis closed Bruno's open locker with his balled fist.
"Weren't no joke, Bruno. I take my nuts pretty damned serious." The statement brought the two men face-to-face; the
loud clatter of the closing locker shifted all eyes to where they
stood. Weare straightened from tying his cleats. "And you'll
be the one choking on my chocolate, big mouth."

"You think," Bruno said. All joking left his expression. A
mean-looking game face replaced it.

Ellis, this time, smiled. "I know. I seen what's been going on
with this team in the last six months." He turned toward Weare,
flashing the rookie a cocky grin. A moment of awkward silence
settled over the bench before Ellis broke it. "But I don't give a
fuck. Whatever's making this team play .600-plus ball is fine so
long as it doesn't affect me. Like the contest, Bruno," he said,
turning back to the veteran center fielder. "My balls. My reputa-
tion. The contest ends now, and it's time for me to collect."

Bruno didn't say anything at first. He didn't have to. The grim look on his face spoke volumes. "You're serious?"

Ellis answered by hauling down the zipper of his Top Socks uniform. Bruno watched as the first baseman fumbled in his jock, tugging it aside. Two bloated, fat balls in a black silk pouch spilled out, looking suddenly huge. "Dead serious."

☆   ☆   ☆

Catalano slowly went down to his knees. The batboy nervously fumbled with the tape measure, blowing hot air on the metal tip. Before moving toward Ellis' low-hangers, he looked up. Scott Bradley, the Werewolf, and Tuc Vandercastille flanked Ellis, watching him with edgy looks on their faces in anticipation of the final outcome.

"What the fuck's this?" Roger Twain demanded, strutting up to Bruno's locker. The Thunderbird broke the tight wall of solid bodies in time to see Cat place the quivering tip of the tape measure against the root of Ellis' cock. Cat nervously pulled back, until the team's first baseman again demanded to be measured.

"He's proving I got bigger stones than Bruno," Ellis said in a voice that sounded like he was full of himself.

"That dumb contest?" Twain chuckled. "You fixin' to win, Curly Joe?"

"Sure 'nuff."

Twain glanced at Bruno, then lower, between the big center fielder's legs. "I dunno, Curly. Big Bruno's pretty big."

"Yeah, but not big enough. Cat," Ellis bellowed. "How big are my fuckin' nuts?

Catalano resumed. With shaking hands he twisted the tape measurer around Ellis's hairy ball bag. At the opposite end of the first baseman's root, the tape measurer came in just shy of the eight-inch mark. Curly had put on nearly an inch of come in his nuts since making the bet.

After Cat announced the measurement, Ellis proudly hauled his big black balls back in jockstrap and strutted near the lockers. His new position provided an unobstructed view of the competition. The batboy knelt down in front of Bruno.

The first few seconds as Cat placed the tape measure on the base of Bruno's cock seemed to draw out. Cat could only stare at the big guy's bat. Bruno and Weare exchanged a nervous look. Nobody spoke, until the Werewolf whistled out a wolf call.

"Come on, Bruno," Thorne hooted. "You got the big and meaties—the biggest and meatiest in the clubhouse!"

Bruno forced a smile that looked just as cocky as Ellis's. He focused down on cat, who was putting the tape in place around his balls. The batboy tucked the measurer into the coarse shag at the root of Bruno's limp cock. Cat's lower lip quivered like his hands. He took a heavy swallow that moved his Adam's apple. Squeezing Bruno's balls, thumbing the head of the big guy's cock to nudge it out of the way, Cat finally had the measurement. It read six and a half inches.

"What?" Weare sputtered.

Twain, Vandercastille, and the Werewolf added their voices to the fracas that followed.

"You gotta be shitting!"

"No fuckin' way!"

"Do it again!"

Cat retook the measurement. The men assembled took turns looking at the results up close, mere inches away from Bruno's limp cock. Each time, the result was the same; Ellis's ball bag had gotten bigger, fuller with come, while Bruno's had shrunk. The first baseman had won.

The veteran center fielder had lost.

Ellis moved victoriously toward the bench. Once there he put one leg up, undid his fly, and pulled out his balls. "I've been looking forward to this all season," he said. "Months of not jackin' my dick, just fuckin' my girlfriend when we was back in Seaside for home games. It was all worth it just to see your face on my knob."

Bruno watched, horrified, as Ellis freed the fat black monster out of his pants. The pink-tipped dark-meat bat got harder with each passing second. "You fuckin' crazy, dude?"

"Not crazy, just the winner, hot shit," Ellis said. He gave his prong a few stiff tugs, making it stretch out farther. "Get down and pay me some respect."

Bruno sighed in disbelief. "You expect me to put my mouth on your fuckin' nut bag?"

"Yeah, Curly," Weare interjected. The tension in the locker room had grown as thick as thunder. "Come on. You can't be serious—"

"I'm serious all right, pretty boy. I'm also a man of my word. I told your boyfriend here," Ellis said, thumbing Bruno's direction, "he had nothing on me. If he had, I'd follow through with it like a real man."

Ellis gave a deep, disgusted huff and said no more. He reached for his rod, shook it again, and stuffed it in his jock. Bruno put a hand on the first baseman's wrist and gave it a firm tug. "You won, and I am a real man, you arrogant asshole. I'm also a man of my word." The veteran center fielder's grip on Ellis's arm tightened to the point where the first baseman winced. "And don't ever cast doubt on our rookie's manliness. He's got more of it than you'll ever have."

Saying that and no more, Bruno sank to his knees. Eyes wide, a stern, determined look on his face, Bruno surrendered.

Twain glanced at Weare before adding his protest. "Don't do it, man!"

Weare agreed. "Yeah, dude, don't!" Bruno shook his head and sighed. "If somebody has to pay," the rookie persisted, "let me do it." He crouched down on his spikes beside Bruno. "I'll suck it for you."

Bruno glanced deep into the rookie's eyes and shook his head again. "Not this time, kid. This is my pain in the ass. But thanks."

Their eyes remained locked a second longer. Bruno had admitted his defeat. The rookie reluctantly backed off, and as the veteran center fielder leaned in, so did all the others—all except Weare, who gave the hungry pack of baseball jocks his back.

"That's it, tough guy," Ellis growled. "Get your mouth on my big black nuts. Show 'em some respect!"

Bruno slowly, carefully, buried his mouth in the clean-smelling, silky skin of the first baseman's nuts. He licked the soft pouch, rolling both of Ellis's balls on the tip of his tongue. He nibbled the skin while Ellis fisted his cock. The fleshy foreskin snapped up and down the excited pink-headed bat, discharging a trickle of precome out of its straining piss hole.

"That's it, Bruno. Suck those nuts. Fuck, that feels good, you macho fuckin' jock."

Bruno sucked on Ellis's black stag nuts while the first baseman beat faster and faster. The audience of teammates watching him break Bruno's spirit seemed to make him pump himself closer to the moment he'd been fighting for months. Ellis knew that with all the guys witnessing his triumph, it wouldn't be long, not long at all.

☆   ☆   ☆

A hand clapped Weare's shoulder. The rookie was so tense, he jumped in place. He spun around to see Damon Thorne standing with his back to the humiliation.

"You OK, dude?" the Werewolf asked.

Weare shook his head. "Bruno shouldn't be on his knees in front of Curly's prick."

Thorne shrugged and scowled. "What do you mean?"

"Yeah," Roger Twain added as he and Hector Valenza took flank on either side of the Werewolf. "I don't see nothin'. You see anything, Hector?" Twain gave the shortstop a good-natured butt slap.

"Me? Not a thing, big guy. What about you, Scotty?"

Bradley and Vandercastille followed suit. Even Ricky Catalano turned away from what was happening. The Cowboy was one of the last men to form the circle, all with their backs to the ball sucking going on at Bruno's locker. "What were we discussing?" he asked in his sexy Southern drawl.

"We're talking about what studs we all are. A big bunch of ball-playin' bulls," Twain answered. "Good guys out to win the game. The best and toughest team in all the majors!"

"I'll second that," a familiar voice announced from the doorway. Mitch Hudson strolled in. "What's going on here?"

"Nothing," the Cowboy answered. He pressed in close to Twain and Bradley, forming a wall to prevent what was happening behind them from being seen. "Just a little pregame bonding is all, coach."

Hudson clapped his hands sharply together. "Good. When

you guys get done buttering each other's balls, let's play some. We still got a game to win if we want the rings. Hustle!"

Hudson did an about-face from the locker room, leaving them all alone with their last-minute jitters. Nobody saw the ribbon of thick come flash across Bruno's cheek, spilled out of Curly Ellis's long black cock as the veteran center fielder sucked on his nuts. Whatever sense of pride Ellis might have gained in besting Bruno went unnoticed when his conquest rose from the floor, wiped his face, and staggered back to his locker, where a long line of congrats from their teammates began.

"Hey, buddy," Thorne said. "You're late. Coach wants us to hustle!"

"Yeah," Twain added. "Where you been the last half hour?"

"We need you out there on the field," Hector Valenza chimed in, rubbing Bruno's bare shoulder. "Stop playing with your own *cajones*, man!"

Bruno looked around, one to the next, the line of handsome faces smiling in a huddle, veterans to rookies, Twain to Weare.

"We got us a game to win, big guy," Number 13 sighed.

Bruno passed a hand over his cheek and wiped what was left of the cooling, sticky string of Ellis's come off his face, then nodded. "And we're gonna win it, my friends."

When he glanced back, Curly Ellis had a distant, embarrassed look on his face instead of the cocky smirk he'd earlier flashed.

☆   ☆   ☆

Approaching Tom Jr. before game 7 was one of the hardest things Bruno had ever done. He attended all the press interviews he could stand, then found his handsome son, who looked so much like him, in a huddle on the field with Ricky Catalano.

Tom Jr. gave him a hard bear hug, a happy smile on his handsome face. "Hey, dad," he growled.

"Buddy," Bruno said, hugging back. Catalano, getting the hint, bugged off and continued to the dugout. Bruno ran a hand through Tom Jr.'s hair and looked around at the blue sky, the greener-than-green grass of the playing field, all the media attention, the players, everything.

"I can't believe it, that we're here," he sighed.

Tom Jr. folded his arms and shook his head. "I can. Dude, you guys are the nuts! You look real good out there on the field."

"You been watching?" Bruno asked. He still had Tom Jr.'s head pinned in his left armpit.

"Yep," Tom Jr. said.

A rush of warmth tingled through Bruno's insides. There was no denying it: Today was the final day of the baseball season, no matter who took home the title.

"Having you here," Bruno sighed, "playing this game at McKinsey...shit, son, it don't get any better."

"I know," Tom Jr. sputtered from the armpit Bruno had mashed him into.

When Bruno released him, they faced each other. "Cat's a good guy, son," he whispered.

Tom Jr. blushed a little, enough to be seen in the bright sunlight spraying over the grand old ballpark.

"It's cool, son. I mean it. You got him like I got Timmy Weare. Cat's lucky to be hanging with a Bruno."

Tom Jr.'s face broke in a cool smile. "No, I'm the lucky one. Damned lucky. I've got Cat, and I've got one hell of a dad."

Bruno pulled Tom Jr. back into a buddy hug for all the media to see. "We're both the lucky ones, son," he said.

Tom Jr. slapped Bruno's ass. "Go out there, you big stud, and whip their unlucky butts!"

☆   ☆   ☆

Whatever it was that day that galvanized the Top Socks after their most incredible season—the united front of friendship before the game, Bruno and Tom Jr. out on the field—whatever its origin, it emerged in the sixth inning and followed them into the ninth. Down two in the sixth, Twain pitched a one-two-three inning to get Valenza up at bat next. His pop fly seemed a sure out until the Cougar's shortstop misjudged the play, bobbling the ball for an error that let one man on base. Two sac flies and a base knock later, Valenza crossed the dish, making it a one-run game.

In the seventh the Socks rallied with one more run. The Thunderbird pitched into the eighth. Vandercastille, assuming relief for the ninth, kept the game at a tie. In the bottom of the inning, Bradley and the Werewolf went down quickly. With two out, Tim Weare blooped a single through the gap in left field. Bruno moved out of the on-deck circle and into the batter's box to a deafening round of cheers from the crowd. They were chanting MVP.

It was their last chance to pull it off in nine innings, the hopes of an incredible season pinned to the one man the rest of the Socks respected above all others.

Bruno fouled the first pitch out of play. The second drew a ball.

Werewolf, Thunderbird, Bruno thought. The third pitch was ball two. *Bradley, Cowboy, Valenza, Vandercastille...*

Bruno chopped the next pitch foul. The home plate ump

held up two fingers on each hand.

Two balls, Bruno thought. *And mine don't itch no more, thanks to him. Timmy…*

The Cougars' pitcher tried to slip one by him, up and in.

Tim…

Bruno swung his bat, muscling everything he could into the effort. The unmistakable thunder crack of hardball hitting lumber shattered the breathless calm. For one moment of total silence, nobody spoke, no one moved. It was as if time froze.

But then Bruno looked up to see the baseball sail over the outfield wall, into the bleachers, and sound came flooding back in the deafening roar of 50,000 voices cheering and clapping all at once. Bruno's home run brought the fans to their feet and a throng of uniformed Top Socks bodies onto the field.

Bruno stood paralyzed, still not believing it, still not believing the amazing season, the rush of memories from that summer, the confrontations, the friendships, the games.

Weare was halfway around third before Bruno's paralysis broke and he began his slow, steady trot around the bases, pumping his fists. By the time he reached first, most of the Cougars had left the field, and the media had begun its frenzied attempt to get beyond the barricades. Circling the bases seemed to take forever, but suddenly Bruno found himself there at home plate with his teammates. The men he loved and who loved him were upon him in a tide of home-field white and black.

Weare was on top of him first, screaming and jumping in a reverse leapfrog that knocked Bruno to the ground. The noise level robbed Bruno of his hearing. The sudden deluge of howling teammates stole his vision. In a rapid flash Bruno found himself at the bottom of a tremendous buddy-buddy pig pile.

"You did it, Bruno!" somebody yelled. "You fuckin' did it, big guy!"

Bruno shifted under the pile of sluggers and pitchers, hugging and howling, to see the rookie's handsome face. Meeting Weare at the safe center of all their friends made everything so clear to him. For one brief, unrivaled moment, it wasn't rookie or veteran—and something more than buddy, boyfriend, lay, or love.

The veteran center fielder knew he was hard even before the rookie reached through the tangle of arms and legs for his zipper. Weare had it down and the head of Bruno's straining, sweaty cock out in record time.

Bruno didn't worry about being seen or discovered. One to the next, Twain and Valenza, Bradley, Vandercastille, the Wolf—even Curly Ellis—all of them pressed in close, forming the same protective wall they'd shielded each other with in the locker room before the game. It was the reward for their effort, the end to an amazing season, one last unforgettable moment for an unforgettable team of baseball players.

Weare sucked Bruno fast and wild. The noise, the danger, worked Bruno to the most intense and quickest load he had ever shot. There, so protected by teammates and the cheers from the crowd, Bruno squirted four steady shots down the rookie's throat. It happened so quickly, Weare had Bruno swallowed and zipped up before the media streamed onto the field. The furor that happened next, when Bruno was hoisted to the shoulders of the now-standing Top Socks, went off without a hitch. Fireworks erupted in the sky, so many it seemed like they would never end, as Bruno was carried around McKinsey Field for the crowd who kept chanting his name.

"Bruno! Bruno!"

In all the heat and excitement of their winning the World Series, Bruno momentarily forgot it wasn't summer anymore or the last game of the year in what had been the most amazing baseball season.

Some hours later the heat and noise faded, and the lights dimmed. A cold October wind blew in, and McKinsey Field went silent again, until spring brought a new team, a new season, and new changes.

Weare found Bruno standing on the dark diamond, squatting near home plate, long after the last of the locker room celebrations had ended.

"Hey, 31," the rookie said.

Bruno sighed and smiled. "Hey, 13."

"Yeah, feeling pretty lucky right now." Weare brought up the top of his right hand. A flash of gold glinted in the broken darkness. "It's just the dummy till they engrave 'em, but that gold championship ring is worth a million times its weight." He knelt down beside Bruno. "None of it is worth more to me than you, though. I'm so lucky."

Bruno glanced up. Weare noticed the trace of tears in his eyes. The rookie knew instantly they weren't sad tears but just the opposite. Bruno had the happiest, most peaceful look on his handsome face.

"It's funny," the veteran center fielder said. "My son said the same thing before the game."

"I ain't surprised," Weare said with a Cheshire-cat grin. "Dude, you're the balls. I mean it, man. You are tops—in socks and in every other way."

"I fuckin' love baseball," Bruno growled as the next drops

slid down his cheeks. He wrapped an arm around Weare's neck. They rose together, and Bruno pulled the rookie into a close bear hug. "Just like I fuckin' love you."

They moved closer, lips crushing one to the other, kissing tightly, deeply. The taste of champagne and cigars on their mouths brought back a million magnificent memories of great times and a love unlike any other. When they parted, Weare focused on Bruno's intense thunderhead eyes.

"Same here, big guy," was all Weare could think to say. The closeness of their bodies made him fidget in place.

Bruno sensed the rookie's erection pressing against his cup. He gave it a playful knock. "Come on, pal. I owe you one. Let's go home."

He slung his arm around the rookie's shoulder, and as had happened so often in the season since they'd met, they walked off across the field together, with the knowledge they'd won and the certainty that after a winter spent with each other in Seaside, they, like the game of baseball, would return.

alyson
books

FRICTION, *edited by Gerry Kroll.* Friction creates provocative sparks in this first-time collection, which includes the most well-known writers of gay erotica today. Gathered within these kinky, passionate pages are the best erotic stories that have appeared in many of the nearly 60 gay men's magazines across the country.

HEAT: GAY MEN TELL THEIR REAL-LIFE SEX STORIES, *edited by Jack Hart.* Sexy, true stories in this unbridled gay erotic collection range from steamy seductions to military maneuvers

THE LORD WON'T MIND, *by Gordon Merrick.* In this first volume of the classic trilogy, Charlie and Peter forge a love that will survive World War II and Charlie's marriage to a conniving heiress. Their story is continued in *One for the Gods* and *Forth Into Light*

MAKING IT BIG: SEX STARS, PORN FILMS, AND ME, *by Chi Chi La Rue with John Erich.* The classic American rags-to-riches story—with a twist. A young lad from Minnesota travels to California to become part of an industry he loves with all his heart: gay porn.

MY BIGGEST O, *edited by Jack Hart.* What was the best sex you ever had? Jack Hart asked that question of hundreds of gay men, and got some fascinating answers. Here are summaries of the most intriguing of them. Together, they provide an engaging picture of the sexual tastes of gay men.

MY FIRST TIME, *edited by Jack Hart.* Hart has compiled a fascinating collection of true, first-person stories by men from around the country, describing their first same-sex sexual encounter.

WONDER BREAD AND ECSTASY: THE LIFE AND DEATH OF JOEY STEFANO, *by Charles Isherwood.* Drugs, sex, and unbridled ambition were the main ingredients in the lethal cocktail that killed gay porn's brightest star, Joey Stefano. He was a child from the country's heartland, but Joey's rise and tragic fall in Los Angeles's dark and dangerous world of gay porn paints a grim portrait of American life gone berserk.

These books and other Alyson titles are available at your local bookstore.
If you can't find a book listed above or would like more information,
please visit our home page on the World Wide Web at **www.alyson.com.**